The Boy Next Door

KATIE VAN ARK

Swoon Reads   New York

A Swoon Reads Book
An Imprint of Feiwel and Friends

Swoon Reads books may be purchased for business or promotional use. For information on bulk purchases, please contact the Macmillan Corporate and Premium Sales Department at (800) 221-7945 x5442 or by e-mail at specialmarkets@macmillan.com.

Library of Congress Cataloging-in-Publication Data Available

ISBN: 978-1-250-06146-1 (paperback) / 978-1-250-06178-2 (ebook)

Book design by Ashley Halsey

First Edition: 2015

10 9 8 7 6 5 4 3 2 1

swoonreads.com

For my mother

Prologue

The skates were beautiful. They weren't the plastic kid kind, all pink and princessed up like they belonged in some cartoon. They were the real kind, just like Mrs. Nielsen's in her scrapbook. Just like the skaters on TV. White leather, brand-new, and *mine*.

I sat on the bench as Mrs. Nielsen laced them for me. Sitting next to me, his own black skates already tied, Gabe squeezed his helmet against his chest. "What if I fall?"

Mrs. Nielsen snapped his helmet on. "Didn't you fall when you were learning to ride your bike?"

"On grass," he said. "*Soft* grass."

My bike still had training wheels. But I looked at that shiny surface. Looked at the big girls in the middle by the orange cones. Twirling, their skirts fluttering up just like Mrs. Nielsen in her pictures.

Mrs. Nielsen stood us up on the foam floor mats. "It's okay, Gabe. We'll start here where it's soft, and practice falling."

Gabe made a face at his mom. "Practice falling?"

"Yes." She smiled. "Put your arms out and think about something that's really important to you. You're going to grab it in your arms and hug it tight."

I looked sideways at Gabe. He looked at me. We turned and grabbed each other, helmets clunking as Gabe's tight hug lifted my skates right off the mat.

Mrs. Nielsen laughed. "I meant like a teddy bear." She showed us how to pull our arms to our chests so we wouldn't hurt our hands or get our fingers run over by other skaters, how to go with the fall and land on our hips. "That's it, Maddy. Just relax into it. Fighting a fall is what hurts. All right, kiddos. Ready for the ice?"

I took off for the door to the rink. The latch was heavy but I got it. And there I was, on that smoothness. Stepping forward and—Whoa!

I pulled my arms in tight and let my hip hit first. It was okay. I got back up, put my arms out for balance this time and took a couple careful steps. All of a sudden I was gliding. I took a couple more steps. I went faster and faster. "I'm flying!"

No one answered me and I turned around. Not even on the ice yet, Gabe stood in the doorway with his mom coaxing him.

I skated back to him. "Come on, Gabe."

He looked at me. "You already fell."

I held out my mittened hand. "It's worth it." Ever so slowly, he reached his own hand toward mine. Hand in hand, we made it to the middle. We were standing by the cones when I looked at Mrs. Nielsen. "Show me how to spin? Please?"

"Of course." She bent her knees, then pushed up as she turned, pulling her arms into her chest to spin herself around and around.

I copied her, winding up my arms. I bent. I pushed. I twirled. And I fell . . . in love.

1

The early August heat is melting the make-up right off Dad's face, but his eyes are soft behind his thick-framed glasses, his voice calm. "You can get this, Maddy. Just ease your foot off the clutch."

The stench of burning rubber makes my eyes water as I grip the steering wheel. I blink and give it another go, but we don't *go* anywhere. My timing's off again and the ancient Dodge Neon shudders like a bug in the last twitch of death.

Gabe makes this look so easy; why can't I do it? The heat flares in my chest and I want to throw something. Release my frustration in some sort of primal battle cry. But I don't do those things at practice and I won't do them here, especially not with the camera crew sitting in the backseat.

Dad squeezes my shoulder. "It's all right."

In the rearview mirror, I see the face of the aide who offered up his car for this driving lesson because Dad thought lessons in a stick shift would be more interesting. He doesn't look *all right*. There's a big toothy smile on his face but his eyelids are tilted up toward his forehead in a way I didn't even know was possible and his eyes look like they're about to pop out of their sockets. I need to think win-win here. What do the aide and I want? Me out of this car, right now. What does Dad want? Footage for his campaign ads. I smile, half at Dad and half at the camera. "Thanks for always believing in me, Daddy."

The petite woman in charge of our little publicity shoot has tears in her eyes. Maybe from my sappy statement, but more likely from the stink of the burnt-out clutch. Either way, she announces in a singsong voice, "That's a wrap. Harold's going to *love* it!"

A teensy bit of film editing will obscure the minor detail that I still haven't managed to actually drive the car. I give Dad a peck on the cheek. "I love you."

"Love you, too. See you later, figure skater."

Halfway out of the car already, I pause and smile. "Out the door, Sena-*tor*." And I run from the parking lot into the arena.

Taking only a split-second peek in the locker room mirror to check that my hair's still camera slick, I change at superhero speed. Then I dash out of the locker room and finally I'm cleansing my lungs with the smell of the ice, the scent of fresh snow with just a hint of fuel from the last Zamboni pass. As soon as I inhale, I feel the anticipation tingle in my body. Hip-hop beats thump from the speakers overhead and, like the music, I'm cranked.

I'm pulling off my skate guards when there's a tug on my ponytail. "Hey, Mad."

All of a sudden there's a completely different tingle running through my body and I'm breathing in the only other smell that can compete with the ice. Irish Spring soap. I turn to face Gabe.

Forget melting in hands or mouths, all Gabe has to do is look at me with those milk chocolate eyes and I'm slush. Add his gorgeous blond waves, and, sadly, so is every other girl at Riverview Prep. Drool-worthy as always in tight black skating pants and a fitted Under Armour mock tee that shows off the upper body he owes to lifting me, he ditches his own guards and steps onto the ice. "How'd the lesson go?"

I follow him. "If it'd been a skating test, I would've gotten marked retry."

"That bad?"

Gabe takes a swig of water, but I take off down the ice. I need the feel of it beneath me, smooth and sure. As I fly toward him again, already headed for lap two, I grin and holler, "It was like practicing triple Axels. Crash and burn, over and over again. Well, no actual crashing but the clutch is burnt toast." I turn backward to face him as I whip past, and pinch my nose at the memory. Gabe laughs.

He catches up to me, but only because I let him. I step forward to match his strokes, easy as breathing. I know I should want my driver's license. My sixteenth birthday's so far past that I turned seventeen last month, but I shrug. "Like I need to drive, anyway. Anywhere I need to go, I can ride with you."

Gabe doesn't answer but as we round the end of the rink, he takes my outstretched hand. We don't need words, anyway. We've been pair skaters since before I cut off most of his hair playing beauty parlor in preschool. Our senior year of high school just started, but we already know we'll be going to Riverview Community College or Wichita State together. Skating and school, that's my life, and Gabe's, too. Since he's the boy next door and has had his license and his own car for almost two years, the bumming-rides deal works out pretty well.

Because he really does live next door, it's also hard to ignore that he goes plenty of places without me, but I shove the thought from my mind and start thinking about triple Axels again. I feel the smile creep over my face. I haven't made any progress with the driving lessons, but I'm going to land a triple Axel. Soon. Our coach, Igor, and I have a secret plan. We've been doing harness lessons to work on a throw quadruple Salchow and, because he knows I like the challenge, Igor's been letting me work my triple Axel in the harness, too.

Gabe and I finish our warm-up and head for the boards. I dart out of the way just in time, and the ice shavings from Gabe's hockey stop miss me. I circle around and send a snow shower of my own across his skates. He laughs and tosses me my water bottle. I take a sip, but I'm drinking in more of his grin than my water.

That is, until the slam of the metal latch behind me. My unexpected jump leaves my jacket soaked from the water I've spilled down my front. Smooth as ice, that move. I turn away quickly before Gabe notices and see Chris and Kate coming into the hockey box. Their faces are in perfect unison, the same stony expression.

"Weren't even going to tell me, were you?" Chris's bicep bulges on his wiry arm as he throws his skate guards on the floor of the hockey box. "Happy two-year anniversary to you, too." His face clashing pink against his fiery orange hair, he stomps past me and onto the ice.

Gabe turns as though he's about to say something, but his mouth hangs open, silent, and then he closes it again. Now on the other side of the rink, Chris rips the edges of his cross rolls purposefully hard. As his skate blades flash across each other, slashing the ice, the grinding noise competes with the music.

I glance back into the hockey box. Kate is sitting on the bench, her body bent forward as she fidgets with her skate laces. She tucks the loose strands of her white-blond bob back into her barrette with shaking hands.

Gabe beats me to my question. "You all right?"

Kate sits up but looks past Gabe. "Yeah." She pushes herself off the bench. "You guys want your music on?"

Gabe hands her our practice CD, tucking behind it a tissue from the box we always keep on the barrier. I ditch my wet jacket, tossing it onto the hockey bench. As Kate heads for the music box, we skate for center ice.

With the hip-hop beats silenced, there's only the *rrrip*, *RRRIP* of Chris's blades. I crouch down, pulling my body as tight to my skates as I can. Even though Chris and Kate are ice dancers and don't do jumps, Gabe jokes about when they're going to land their Axel. He means that their relationship is like us attempting our Axels: up, then down. Hard. Over and over and over again. But— "It's worse than ever this time."

"I'm so glad we're not like that." Behind me, Gabe takes his time covering my body with his own. "Classic why-you-shouldn't-date-your-partner."

I ignore that last part, taking the second to enjoy the closeness instead. Our music starts and we explode into movement, a fast routine from the soundtrack of *The Incredibles*. We sail across the rink in perfect unison, completing side-by-side triple toe loops before launching into flying camel spins. As we soar down the ice for our spiral sequence, stretching our free legs up behind us, we're at warp speed. In our pair spin, I pull my leg over my head. I *am* Elasti-Girl.

I rotate around Gabe for the death spiral, my body arching until I'm face-to-face with the ice. Our last move is a throw triple Salchow. Gabe's hands are firm on my sides. I spring from the ice, feeling the release as he launches me. My arms cross tight against my chest, elbows down, ankles crossed. I'm spinning through the air, my ponytail flying out from the force of the rotation. My toe pick hits the ice, then I'm gliding backward, arms checked out and a smile on my face. That landing was demo-video smooth.

We hit our end pose as the last note sounds. I gasp for air, but the smile on my face isn't for the judges that our coach insists we pretend are watching every practice. It's for real. We nailed that run-through. "That . . . was . . . *incredible*."

"Drop," Gabe manages, and we lose the pose. He's breathing hard, too. He drapes an arm around me, half leaning on me, half hugging me. "We're . . . gonna win."

I grin, too, leaning back into him. If we skate like we just did, he's right. Forget last year's pewter pity medal, the Junior Grand Prix is ours this year.

Gabe releases me so fast it's like I've sprouted toe picks on my shoulders. He snaps to attention, military style, except his hands are clasped behind his back instead of saluting. This means one thing, and I straighten up, too. Igor glides across the ice toward us, his long black coat floating behind him. It's his job to pick our skating apart but today, even though my face is hiding my gloating, I'm daring him to find even one thing wrong.

Igor stops right in front of us but he doesn't smile. He doesn't even nod. His mouth is a thin, straight line and his forehead has a matching thin, straight line creased into it. "We skate like so?" His dark gray eyes stare at us from under furry, silver eyebrows that match his furry, silver cap. "We lose."

I don't flinch, but I feel like the little air I had left has been sucked right out of me.

Igor's eyes pierce mine. Then I see his face smooth out, the steely eyes soften. "Technically, is perfect. But . . ." He tilts his head. "Is time. Gabriel is no longer a boy. Madelyn is no longer a girl. We do new long program this year, *Romeo and Juliet*. We are needing . . . *passion*. A love story."

My heart does a split jump in my chest. I can do passion. But it crashes down as I look at my best friend, because Gabe doesn't even look at me.

2

Gabe

Shit, double shit. If my coach were on TiVo, I'd be hitting rewind. A love story? This is some sort of deranged joke. Except Igor doesn't crack jokes. He barely knows how to smile.

I glance at Mad going all starry-eyed next to me. I've heard correctly. I look back at Igor and hold my eyes steady on him, but my insides are shaking worse than when I told Kurt I was quitting hockey just before the bantam travel team championships.

Igor nods his head toward our water bottles at the boards. "I leave copies of music there. You listen at home tonight, yes? For today we see what we have to begin." He cracks his knuckles under his leather gloves. "Death spiral again. Before, you skate for audience. This time? No audience. Only Madelyn and Gabriel. You understand?"

"Yes, sir." I understand, but there's an ice rink's chance in hell that I'm actually going to do what he wants. I take the lead and set my pivot, looking at the empty bleachers. It's been *Madelyn and Gabriel* for longer than I can remember. I let her hack off all my hair in preschool. I quit hockey for her. I broke my arm for her. There's nothing I wouldn't do for her . . . except this. She's like my sister, the way we read each other so well. Sib closeness I can deal with. That's where it stops.

On the exit, I push out so my back is facing Igor and I stare over the top of Mad's head. Epic fail on my mission to fool our coach. "Again," he says. "You must look, Gabriel."

This time, I watch the skate on Mad's free foot as she circles around me. Igor is skating toward us before we've even finished the move. He nods at Mad. "Good, Madelyn. I have changed my mind. We listen to music now. Put it on."

Mad skates off, leaving me alone with the KGB. "I do not believe," Igor says. *"Make me believe."*

I kick at the ice with my toe pick. Disrespectful, yeah, but a trip to the penalty box is sounding like a winning idea right now. I've known this day was coming. Known it since I first made myself look away from Mad's arched chest and . . . "I can't."

Igor steps closer, and I stop. I'm not sure what he'll do if I accidentally kick *him*, but I'm sure I don't want to find out. His breath makes warm puffs of air in my face. "Do not tell me, 'I can't.' 'I can't' is not part of plan."

For years I've trusted Igor's plans. For good reason. He's coached me and Mad to the national junior pair title and three Junior Grand Prix medals, including a fourth-place finish at the final last year. But . . . "This is Mad."

Igor's stainless-steel eyes glint at me. "You want to win, yes?"

"Yes," I whisper. Mom's medals gleam in the back of my mind. I *need* to win.

"So you pretend. You need me to, what do we say, write it out?"

I don't need Igor to spell it out. I know how to get a girl going. Trouble is, I'm not so hot at *keeping* things going. Mad returns and I ease her into the move once again, this time to the long desperate notes of the music. I look at her face. *Sister, sister, sister,* I chant in my head. But there's a cartoon red devil on my shoulder reminding me I'm an only child. Okay then: *Friend?*

My feeble attempt only spawns another devil. They slap each other five. "With benefits!" they chorus.

Where the hell are my angels? "No."

I must've said it out loud, because Mad startles. She slips off her edge and falls out of the spiral. She was only a few inches from the ice, but still. Stupidest move in the world to fall on. Even juvenile pairs do it in their sleep. I help her up. "Sorry."

"Madelyn," Igor says, his voice as sickly as a tornado-warning sky, "please go work on your brackets for a moment."

Igor's temper usually blows on Chris's shenanigans, but today I get the twister-cloud eyes. "I see you. All those girls, under bleachers at hockey games. What is problem here?" His gloved fingers curl, now black claws.

I look at Mad, zipping through her brackets. She attacks the twisty turns, the determination fierce on her face. She puts so much power into the pattern that she almost slams into the barrier at the end. That's the problem. I've compartmentalized my life for so long but Mad has no fear of the barrier.

I look back at Igor, watching me watch Mad. His fingers have relaxed in his gloves. "Is pretend," he says, cajoling now. "But we are needing under the bleachers. Mind in storm drain."

If I let my mind go in the gutter, I'll never get it out.

"Madelyn," Igor calls. "Get a drink. We resume."

I skate over for a drink, too. Anything to stall.

Mad plunks her water bottle down on the barrier. She keeps her chin up but she doesn't look at me. "Am I that disgusting?"

"What?"

"You won't even look at me."

"No." Shiny, dark brown hair. Eyes as wide and blue as summer sky. Cheeks splashed with such tiny freckles that I want to lean in close just to see them. Barrier. I need that barrier. "Mad. No."

"Forget it, forget I said anything." She skates back to Igor.

I follow, but this time it's me stretching my hand out to her. Once more, we set up for the move. I do what Igor wants. I watch the white of Mad's neck as her head dips backward, let my eyes trail from that perfect collarbone over the bloomed arch of her chest. Mad's circling smoothly around me but my whole world is waterfalling down the storm drain.

On the exit my heart is pounding so loud I can't even hear the music. We present, arms locked out, free legs extended. But I can't stop. I take an extra stroke toward Mad, my face right up to those barely-there freckles. "You're disgustingly beautiful." With my eyes locked on hers, I miss Igor's reaction. But I don't need even a nod to know this time was exactly what he wanted.

"Dismissed," Igor says. "You practice jumps alone now."

I look at the clock on the scoreboard. An entire hour has slipped by.

Mad raises her eyebrows at me. "Want to play triple Axel contest again?"

Neither of us has ever landed a triple Axel and practicing them is a bruise cruise. I'm still feeling unsettled from our lesson, though, the truth making my dance belt uncomfortably tight. I *have* been thinking about Mad. For a long time. Now that Igor's ordered me to unleash those thoughts? It's like trying to stop after eating just one Dorito. Maybe knocking into the ice a few times will knock some sense back into me.

I gesture toward an open space. "Ladies first." Mad takes a couple back crossovers, pushes forward onto her left outside edge, and launches herself into the air. Three revolutions and she's on her butt on the ice but damn, that was close. "You been practicing off ice?"

She stands, brushes the ice shavings off her hip, and . . . busts me looking. She smiles. "Your turn."

I set up my own takeoff. I don't crash, but I pop the jump into only a single. I should be able to get this jump. Mad doesn't say it, but we both know I'm chickenshit. She's the fearless one, and now she's grinning at me as she goes for it again and makes three and almost a quarter revolutions this time, touching her hand down on her landing. And I know, then. It could happen. Today. *Now.* "You got this, Mad," I whisper to her. "Do it again."

She nods, and her face reminds me of her dad, the way he looks on his campaign billboards. Eyes focused, chin set. A look that says you can trust him to get whatever job needs doing done. Mad takes her crossovers. She pushes. She jumps. One-two-three and there's the extra half rotation and on the landing her knee's bent so low she's almost doing a backward shoot-the-duck but by some miracle of anything and everything holy—

She. Stands. Up.

I have officially lost the triple Axel contest. I will never live this down, but I'm so psyched for Mad that I don't give even a bucket of Zamboni sludge. Mad's screaming and I'm screaming and Chris and Kate have forgotten whatever the hell they were fighting about this time. Mad throws her arms around me and I hug her back. Over her shoulder I see Igor watching, *smiling,* as our club mates pile on us in a massive group hug. Mad's landed her triple Axel. I'm not worthy to tie her skates, but for some reason she's still my partner.

No, not some random, unknown reason. In the middle of the celebratory huddle with Mad, her body pressed against mine with her arms around me and her face buried in my neck, I know the reason she's still my partner. And I also know that whatever I do, I can't lose Mad.

3

In the girls' locker room, I turn the shower as hot as it goes and step in. Clouds of steam rise from the spray and I feel like I could rise with them. I landed my triple Axel today. My. *Triple.* Axel.

Once, my brain reminds me. *It's not consistent. And you'll never get credited for it because Gabe can't do one so you won't ever . . .*

It's too late. I'm already lost in my favorite daydream, the one where Gabe and I are on top of the podium at the Olympics, our arms wrapped around each other. I wrap my arms around myself now and lift my chin, pushing my neck forward into the warmth, and I remember the rest of today's insanely awesome practice. So maybe Gabe wasn't sure at first, but it didn't take him long at all to warm up to the idea of *us.*

Don't get ahead of yourself, my brain warns me again. *Gabe hasn't said anything about—*

I freeze the thought out, then rub my shower scrubby over my body the way Gabe's hands touched me today. Some things don't need to be said.

I step from the shower and wrap the softness of my towel around me, blissed out. Then I see Kate huddled on the bench in front of our lockers and I remember how practice started today. I scoot over next to her.

Kate's my best girlfriend and I'm hers, but we're both smart enough to know that a serious skater's true BFF will always be the ice. We don't share everything. Some stuff, especially partner stuff, is better left on the ice. I check in anyway. "Want to talk about it?"

Kate looks toward the showers, but our club mates Regina and Lucy are still going full steam. "You and Gabe are getting a new program. What's your music?"

"*Romeo and Juliet*. But—"

"Fitting." Kate looks at me with red-rimmed eyes. "You've read the play, haven't you? Seen the movie at least?"

"Sure, but—"

"Maddy." Her voice pleads. "Don't forget how it ends."

What, like I'm going to kill myself? Not like Gabe and I are even from feuding families; our moms were college roomies.

"Seriously. Dating your partner is a bad idea."

Didn't stop her from doing it. I turn away, thinking of Gabe's words, how he says their relationship is like learning an Axel. Well, guess what? I landed my *triple* Axel.

When I beat Gabe to the car, I'm surprised. I think about my shower and smile. Probably he's just running behind, enjoying his own steamy thoughts. I lean against his Viper, which must've been waxed recently because it's looking candy-apple shiny, and close my eyes.

The chirp of his car remote startles me. He pops the trunk and I heave my skate bag in next to his. We climb in and he lowers the convertible top but he doesn't say a single word to me. My jacket's still soaked and the summer sun isn't warm enough to cover the breeze as we zip past the cornfields back toward town. I watch the blur of green and gold outside my window and shiver until I can't stand the silence anymore. "Good practice today."

"Unbelievable," Gabe says, so quiet I can barely hear him over the rush of wind.

Then it hits me like a block of ice. I landed my triple Axel first and he's— "Jealous much?"

"Hell, Mad. We're all jealous." Gabe glances at me, then back out the windshield, but I've caught the sad attempt at a smile on his face. My stomach twists. This conversation isn't about my Axel. "It's not you," he says.

I feel like I'm on camera again. But this time, instead of publicity ads for Dad, we're filming a cliché break-up scene. "It's not me," I echo dully.

Gabe's phone jingles a poor imitation of *Let Me Down Easy*. "Get that, please? I'm driving."

Of course he's driving. The Viper isn't a Batmobile with auto-pilot, and it's not like I can drive. But I sit up straight again because I know what that ringtone means, the real reason Gabe wants me to answer his phone. This explains the quiet; he's going out with someone. *Was* going out with someone, anyway. I pretend to gripe. "Seriously? What does this make? Six?"

"Please? She wanted to wear matching outfits so people would know we were a couple. You know I don't do that for anybody but you."

I sigh but we both already knew I was going to answer his phone. I summon my best cheerleader giggle. "Hello?"

Usually, that's enough. There'll be a choked sob, then only the silence of an ended call. The first time it happened, freshman year, it was an accident. Gabe and I had the same ringer on the same phones then and they'd gotten mixed up. Gabe said not to worry about it, that he'd call Kristen back later and explain. I don't think he ever called Kristen back, but somehow our phones magically got mixed up again after Anita.

This time, though, the cheerleader giggle isn't the death kiss. A hesitant girl's voice says, "I'm sorry, I must have the wrong number? This isn't Gabe Nielsen's phone, is it?"

My stomach twinges. Ugh, this one is going down hard. *Why* do they prolong the torture? "This is Gabriel Nielsen's phone." I force another giggle. "Ooh, Gabe, stop it."

The caller hangs up.

"Thanks," Gabe whispers, then goes back to mute.

I flip his phone over and over in my hands. My hip is starting to ache from the first fall I took during today's Axel challenge. But if I'd given up then, I never would've landed the jump. I take a breath and vault my heart into the air. "What do you think of the new program?"

Gabe doesn't look at me. "I think Igor knows what he's doing."

The many cases of medals I have at home think so, too. I narrow my question. "It makes you uncomfortable, doesn't it?"

"It doesn't change anything off the ice."

But it already has. "It's a pretty big change on the ice."

"It won't be the fast, flashy footwork of our last program. The elements Igor had us run through today, the music . . . This is going to be a lot more sustained edge work."

"That's not what I meant."

His eyes still on the road, he says, "I can handle it." He pulls into the shared driveway between our houses and parks in his garage. "Can you?"

My palms are sweating like a Zamboni pouring out water for a wet cut but if that's how he's going to play it, I'm going to have to make a move. With my own belt already unfastened, I lean over and put my hand on his leg, as close to his lap as I dare. "I think you should take me to the back-to-school dance and we'll find out."

Gabe pulls away from me. "We can't do this, Mad."

He wasn't having such a hard time with it an hour ago. "Why not?" I've never seen Gabe get out of the car so fast, and then I see.

Dad is walking into the open garage bay next to the Viper. There's a smile on his face but he clears his throat. "Did you forget something, Maddy?"

Oops. Today wasn't the day for a long shower. I'm late for another publicity shoot with Senator Spier.

* * *

In our kitchen, I spread my textbooks on one side of the island. Even though it's the first week of school, my impressive array of homework isn't an uncommon sight at our house. Dad's crazy proud that I earned an academic scholarship to Riverview Preparatory Academy, but the status means the little time I don't spend at skating practice or school I spend studying.

What is uncommon? Dad standing on the other side of the island, helping Mom chop vegetables for our dinner salads. Behind them on the stove, a pot of fifteen-bean soup simmers. Darting around us, a photographer snaps shot after shot of wholesome American family values.

At least, distracted by the shoot, Dad didn't notice my little stunt with Gabe in the car. For once, I'm glad for his obsession with presenting a picture of our family that could rival John F. Kennedy's Camelot years. I open my calculus book and chew my lip, but I'm not puzzling over integrals and differentials. Even if I could work with the constant clicking and flashing, the ache forming just behind my forehead tells me there was more to Gabe's hasty exit this afternoon than Dad's arrival.

"Chin up," says the photographer, and he adjusts my jaw for his next shot.

I stop biting my lip but I still don't get any work done or figure anything out about Gabe.

The photographer follows us to the dinner table, too, capturing a sight almost as unusual as the kitchen scene. It's not like we eat in front of the TV; family time is pretty important at my house. It's just that usually family time means me and *Mom*. Between legislative sessions in D.C., constituent meetings across our grand ol' state of Kansas, and party conventions, Dad doesn't make a lot of family time anymore.

I don't blame him. When he first won the national Senate seat, we had a big family meeting about where we were going to live and if Mom and I would do some traveling with him. But he understood that I couldn't leave Gabe and Igor. Lots of skaters end up having to relocate to be closer to better coaches or training facilities with more freestyle time, so I'm lucky that I have Igor here. I know my parents would support me if I needed to move for skating, though. Dad doesn't know as much skating trivia as I know political trivia, but he gets it all the same. Sectionals, Nationals, Worlds, just like nominations, primaries, and the final election. Dad's reelection isn't up until next year but already his chances of holding his seat are looking very good.

I keep my chin up through dinner. Across the table from me, Dad picks at his food. I give him my best smile because I know what it's like to have to perform in front of cameras. He's always believed in me and my dream, made me believe I could be Madelyn Spier, world figure-skating champion. I want to support his dream, too. Senator Spier now, President Spier someday.

I'm snuggled in bed later when Mom comes tapping at my door frame. She walks over, smooths my quilt, and sits beside me. "With our big photo shoot earlier, I didn't get a chance to ask about your day."

How ironic—our "family time" photo shoot gave us even less actual family time. I curl on my side facing her, my hands tucked under my pillow. I can't believe I forgot to tell her. I feel the grin stretch over my face and remember how it felt, every muscle in my body fighting to stand up. "I landed my triple Axel."

Mom's hands fly to her face. "You didn't."

"I did." Laughing, I sit up and grab her in a hug.

She squeezes me tight. Mom knows this is a major deal, that even though lots of the top guy skaters do the jump, only two American ladies have ever landed a triple Axel in competition. "I can't believe I missed it," she murmurs into my hair.

"It's okay." It is. I know Mom feels bad that her long hours at her dress shop keep her from watching my practices the way a lot of skater moms do, but I don't want her hanging over everything anyway. I press my face into her shoulder and breathe in the light flowery scent of her perfume before lifting my head and smiling at her. "I'll just have to do it again sometime."

Mom laughs now, a big laugh that sets us both shaking. "Well, I'll have to do something special to commemorate the event. Maybe a new skating dress?"

My other big news. "I'm going to need one. Igor gave us a new program today."

Mom sits back. "No more Mr. and Mrs. Incredible? Are you okay with that? I know how much you loved that program."

Getting to play at being Gabe's girlfriend for more than

ten seconds on the phone? I'm A-plus okay with that. "The new program is cool. It's *Romeo and Juliet*."

Mom smiles again but this time her lips are pressed together funny. She takes a breath. "Maddy, you know your father and I both adore Gabe, but . . ."

Here it comes. There's only one red Dodge Viper in our little town, and I'm not the only one who's been following its traffic patterns.

"He's had a lot of . . . girlfriends," Mom finishes.

Gabe has never stayed with a girl longer than two weeks. Girlfriend isn't the right word, but I don't correct her.

She leans in close and tucks my hair behind my ears. "Don't let him break your heart, okay?"

"I'm not six years old anymore," I tell her. I'm not. But I'm still in love with the boy next door.

Dad walks by in the hall and Mom calls out, "Will, Maddy has some *Axel*-lent news."

Dad peeks around my door frame. "Some triple *Axel*-lent news?"

"So punny, guys," I say. But I'm smiling.

Dad smiles, too. He joins Mom on the edge of my bed. "Can't say I'm surprised, really. 'Courage and perseverance have a magical talisman, before which—' "

" 'Difficulties disappear and obstacles vanish into air,' " I finish for him. "John Quincy Adams, oration at Plymouth, 1802."

"That's my daughter," Dad says.

I kiss my parents good night, fluff my pillow, and settle

down. As I slide into dreamland, there's one thought etched in my brain.

I am my father's daughter. Courageous and persevering, yes, but also determined, dedicated, and driven, just like his campaign slogan. No matter how many times I fall, I get back up and try again. And Gabe's always been right there, ready to catch me. We were meant to be a pair, and I know Gabe knows it, too. All I have to do is get him to see what's already there.

4

Gabe

I'm in bed by nine. Total waste of time; I'm not the slightest bit tired. I toss and turn until I'm so tangled up I can hardly move anymore.

My gut is as twisted as my sheets. Because Igor's right, dammit. As long as I've spent suppressing my thoughts, trying to fool myself into believing it, Mad isn't my sister. If we want to be serious contenders, we can't keep playing around with kid-themed programs. And that's all this is. A program.

Lace your skates right, purrs the devil I haven't been able to shake since practice, *and you might win in more than one way. Have Mad for your skating partner and have . . .* Wrenching myself loose from that thought and my sheets, I get out of bed. I've never stayed interested in a girl longer than two weeks, and I can't break up with Mad.

I grab my history book from my backpack, flip to a random page, and start reading. In class, this gets me from zero to *zzzzz* in under four seconds. Here in my bedroom, I get bored but not tired. Staring out my window, I see Mad's light on behind her curtains and suddenly I'm feeling her hips pressed against mine during our spread eagle. I snap the book closed and flop back on my bed. Me and Mad. How bad would it be, really?

Well, croons my little red cartoon un-friend, *you'd never have time to hang out.* Except for the five hours a day we spend training together. With her living next door and our families' Saturday night tradition, it's near impossible to avoid her. *But she's not that much to look at.* Thin, sleek, and all muscle underneath? She's got the body of an Abercrombie model. *Well, too bad she's not interested.* Yeah, that hand in my lap after practice? Complete coincidence.

I smack myself across the forehead. I've just let the devil play devil's advocate with me. "Senator Spier would slice my balls off with my own skates," I argue with myself.

The mental image is all too clear as something as sharp as toe picks digs into sensitive territory. There's a searing pain in my groin and I crunch up, my hands scrambling for the ball of white fur. I shove my cat, Axel, from my lap.

Axel jumps on the windowsill and nuzzles his face against the glass, purring. "Yeah, you and Mad didn't work out either," I tell him. "You're stuck with me." I pull on a pair of shorts and my athletic shoes, and head downstairs.

As I round the big oak post at the bottom of the staircase, there's blue light spilling out of the living room, beeping machine and rolling gurney noises coming from the TV. I scrunch my nose. Don't Mom and Dad get enough medical drama at work?

"Gabe?" Mom asks as I walk past the doorway. "Shouldn't you be in bed?"

I stop myself from making a snappish remark I'll regret later when I haven't got ice in my tights over this mess with Mad. Mom's right anyway, I have to be up at five. I turn and answer her. "Couldn't sleep."

"Excited about the new program?"

That would be one word for it. "Yeah. My mind keeps running through the new stuff Igor gave us today."

On the other end of the couch, Dad's eyes have glazed over, but Mom smiles. "I always loved learning choreography, too. "

Mom was a junior national champion for Denmark before she traded her skates for a speculum, so she gets it. Usually, that's cool. But choreography isn't what's on my instant replay just now, and even though Mom's the one who paired Mad and me up years ago and would probably be thrilled if I wanted to go out with her, I don't want to share these thoughts. I hold my sigh and start for the basement again. "I'm going downstairs to work out, see if I can tire myself out enough to sleep."

"Gabe?"

I turn back again. "What?"

Mom mutes the TV. "You and Maddy . . ."

Too late. "It's a program, Mom. We're not getting married."

Mom smiles at me. "You already did that, didn't you?"

Stupid six-year-old self. I cut her off before she decides it's a good idea to give me a sex chat again. Once was educational but embarrassing. Even if her specialty is gynecology and she's an expert on girl parts I have no desire to repeat the experience again. Ever. "Make believe." I take my footwork in a straight line for the basement door. Behind me, an ambulance siren screams as Mom turns the TV back up.

Dad installed a sweet gym in our basement with weight machines. They mostly gather dust since I do my strength training at the arena's fitness center or at school and my parents are too busy doing breast exams or brain surgery to work out much. I like free weights better; they require more core work. But machines at home mean I don't need a spotter.

Looks like I get one anyway, though. I'm just finishing a quick warm-up on the treadmill when I see Dad amble down the stairs in a pair of sweats and a T-shirt. "Want some company?"

Even though Dad's voice rose at the end, it's ice clear that wasn't really a question. I shrug an okay and get started with leg presses. I glance over at my dad walking on the treadmill. The rare times we work out together he hits me up right away, wanting to talk hockey or football, but tonight all I hear is the clink of my weights and the hum of the treadmill motor. Dad's not even moving hard enough for me to hear his footsteps and I think I catch him yawning out of the corner of my eye. Yeah, don't need a technical specialist to call that move. Totally un-hidden agenda. "Mom sent you down here to talk to me about sex, didn't she?"

"Who said anything about sex?" Dad continues strolling, but a hint of a smile stretches his mouth. When I don't dignify his question with a response, he shrugs. "Well, if you don't want to talk about sex, what do you want to talk about?"

"Mad landed her triple Axel today." The words blurt out before I even knew I was thinking them.

"Is that a big deal?"

It's the jump *I* should be able to do, not her. But single Axel, double Axel, and now triple Axel, Mad's always been able to do them first. Even Axel the cat was hers first, until he ate a bunch of her mom's sewing supplies. Landing the triple Axel is a major deal. "Most girls don't even try it."

"Sounds like she's a keeper."

"I'm not pairing up with Mad off ice. I don't care how cute Mom thinks it would be."

"Good," Dad says. "That's what Mom's worried about."

Wait a sec. I let the weights clank down. "Mom doesn't want me to go out with Mad?"

The treadmill whines to a halt, then Dad walks over and sits on the bench of the machine next to me. "You and Maddy have been training for, what? Ten years now?"

"Thirteen."

Dad whistles and shakes his head. "Lucky thirteen. You've got more time invested in this partnership than Mom and I spent in med school." He looks at me, thinks for a moment. "Business partners."

"What?"

"You and Maddy are like business partners. Being friends with a business partner is a great thing, but dating?" Dad doesn't finish, but I know what he's thinking. What he's probably been thinking since my freshman year. If I gave up a place on a championship hockey team for figure skating, I damn better be a gold medalist. I might be able to bench 250 pounds, but I'm still the weakest link in this partnership. If Mad leaves me, me and my sorry ass will be a figure-skating nothing.

"I get it. Don't worry."

Dad adjusts the weight pin and swings his legs onto the machine. "So, who are you taking to the back-to-school dance?"

"Alyson," I lie. After Mad answered my phone today, I'm pretty sure Alyson doesn't want to go with me anymore. Dad nods and starts talking football as we rotate through the rest of the machines. Our little chat has put him at ease. But as I mutter "Uh-huh" and "Yeah," I'm thinking *Oh, no.*

I tumble into bed exhausted and sleep like a rock until I wake to the smell of her. I roll over and Mad's here. In my bed. I plant a kiss on her shoulder blade, breathe in the cherry candy scent of her shampoo. She nudges me onto my back, then crawls on top of me. Her hair brushes against my face and she starts kissing my ear.

Beep. Beep. Beep. I swipe at my alarm. "Let's just be late to practice today," I urge.

Mad doesn't protest but keeps kissing my ear. No, licking my ear. I open my eyes wide and see Axel, who slicks my nose with his sandpaper tongue as I turn my head toward him.

I roll onto my back again and groan. A dream. Should've known. Mad would never be cool with being late for practice.

I groan again. Practice. I drag myself out of bed and start getting dressed. In a few minutes, I have to drive Mad to our morning practice. What am I going to say to her? "Why not?" she asked me yesterday in the car. As I finish grabbing my stuff, I make a mental list of why nots:

1. Because my parents told me not to.
2. Because her ex-Navy SEAL father would hurt me.
3. Because I don't want to hurt her.

When I get to the car, Mad's waiting. But she doesn't ask me again. She doesn't say anything about yesterday at all. So I don't, either.

At the rink, I half expect her to pounce on me at any second. She peers at me over the top of her water bottle, a cat debating eating or playing with its food. Her mouth doesn't move but I see her question in the arch of her eyebrows: *Thought you could handle it?* I've never been so excited to see the KGB in my life.

It's not something I'd brag about to the guys at school, but I usually do like the choreographic process. Something about making movement more than movement, arranging motion into style. Taking the blueprint of how Igor wants us to utilize the ice and building it in levels, getting every body line just so.

Today, though, I'm beyond *liking*. We chunk together the new pieces of the program. Hormones, lust, whatever those urges I've got for Mad are, this is my chance to remove them from my system. I let everything out. She soaks it all up. By the end of the session, we have a complete frame of the program. Igor's as close to psyched as it's possible for the KGB to be. "You work hard, this I know, but is looking very natural already."

It's feeling very natural already. But as much as I let out at practice, even more has built up behind it. Thirteen years. I've got to shut this down. Now.

In the car on the way to school, I score myself like I'm performing a program. I give myself plus-two grades of execution on the staring out the windshield element because I don't check out how many buttons Mad's left undone on her uniform blouse. I'm doing really well until I park in the school lot and Mad and I reach for our backpacks at the same time. Her wrist brushes against mine and I have the sudden urge to pull her up against the car. Shaking the Romeo act isn't going to be so easy.

Inside, I slog for my first period class. I could've opted out of PE with a note from Igor, but I like sports. Usually. After last night's workout and this morning's practice, my legs are Jell-O jigglers.

"Hey, Gabe," Chris calls as I waddle to my locker. "I've got a joke for you."

Great. Chris and I have each other's backs. As male figure skaters, we have to. He *is* funny and usually cool to hang around with. But if he's telling a joke, it's guaranteed to be about the last thing I want to think about right now. I bend toward my locker so its door will block Chris's view of me. I plug my ears, reducing his voice to a mumble, and laugh in what I hope are appropriate places.

I miss the punch line. Chris leans around my locker door and catches me with my fingers still in my ears. "You're not even listening!"

"Bug off." I swat at him.

Chris only changes tactics as we check in with the teacher and jog toward the track. "Two words for you, man: *Try it!* You might like it."

My legs are screaming for mercy, and without Mad in them, my arms tingle, too. I liked it the way things *were*. Chris and Kate are recreational skaters. Both of them were struggling with their doubles when Igor paired them up two years ago, not the place to be at age sixteen if you're planning a serious singles career. All of us have a solid foundation in ice dancing. Igor believes the extra edge work gives us a real edge in competitions. He convinced Chris and Kate to make it their primary discipline, but they're still only in it to see how far they can go. They'll never be national medalists.

I shake the prickles from my hands. Mad and I fit each other like perfectly broken-in boots. If one of these times Chris permanently blows things with Kate, he could find another partner easily. I could find another partner, too, but she wouldn't be Mad.

Making an excuse about asking another classmate for the notes from history, I force my aching legs to sprint ahead, leaving Chris and our conversation behind. When Mom warns me about something, I don't worry too much. She's a mom. When Dad warns me, too, I don't know. But if Chris thinks it's a good idea, I might as well go jump off a bridge. Onto a frozen lake.

As my feet pound away on the track, I let my thoughts echo their rhythm. Two weeks. Two weeks. Two weeks. The urge will be gone in two weeks.

5

I shove my skate bag into the hall closet so hard that it tips over.

"Maddy?" Mom calls from the kitchen. "How was practice?"

I right my bag and head for the chopping noises, then pull a bar stool up to the island and raid the diced vegetables on the cutting board. "We've got a couple problem areas to work on." At least one problem area anyway. Once again, Gabe and I practically groped each other for two hours and then I spent the car ride home texting Kate just so the tapping of my fingers would break the silence. He still hasn't answered my "why not" question, but taking the direct approach didn't get me anywhere. I'm not giving up but I know better than to keep practicing with bad technique. "Is Dad eating with us tonight?"

"No, he's doing another Honest Bill segment."

Dad's "Honest Bill" webinars have put him at center ice in the political arena. They're sort of a modern-day version of the famous fireside chats of Franklin Delano Roosevelt, Dad's political idol. Honest Bill, aka my dad, William, posts videos where he explains current legislation on the Senate floor, minus the legislative crap, and tells people honestly what they're trying to accomplish with the bills. Just like FDR had the perfect voice for radio, Dad has the perfect voice and look for video. And maybe I'm bragging on my dad, but the man knows how to dress. He's got this trendy Midwesterner style that somehow makes him still look like just one of the guys, the guy everyone goes to for advice. Thinking I could use some advice right now, I reach for more veggies. "Need any help?" I ask Mom.

"No, I just need to add these to the pot," Mom says as she swats my hand away, "and let it simmer a bit longer. I'm sorry dinner's going to be late today. Things were crazy at the shop."

Crazy at the shop or not, dinner's always late when Dad's away. My stomach grumbles and I sneak another slice of zucchini. "We could always get—"

"A housekeeper, like the Nielsens?" Mom reaches over and ruffles my hair. "We've been over this before. Your father and I want you to develop a good work ethic. And speaking of work, any homework?"

"Always." My stomach grumbles louder. After two hours of practice, diced veggies aren't enough. I grab a yogurt from the fridge.

Mom looks at me, a small smile on her face. "Need a break first?" She nods toward the pile of mail on the counter behind her. "Your magazine came."

"Thanks, Mom." I tug my copy of *Seventeen* from under the stack of envelopes and scan the article titles on the cover as I rummage in the drawer below for a spoon. "Tons of Cute Shoes," "The Best Trends For Your Body." Meh. I think Mom hopes the subscription will inspire me but between skating and school, I don't have much time for fashion, make-up, or hair styles. Then I see the tiny letters across the top: "Love Quiz Blowout!" I tuck the magazine under my arm. "I'll be in my room."

Upstairs, I flop on my stomach on my bed and turn to page eighty-seven. I pour over the article, but the love quizzes aren't what I was hoping for. Who cares what my kissing style is if I'm not kissing anybody? I flip through the rest of the magazine while I eat. There're some cute ideas for sprucing up your room decor and a scary article on eating disorders, but nothing that will help me with Gabe.

There's still at least half an hour until supper, so I turn on my laptop and log on to seventeen.com. Bingo. I click on the "How To Get Your Crush" article. At first there's not much help there, either. "Get to know his interests," advise the Hot Guy panelists. I already know Gabe's hobby inside and out. "Be friends first." Been there, done that. Most of the guys advise girls to play it bold, but I've already tried that and crash-landed.

I'm about to ditch the article when I come across something different. "Play it cool," this panelist cautions. "Never start by showing interest." The next slide explains that most guys like a challenge. Is that my trouble? Could it be as simple as playing hard to get?

I've never liked those girls at school who play mind games, but how many years have I spent waiting around for Gabe while he dates other girls? One of Dad's FDR quotes floats through my brain. *"It is common sense to take a method and try it. If it fails, admit it frankly and try another. But above all, try something."*

Mom calls me for dinner, and I head for the stairs with a little bit of skip to my steps. Maybe playing hard to get will work, maybe not. But—*"One thing is sure. We have to do something. We have to do the best we know how at the moment. If it doesn't turn out right, we can modify it as we go along."*

Our school cafeteria is more of a food court than a lunch line. I take my time at the salad bar and scan the sea of navy blue blazers for Kate, finally spotting her already sitting with Chris. I know I should be happy they're getting along for a change, but it's bad timing for them to be on speaking terms.

I groan. My training schedule doesn't leave much time for friends and spending most of my lunch periods studying in the library doesn't help. It's not like the other girls treat me like mystery meat. Being on TV, even if it's just local news, is a definite popularity boost, but right now I don't want a fan. I want a friend.

My stomach twitches, the way it does every time I try a new jump. I only have to walk across the cafeteria, but still. Do I dare saunter over to Gabe's table alone? What's another day or two? It won't take long before Kate and Chris start giving each other the silent treatment again. I head for the closest cashier.

At the end of the line ahead of me, there's a familiar Celtic-style barrette nestled in long brown waves. That girl sits in front of me in calculus. What's her name again? I realize she's hunched over her lunch tray and, beneath those waves of hair, her shoulders are shaking. She's crying. I step toward her. "Are you all—"

An oversize messenger bag slams into my tray as another girl rushes in front of me. I grab my tipped glass before it smashes onto the floor but the second girl doesn't notice me. She throws her arm around the crying girl. "Alyson, get it together. He's not worth it."

Alyson, that's her name.

Alyson tips her head onto the other girl's shoulder and lets out a wail. "But we had, like, this amazing connection. . . ."

"Uh-huh. The same *amazing connection* he had with Anita. And Kristen."

I step back, not sure I want to hear the rest of this conversation. I've never had to actually see the wreckage from the other end of the phone before. Half of me wants to explain to Alyson; the other half isn't sure it would be any comfort.

Even Alyson's comforter stops making any effort in that direction. The other girl's voice rises in indignation. "Piper. Lisette. And whoever he was with two days after you. You couldn't resist trying the cookies, I get it. We've all heard how good—"

I jet for the other line, the twitch in my stomach growing to a jerk. Alyson maybe should've known better; Gabe's reputation is hardly a secret. Maybe I should know better, too. Do I dare do this at all?

I take my lunch to the library, but I can't study. Instead, I sit at a table by the window and stare out into the courtyard. Wind ripples the leaves on the maple tree and I have a flash of another maple tree. A crack. Tumbling down through the branches, grasping for anything. And then Gabe's arms around me, catching me. Holding me tight even after we hit the ground, his arm bent in a way that an arm should never be bent.

It doesn't make it right, what happened with Alyson, but I'm not Alyson. I'm the girl Gabe's always been willing to wear matching outfits with.

That afternoon after our lesson, I jump triple Axel after triple Axel. I miss a lot of them. The shock of my falls rattles my bones even through my hip pad. I get a wet spot on my tights the size of Wichita, but I don't give up and I land *three* triple Axels. I am fearless. I am not a chicken.

Gabe only tries five, and he doesn't come close to landing even one. Without Igor there to make him do it, he gives up and goes to practice spins instead. He's never going to make a move on his own.

I can't be a chicken.

The next day at lunch, I'm about to head for Gabe's table when I see the corn silk hair and tight red curls. Gabe's cousins, Sara and Louisa, are standing at the condiments station.

I won't be a chicken, but I won't squawk about company, either. I walk over to them.

"Hey, Maddy." Sara waves a ketchup packet at me.

I nod back. "Where are you guys sitting today?" I tilt my head toward Gabe's table. "Want to go bug Gabe?"

Louisa grins. "Always." She looks at Sara checking out Gabe's company and her grin grows. "Gabe's sitting with *Andy*. She's in."

Our school is above having plastic silverware and my fork rattles on my tray as I follow Louisa and Sara across the expansive stone floor. I hold my tray tighter to steady it. Gabe sees Louisa coming first and cocks his head. "What do you want?"

Louisa tosses her curls over her shoulder and laughs. "Nothing from you."

Sara beelines around the table toward Andy, and Gabe's eyebrows arch. He's seen me. I haven't eaten lunch with him at school since sixth grade. He begged off then, embarrassed about the teasing from the other boys that I was his girlfriend. He was over it by seventh grade, but I'd started studying in the library by then. And speaking of studying . . . My chem partner, Jonah, is sitting next to Gabe. The setup couldn't be cleaner. I flash Jonah a gold medal smile. "Mind if we crash your table?"

The result is more than I hoped for. As I slide into one of the two empty chairs next to Jonah, two of the other boys tussle to switch to the remaining seat.

Jonah brushes his straight brown hair out of his eyes. "*Ma chère,*" he says to me.

Louisa swoons a little as she slides into the vacant seat, but Jonah calls all girls *ma chère* and I'm not sure he's actually interested in any of us. He is, however, very interested in being our class valedictorian.

Slipping from French to English as easily as he alternates vacations with his mom's family in Paris with schoolyears here, Jonah continues. "You never called me about—"

"Sorry," I interrupt before Gabe finds out what I was supposed to call Jonah about. I take my phone from my purse and hand it over. "I realized too late I didn't have your number. Put yourself in my favorites list."

As Jonah enters his contact information in my phone, I glance over at Gabe and have to stop myself from flinching. The look on his face—it's like I've thrust Romeo's dagger right between his ribs. For a second, I consider telling him it's just about a school project. But it's for his own good anyway. How can he see how great we are together if he never gives us a chance?

I ignore the twisting deep in my gut. I'm used to putting a smile on my face. I can do it on the ice, sprawled on my rear with my hip screaming in pain. Even though I feel sick, I slap one of those automatic smiles on now and, for maximum effect, turn to the boy on my other side. "Are you going to finish those fries?"

"I'll share." The boy holds a fry out to me at mouth level and I let him feed it to me.

It's squishy and cold and I have to force myself to swallow, but Gabe stands up. His face white, he mumbles something about needing the restroom. Except he takes his tray with him.

I've won this segment, but there's no joy in my victory. Feeling pukey myself, I let Louisa pick up where I've left off with fry guy and I clear my own tray. That went about as well as FDR's court-packing scheme. There's got to be a better way.

6

Gabe

I stare at the blue stall door, pissed at myself for being pissed, and try to chew my bite of sandwich. I dumped my whole lunch before realizing there's no way I can skate the afternoon practice after skipping a meal. But I don't feel like eating the PB&J that our housekeeper, Helen, packed me for an after school snack any more than I felt like finishing my lunch. The peanut butter is sticking to my mouth and the bread tastes so dry I might as well be eating a paper towel from the dispenser.

I shouldn't care if Mad goes out with Jonah. He's a nice guy, and Andy and I've been trying to fix him up with someone. Mad and Jonah should be exactly what I want—then she'll leave me alone. I was never going out with Mad. All the same, this is the closest I've been to the dumped side of the fence. I'm getting a taste of my own medicine and it isn't cherry flavor.

I bang my head against the door and squeeze the plastic bag in my hand. There's a pop and—*splat*—there goes the rest of my sandwich. Headmaster Kohn was quoted once saying that Riverview Prep was so clean you could eat off the bathroom floors.

Well, the Kohn-head can say whatever he wants. I still don't think the two-second rule applies to bathrooms. Screw it. Like I was going to eat it anyway. I pitch the sandwich in the trash.

Outside the bathroom, I almost run into Chris and Kate, tangled together against a row of lockers. Whether or not they're on speaking terms again they're definitely on make-out terms.

I brush past, headed for my own locker because there's no place else to go. When school started, I was bummed that Mad and I only have one class together this year. It's easier doing homework at competitions when we have the same assignments. Now even one class is too many. I feel like skipping, but where would I go? I'm not hanging out in the bathroom for another hour just so the school can call my parents, I can't walk off campus in uniform, and even with the mass of expensive cars in the parking lot the security guards are going to notice if I take the Viper anywhere.

"Gabe?" I turn toward Jonah. "*Eh*, can I talk to you about Maddy? I just—"

I hold my hand up to stop him. "We're skating partners. That's all. Have fun. Go out."

His forehead scrunches and his eyebrows rise. Confused? Nervous? Both? "You think—"

"Yeah, whatever. It's cool." I wave him away. He doesn't leave. I still don't want to go to class but I don't want to stand here looking at Jonah and thinking about him going out with Mad, either, so I trudge off.

Chris catches up to me in the stairwell. "Think this'll be the day she figures it out?"

As quick with this as she is with everything else, Mad's

already figured out how to push my jealousy button, but how would Chris know anything about that?

He waves his hand in front of my face. "Hello? You think Xander's going to give us assigned seats today?"

I relax. "Hell, no. I bet it would take her a month. Think she's going to give us an actual assignment today or just more of that ice-breaker crap?"

Chris rubs his hands together as we hustle up the last few steps. "I hope more ice-breaker crap."

As we enter the classroom, Mad's sitting at a table on the far left side. Her nose is buried in a book. I glance around. No one else is reading, but there are books at every seat.

Chris frowns. "Looks like we're done with the ice breakers."

I point to the back right corner of the room. "Let's grab that table quick before we get stuck in the front."

We dump our book bags and slide into our seats as the bell rings. Chris picks up the book in front of him. "At least this one's been made into a movie."

I look down at my own copy. Clouds cover the front, with boats at sea near the bottom of the picture and what looks like a city behind them. The author's name is printed in capitals across the top: William Shakespeare. My stomach drops. But it can't be, there aren't any boats in . . . Slowly I let my eyes travel down to the title. No. I read it again. It hasn't changed. *Romeo and Juliet.*

"All right now, class. Settle down, please?" Miss Xander stands at the front of the room with her hands clasped on the book in front of her. Her flushed face matches the pink of her sweater. We ignore her request. She repeats it only to be ignored again.

I flip my book upside down. On the back is printed: *This collection serves as a vessel to carry forth the light shed by the greatest writers our world has ever known.* That explains the damn boats. I shove the book to the corner of the table with one finger, then I tip my chair back and rock it on two legs. The longer it takes to get started today, the better.

Chris puts his fingers in his mouth and whistles. "Everybody quiet down!"

The class goes silent, every head swiveling to look at our table. Staring at Chris, I forget about my rocking. My chair tips too far backward and dumps me on the floor. Feeling everyone's eyes on me, I scramble to fix my chair. What the hell? So far, we've gotten at least five minutes of extra chatter a day while Miss Xander tries to gain control. Yesterday, we managed ten.

Chris clutches his book against his chest in a passionate embrace similar to the one he just gave Kate in the hallway. With a smile that stretches so wide it surpasses his ears and threatens to escape his face, he looks at our teacher. "I'm real excited to read this play." And he sounds . . . sincere?

My eyes dart from Miss Xander to Chris and back again. Something's rotten here, even if we're not reading *Hamlet*.

Miss Xander doesn't even correct his grammar. She beams at him. "I'm glad to hear that, Christopher."

Chris stretches his hand straight above his head as the rest of the class continues to stare.

I feel the bits of sandwich I managed to swallow clumping together in my stomach. *No. Please, no.*

Miss Xander is now almost glowing. "Yes, Christopher?"

"Did you know that Gabe and Maddy are skating to music from the ballet of *Romeo and Juliet* this year?"

A veteran teacher would know better than to bite at any bait Chris dangled. Miss Xander? She's filling in for a maternity leave and has a thing or two to learn yet. Her mouth forms a perfect "O." "A teachable moment!" she gushes. "How wonderful, such lovely music! Gabriel and Madelyn, would you do us the honor of reading the scene where Romeo and Juliet meet?" She flips through her own copy, rushing to find the page. "Act one, scene five, beginning with line ninety-three? I'm sure your knowledge of the material will help the class better understand the emotions at play here."

Chris kicks me under the table. "Knowledge of the material? Ha, you want more than knowledge. I bet you'd like to deeply penetrate this material."

I kick him back. "I'm going to kill you," I threaten through clenched teeth. "Right after class, I swear I'm going to beat you to death with this book."

Chris pulls his legs out of my reach, then grins. "Don't be too *hard* on her."

Miss Xander gives us a look over the top of her tortoiseshell glasses. "You may, of course, disregard the stage directions," she says, switching her gaze to Mad.

Chris's hand shoots into the air, but he doesn't wait for Miss Xander to call on him this time. "Can he kiss her if he wants to?"

The rest of the guys howl.

Miss Xander exhales through her nose. "In Shakespeare's

day, the part of Juliet would have been played by a boy. Would you prefer to read for Madelyn, Christopher?"

I slouch in my seat and wish I were an ice cube so I could melt myself into the ground. Two male figure skaters reading a love scene? Sneaking around under the bleachers with his girlfriend, Anita, bought an uneasy ceasefire to Kurt's slurs during sophomore year, but I can already hear him snickering two tables over. If Miss Xander makes me go through with this, not even sleeping with the entire cheerleading squad will keep the hockey players off my back.

Mad raises her hand.

"Yes, Madelyn?"

Mad looks at me. "I think we can handle it."

Miss Xander lets out a breath as big as a gale of wind. "Thank you, Madelyn. Just from your seats will be . . ."

Too late. Book in hand, Mad's already striding to the front of the class.

Mad's move has forced me up against the boards. Now I can kiss her or I can hand Kurt a Sharpie so he can write "Gabe likes boys" on my forehead. The class is so silent I can hear my chair scraping the floor as I stand to follow her.

Focus. Breathe. It's just acting. Just like on the ice. I think of the sports psychologist who did a presentation for our skating club. Can I do this? Yes. I can read. Not like I've never kissed a girl before. I force myself to inhale as I join Mad at the front of the class. The rustling of my book's pages is loud enough to give me a headache, but I find the line Miss Xander indicated. I clear my throat. "If I profane with my unworthiest hand . . ."

I take Mad's hand, lift my eyes to hers, and the hopelessness of my situation slams into me like a full-out hockey cross-check. My mouth is moving, somehow the words are coming out, but all I can feel is the softness of her hand in mine.

Mad's answering, then she isn't. I have to read the next line. "Have not saints lips, and holy palmers, too?"

She smiles. "Ay, pilgrim, lips that they must use in prayer."

No prayer will save me now. "Thus from my lips, by thine my sin is purged." I lean toward her, my heart a traitorous hockey player pounding against the penalty box of my ribcage. I let my lips brush hers. The lightest feather kiss, but I want so much more.

"Then have my lips the sin that they have took."

Mad steps on my toes and I realize the scene isn't over yet. I have to kiss her again. Acting, acting, acting, my mind screams at my body but I've used all my willpower restraining myself on that first kiss. This second kiss is an explosion of energy, a toe pick vault into oblivion, leaving my mind spinning with no thought of checking out.

Mad has to come up for air first. "You kiss by th' book," she says, her words coming out in gasps.

It's not a thunderstorm brewing outside, it's our classmates giving us a standing ovation. "Bal-co-ny! Bal-co-ny!" come the cheers. Kurt stands, too, but his arms hang loose at his sides.

Miss Xander gives us all a silent reading assignment for the rest of the period.

As our teacher pops a fistful of ibuprofen, Chris flicks a note at me. I open it to see the beginnings of a game of hangman with some of the words already filled in: FRIENDS WITH _ _ _ _ _ _ _ _.

I don't bother filling in BENEFITS. I draw myself hanging from the noose. I don't touch my lips. I don't look at Mad. This is lust. Just lust. It'll fade. I'm already four days into my two-week countdown.

I flip the paper over. I make my own game on the back: _. I fill in the answer. ONE WEEK AND THREE DAYS.

Next day, Friday, Chris asks after practice, "What're you up to this weekend?"

I shrug. I've been thinking about a lot of things, but for once the weekend ain't one of them. "Family stuff on Saturday as usual."

"That's right, I forgot. You're going to spend some *quality* time with Maddy."

With Mad and both sets of parents. Yes, that's right. I *want* parental supervision. I need a distraction. Maybe checking out the scenery at our favorite coffee shop? "What about tonight, want to go to Cappi's?"

"Nah, not tonight. I had to give her my gaming system, but Kate forgave me and we got plans. Some more moves to practice, if you know what I mean." He elbows me.

I leave before I'm subjected to any more of Chris's Trojan tales. Mad doesn't say anything about English class on the ride home. She texts while I drive but I hear her new message tones going off over and over and the occasional giggle. What is going on with her? First she pretty much propositions me, then she ignores me, then she flirts with my friends, then she makes me kiss her?

Mad giggles again.

"What's so funny?" It comes out more snappish than I intended.

"What's brown and sticky?"

A poop joke? Are we six years old again? "Shit."

"No." She laughs. "A stick."

"That's completely lame."

"That's the whole point. Why was the tomato blushing?"

"I don't know. Why?"

"I don't know, either."

"Then why—"

"Hold on, Kate's going to text me the answer." Her phone chimes. "Because it saw the salad dressing."

Maybe that was a teeny bit funny; maybe I've just decided it's better pretending we're six again. I let myself laugh. "Tell me another one." I still don't know what's going on, but it's working for now.

When I get home, Mom and Dad are in the dining room talking. "It doesn't look good," Dad says. "I really wish they'd—"

Mom interrupts. "You think we should talk to Cynthia?"

"I think . . ." Dad trails off as he looks up and sees me coming. "Hi, Gabe."

What are they worried about that they need to talk to Mad's mom? If this is about me and Mad—

Dad clears his throat. "I thought you were going to the back-to-school dance tonight?"

Crap, that was tonight. "Um, I was . . . but Alyson's sick."

"Why don't you take Mad?" Mom says. "You can just go as friends."

This is a test or they want me out of here, bad. Either way, "Not going to happen." Double crap. That's what Jonah was so nervous about. No way I'm going to the dance now. "Mad already has a . . . date."

"Why didn't you tell me about Mad's Axel?" Mom asks.

"I forgot, I guess. I'm going upstairs."

In my room, I sit at my desk and stare across our side yards at Mad's curtains. Enough time slips by that I dare to hope I was wrong. Then the car pulls up in front of her house. There's no mistaking Jonah's sky-blue antique boat on wheels. Mad darts out her front door, wearing a hip-hugging skirt and a new, red halter with a sweater cinching her waist. Jonah eases the car door shut behind her but I slam my hand against the window frame. As the smooth hum of the motor fades away, I grab my keys and head for Cappi's.

Even with a school dance competing for business, the place is packed. Guitars and drums from tonight's band boom from the corner. I elbow my way to the counter, order a latte, and stand near the back, surveying the crowd. It's easier than I expected. The redhead sidles up to me before I've taken one sip. With her silver tank top, super skinny jeans, and black stilettos, she looks more ready for a club than a coffee shop.

"Is it always this crazy in here?" she shouts over the noise.

I nod. Tonight isn't going to be about talking.

"You're Gabriel Nielsen, aren't you?"

I nod again, even though only Igor, my teachers, and reporters call me Gabriel.

She flips her long, straight hair behind her shoulder, making her oversize hoops dance, and yells back her name.

I don't catch it and don't care. Tonight isn't going to be about names, either. Half an hour later, she's in my car at Miller's Point, the top up and the windows fogged over.

My arms and hands are stiff. And the part of me that should be? Isn't. This shouldn't be so much work, but I can't stop thinking about Mad. I groan.

"You like that?" Whatever her name is, her hand's on my crotch.

I stop, pull away from the too-tan skin. "I can't do this."

She laughs, making that shiny red hair and those silver hoops shimmy. "So modest." She pulls me back toward her, whispers, "You're doing a pretty good job so far."

No. I sit up. "It's just . . . too fast. I don't want to ruin things."

She sits up herself, reaches for her pants. She pulls them on and frowns. "I think you just did."

7

Maddy

The next morning after practice, I swing my legs into Gabe's car and snag something on my sneaker. I bend over, stretch forward, and see fuchsia. A *very small* piece of fuchsia fabric, emblazoned with the words PARTY GIRL. Panties. There's another girl's underwear hanging from my shoelace.

I blink hard, remove PARTY GIRL from my sneaker with the tip of a nail, and flick it back under my seat. "Guess you were busy last night. At least one of us had fun."

"You went out with Jonah," Gabe accuses. "I saw you leave."

"You were spying on me?"

"I got better things to do."

"Evidently." I wrinkle my nose at the thought of what's under my seat and don't care if I sound as sarcastic as I am. "Not that it's any of your business, but you can be sure I'll be telling all the girls what a rocking good time I had with Jonah—conducting research for our chemistry project in the stacks at the college library."

Gabe opens his mouth, closes it, then opens it again. "Sorry."

"Don't sweat it, I'm not your girlfriend. Though I pity the owner of the underwear under my seat. Because I'm pretty sure, Mr. 'I've got better *things* to do,' that those panties belong to a *person*."

"I know that, Mad."

"Let me down easy . . ." sings Gabe's phone.

Unreal. I watch Gabe's mouth start to open again, sigh, and reach for his phone. I stop, remembering Alyson. No. I'm done.

Saturday night is "families" night, every Saturday night, and for years I've enjoyed the tradition that my parents and the Nielsens started before either Gabe or I were born. Tonight though, I'd rather practice my triple Axel for two hours without a hip pad. It'd be less painful than even being in the same room with Gabe.

Mom gives Mrs. Nielsen a sideways hug as they sit across the dinner table discussing costume possibilities for the new program. "I'm thinking silk chiffon. Layered, of course, with an empire waist?"

"Definitely, it'll be perfect with the music." Mrs. Nielsen sighs. "I always wanted to skate to *Romeo and Juliet*."

I push my chicken marsala around on my plate and try not to gag on the bite already in my mouth. Normally, I'd eat this conversation up. Put on the music, make Gabe do a walk-through of the program with me to humor our parents.

But tonight the program only makes me think of Gabe, and the thought of Gabe only makes me think of PARTY GIRL. "So who's up for Yahtzee?" I ask in an attempt to end the sap-fest.

"Oh, no games tonight, sweetie," Mom says. "Didn't I tell you? Your father and I rented *Shakespeare in Love* in honor of the new program."

In the living room, our parents claim their usual spots, leaving me and Gabe to the love seat. It's a routine we've practiced hundreds of times before, squishing a popcorn bowl between us and sometimes even sharing a throw blanket over our legs. But tonight Gabe sits all the way against the left arm while I press myself against the right. The popcorn sits in the no-man's land between us, untouched.

I pull my legs up tight against myself, wrap my arms around them, and stare straight at the screen, forbidding my usual sideways glances at Gabe. My throat is dry and my eyes threaten to water. I can't get that stupid underwear out of my head. I am. Such. An. Idiot. I'm not Gabe's girlfriend and I never have been. But I know exactly how many flings he's had; I broke up with every one of them for him. And why? Because I was so desperate I was willing to take *ten seconds?* Of *pretending* to be his girlfriend?

Mom pauses the movie for wine refills. With our parents in the kitchen, the silence looms between us like a glacier. I think about Gabe in the cafeteria and am sorry I confessed my "date" with Jonah was only for studying, because right now I want Gabe to hurt like I'm hurting.

Gabe whispers something so quietly I can't understand

him. Whatever. I'm not interested in anything he has to say right now. But he whispers again, louder this time. "I'm really sorry, Mad."

I move to turn my entire body away from him and my backside collides with the popcorn bowl.

"Jeez!"

I twist back to look at him. The entire left side of the love seat is covered with popcorn and it's all over Gabe's lap. It's only the light butter kind but still. Mom is going to kill me. "Hold still." I start scooping popcorn back into the bowl.

Gabe brushes my hands away from his lap. "It's okay, I've got it."

"Don't move, you'll get even more grease on the upholstery." I start picking out the kernels that are stuck in the crack between his legs.

He stands up and moves away from me, dumping a pile of popcorn onto the rug. "Stop. It." His hands are clenched into fists and the entire back of his neck flames.

"Oh, come on. You think I did that on purpose?"

Gabe spins around and glares at me. "Yeah. Putting your hands in my lap, playing Chris's stunt in English so I had to kiss you, pretending you had a date with Jonah. You did all of that on purpose. We can't do this, do you understand? The Romeo and Juliet crap has to stay on the ice. I'm not getting involved with you."

Screw the grease stains. I stand and glare back. "Tell me how you really feel."

He looks away from me and presses his hands to his head, his fingers gripping his hair. "It's not you."

I've heard that line before and I cross my arms over my chest. "Oh, it's not me? That's right, it's not me, it's you. About time you did your own break-ups, you're not half bad at it. Except most people actually *date* before they break up with someone."

He drops his hands and his eyes meet mine. "You see what Chris and Kate are like. You want that to be us? Wasting half our practice time fighting and hoping maybe someday we'll get to Junior Worlds?"

We've already been to Junior Worlds, multiple times, but it doesn't seem the time to remind him. I drop my own arms to my sides. "We're not Chris and Kate," I say softly.

"You're right. We're not. Because we've kept our partnership to the ice." He softens his tone as well. "I don't want to hurt you. Look what happened this morning. We're fighting already. I hurt you already, Mad."

I feel the wet in my eyes again at that name. Mad. Gabe's special nickname for me, because I'm "mad" about skating. Mad about you, too, I want to shout. But I know I won't be able to stop the tears if I so much as whisper those words aloud, and I am not going to cry. Instead I sink back into the love seat and study my hands in my lap. "Who was she?"

"I don't know."

I'm not trying to be smart. "You seriously don't know?"

"Seriously." He tips my face up to look at his, cupping my chin in his fingers.

Can't he feel this? How right this is?

"You know me, Mad. Probably better than anyone."

And he knows me. He has to know we're so right for each

other. I feel his thumb hop along my cheek. His fingers are shaking.

"You know what I do. I'm a screwup. I'm bad news. You deserve better than me." He blinks hard and his voice trembles. "Don't make me hurt you like that."

I pull my chin from his hands, immediately missing the warmth of his touch.

Gabe puts one hand on my arm and I look up at him. He wipes the back of his other hand against his cheek, then extends his pinkie finger to me. "Promise?"

I look at his pinkie, then back into his eyes. "I love you," I whisper.

Gabe's arms drop to his sides again. "Don't, Mad. Please."

"No." I choke back my own sob. "I love you. Enough to let you be, if that's what you want." I stand and link my own pinkie with his. "We'll leave it at practice."

Gabe turns and runs. He crashes into his father in the doorway. Mr. Nielsen looks down at the red wine stain spreading across the front of his white shirt. He spins toward the hall. "Gabe!"

"I think he's going to be sick." My voice is shaking along with my knees. I sway on my feet as Mr. Nielsen turns back to look at me.

He makes it to me just in time. "You look like you're about to be, too. Cyn? Will?" He eases me down to the love seat.

Dad sticks his head around the doorway. "What's going—?" He hurries over. "Maddy, are you all right?"

Not going to cry, not going to cry, not going to cry. "I don't feel good."

Mom appears over Dad's shoulder. "Doesn't look as though Gabe does, either," she says. "You two must have shared some sort of bug. I thought you seemed off."

I let Dad scoop me up in his arms. I nuzzle my head into his shoulder but it doesn't fit the way it did when I was little. Saturday stubble scratches my forehead when I want the feather-light brush of Gabe's waves.

Dad carries me upstairs. It's been years since he's carried me anywhere and, even though he did a stint as a Navy SEAL before college, his arms are shaking by the time he lays me in my bed, clothes and all. He pulls the covers up to my chin and kisses my cheek. "Everything will be better in the morning."

I turn on my side and curl my body into a ball as Dad clicks off my light and eases my door shut. I scrunch my eyelids, but no amount of dark can hide what happened tonight. Gabe ran away from me. So maybe that's his usual act with girls, but not with me. Never with me. After all these years, what if I lose Gabe?

I don't want to go dress shopping Sunday afternoon. On the rare occasion I do need a dress, Mom makes it. But I need to get away from my house for a while and Kate wants to shop for the fall formal. So I grab a couple dresses off the rack and slip into the dressing room next to her. We come out and model in front of the mirror. "What do you think?" Kate asks.

I study myself. "Meh."

"Yeah, that's what I thought, too." Kate looks at her own reflection and pinches her flat stomach through the fabric.

"Not your dress," I say. "Mine. You look great, Kate."

"No, this dress makes me look fat. Next."

It takes me a minute to realize I've gotten the next dress all the way on. It's actually comfortable. I tie the halter, then lift my eyes to the changing room mirror. I draw in my breath. This is why they say every girl needs a little black dress. I look . . . hot. No, not hot. I look sizzling. The deep neckline somehow gives the illusion that I have cleavage and the flare at the hips makes me look way more curvy than I am. I step out and twirl in front of the three-way.

"Oh my God, Maddy," Kate says. "That dress was made for you."

I stroke my hands down the smoothness of the fabric at my sides. "Too bad I'm not going."

"You have to get it anyway. Maybe somebody will ask you." Maybe. But the person I want to go with doesn't want to go with me.

My phone rings in my bag and I scramble for it. Mom was going to call before she came to pick us up. But it's not Mom. Jonah Hvalbard flashes on the screen. "Jonah? What's up?"

He doesn't call me *ma chère* this time. Instead, he pronounces my name in French, making it sound like a song. "*Bien, Maddy.* I had a super time, at the library? And I was wondering, do you, perhaps, want to go to the fall formal with me?"

Smart, cute Jonah, with his fabulous French voice, likes girls. Likes *me.* I look at Kate. "He just asked me to the fall formal," I mouth.

"Go!" she mouths back, giving me a double thumbs-up.

"Okay, sure," I tell Jonah. It's most of the money I've been saving for two months, but I buy the dress.

When I get back from the mall, Dad's packing for D.C. I sit straddle position on my parents' bed and stretch while I watch him line up his socks just so in his suitcase. "Why do you bother? They'll get all tossed around during the loading and unloading, anyway."

He carefully places his electric razor next to the socks and starts laying garment bags on top of them. "Probably because I like to think that anything worth doing is worth doing right." He transfers the rest of his categorized piles into his bag and zips it shut. He leans over toward me and plants a kiss on my forehead, then grabs the bag from the bed and heads for the door. I trail after him. "What if doing something means . . . taking a risk?"

Dad stops and looks back at me. "Every great gain we've made has come from taking risks, Maddy. 'The only thing we have to fear is fear itself.'"

"Franklin Delano Roosevelt, inaugural address, 1933." He smiles at my answer and I throw my arms around him. "I love you, Daddy."

"Love you, too. See you later, figure skater."

And the Sena-*tor* is out the door.

Something's tickling my cheek and I reach to push my hair out of my face. When I pull my hand away, though, a strand of Dad's hair is stuck to it. I look at the brown changing to gray. He just left and I miss him already.

I let the strand fall to the ground, thinking about Dad's words. Jonah is cute and smart. He's a nice guy and a great chemistry partner. I had a better time at the library than I let on to Gabe, but I didn't have a super time. Even with that fabulous French voice singing my name, there's no chemistry between us. It's a big risk, but I still want Gabe. And if I go to the formal with Jonah, I'm not doing things right. I pull out my phone.

8

Gabe

I wobble my way through the week, feeling as though any moment I could lose my edge. But Mad keeps her word. Outside of practice she doesn't touch me, talk to me, or even look at me. The silence is awkward but still a relief. My two weeks are about up. Mad and me, we'll find our balance again.

Saturday, we're all cooling down at the barre after ballet class when Igor walks in. He goes hush-hush in the corner with our instructor. With Igor's hand on her shoulder, Ms. Rasgotra smiles and nods.

Chris slides down the barre, moving next to me. "See that?" he whispers. "Bunhead *smiled*. Ten bucks says good old Igor's tapping—"

"Stop," I hiss back. Like our coach, Ms. Rasgotra's never going to win a medal for her sense of humor. Chris's nickname for her is less about the tight bun she always wears and more about her anal retentivity concerning order in her classes.

"Gabriel!" Ms. Rasgotra's sharp voice cuts through the air.

"Come here." I'm plotting my revenge on Chris when she adds, "You also, Madelyn. Everyone else is excused."

Swinging my leg from the barre, I breathe a sigh of relief. If Ms. Rasgotra needs Mad, too, I'm clear.

Ms. Rasgotra waits for us to approach. "Igor tells me you are skating to Prokofiev's *Romeo and Juliet* this season."

We nod.

"Did you have plans for this evening?"

I wiggle my toes against the worn leather of my ballet slippers. "Our families usually have dinner together on Saturday nights." I clasp my hands together behind my back and bow my head. *Please give me an excuse, any excuse, to get out of it,* I mentally bargain with any higher powers that might hear my plea.

"See if your parents will excuse you," Ms. Rasgotra says.

I look up and send a silent thank-you heavenward an instant too soon.

Ms. Rasgotra looks at me. "Igor would like you both to have a sort of . . . extra practice. The Russian National Ballet is presenting *Romeo and Juliet* in Wichita tonight. He asks that you attend the performance." She holds two tickets out to me. "Enjoy. They are excellent seats."

I take the tickets and, under my breath, the Lord's name in vain.

"It shouldn't be a problem, Ms. Rasgotra," Mad says. "Thank you."

Thanks for nothing. I drag my feet to the car.

At home that evening, my suit jacket is hot and scratchy. I fidget with it for the tenth time. "You're sure I have to wear this?"

It takes a lot to rattle my mom, but I've crossed the blue line into the offensive zone. She looks at me sideways and blows air over her upper lip hard enough to make her bangs rise. "Go and get Maddy already, you're driving me nuts with that squirming."

"She lives next door, she'll walk over like she always—"

"You know, I'm glad that you're not interested in Maddy, but you're still taking her out for a nice evening. Please don't embarrass me, Gabriel Thomas."

My stomach churning, I head outside. I eye the walk to Mad's front door as though headed for the gallows I drew myself hanging from. Then I force my stomach contents back down my throat and my feet up her porch steps. I ring her doorbell.

Mad answers.

I stare. Her little black dress brings new meaning to the word little, its plunging halter neckline accentuated by dangling earrings and a simple diamond pendant that draws my eyes down her body. Her hair's been swept up into a mass of curls, leaving her shoulders temptingly bare. "You look . . . incredible."

Mad ducks her head and bites her bottom lip, the corners of her mouth turned up in the smallest smile. Her cheeks flush. "Thanks."

I bite my own lip. I shouldn't have said anything. The last thing I need is for Mad to start thinking this is a— "This isn't a date."

Mad blinks at me. Shit, I really shouldn't have said anything. "No. No, of course not. It's just . . ." She stops and smiles. "Practice."

Mrs. Spier sticks her head around the corner. "We're going out with Gabe's parents," she says to Mad. "Do you have your key, just in case? We might not be home until late." Mad nods and her mom continues. "Enjoy yourselves, then, you two."

"Sure thing, Mrs. Spier." I hustle Mad out the door, cursing Igor for roping me into this night of torture.

In the car, Mad slides a copy of our music into the CD player, saying it'll help set the mood. Sadly, it does. At least driving gives me an excuse to keep my eyes on the road and off her, and the music means we don't have to talk.

An usher in a black tux shows us to our seats in the theater. I scratch under my collar again. I'm underdressed in this damn suit. The man leads us farther and farther upstairs and finally opens a door and I see a very private, very dark box. Not my idea of excellent seats. At least no one will see me ditch this stupid jacket.

Feeling even more stifled, I undo my top shirt buttons and loosen my noose of a tie. I still feel like I'm choking. As the orchestra warms up and the lights dim, I sit ramrod straight in my chair, hands folded in my lap. I can see just a shadow of Mad's profile against the lights from the stage, but I can smell her next to me. She smells incredible, too.

Mentally, I try to replace her scent with the stench of gym socks. This only makes me think of a locker room and Chris's earlier comment: Try it, you might like it. I don't have to try any more of her to know I'd like it. The brief taste from English was enough.

"Did you see our parents?" Mad asks. "All geeked about going out by themselves? Like it never occurred to them we could stay home without them?"

I don't want to think about being at home alone with

her, either. Vaguely aware that the ballet's started, I study the ornamental details on the railing and try to think of something, *anything*, else.

"Check that out." Mad gestures to the dancers. "Are those guys flexible or what?"

She's quite flexible herself, especially in my imagination.

"You know, Igor told us to come here." Mad leans in closer to me. "Ms. Rasgotra said he wanted us to have an extra *practice*."

Shit, double shit.

Make that triple shit. Side-by-side triple shit. This is about as good of an idea as stepping onto the ice with my skate guards still on, and I can already see the crash coming. I make a pathetic attempt to stall. "I'm . . . too tired."

"You're not tired." Mad finds my face and then my arm in the dark.

In self-defense, I cut back at her. It's for her own good. "Yeah, I am." I fake a yawn and stretch away from her. "I went to Cappi's last night, stayed out too late."

"No." Mad takes my hand. "You're afraid." She pulls my arm around her and nestles her head against my shoulder. "Admit it, I'm scaring you."

It's her who should be scared, always too fearless for her own good. On the ice that recklessness serves her well. But off? I stiffen. "You promised."

"To leave it at practice." She reaches her hand to my leg again. "That's all this is."

The orchestra comes to a crescendo. Suddenly I'm a worn skate lace and I snap. In an instant, my mouth is on hers. Hard. I pull her onto my lap so she's straddling me, that little dress barely covering her. I want to frighten her, but my rough hands on her sides only scare me even more. They have a mind of their own as I pull her tight against me, let her feel what she does to me. "Is that what you want?"

Mad kisses me back, as gentle as I was rough.

I pull my hands from her. "I'm sorry," I say, unsure if even that's the right choice of words.

"Mm-hm. I'm not," she whispers, her lips moving to my neck as she puts my hands back against her hips.

Carefully this time, I let my fingertips revisit where they forced before. The music softens and I mirror it, feeling Mad's skin warm against my mouth. We're not going to see any more of the ballet.

9

The air in the car on the ride home from the ballet feels charged, like I'll light up a static flash if I so much as look at Gabe. As he pulls into the driveway, both our houses are dark except for the kitchen lights that are always left on. Neither of our parents are home yet.

Gabe could walk me up to the front door, where he picked me up, but he doesn't. He doesn't just head for his own house either, the way he does after our normal practices. Instead, walking so close that our hands almost touch, he escorts me to the side entrance to my house. Behind the hedges he lets his fingers graze the side of my hip. His eyes drop from looking at mine to looking at my dress straps, and his other hand slides to where they're tied at the back of my neck. "Mad," he says, his voice hoarse.

Our private box was still in public. If Gabe comes in with me, though, we're not going to be able to stop. I let him draw me closer, bringing my lips within a fraction of an inch of his. "Save it for Monday morning," I whisper, then slip away from him and into my house without even a good-night kiss.

I close the door fast and sink down against the wall, my heart pounding. My insides spin with thoughts of Gabe's hands at the back of my neck and against my hips. Practice, date, whatever tonight was, Gabe clearly wasn't ready for it to be over and every one of my own skin cells is whimpering that I wasn't either. Only—

Give 'em what you promised, Dad says. Since he started his political career as Riverview's youngest mayor, fresh out of college, he's held fast to his campaign rule. And I promised to leave it at practice. *Things do not happen. Things are made to happen.* JFK. It's time for Gabe to make a move.

Sunday, the day of rest. Or, in my case, with five hours of practice on top of a full school day as my weekday routine, the day of homework. And seeing how I skipped Igor's assignment last night to watch the ballet, I need every minute. After church, I rush through my math and skip English because, even though it's my favorite subject, I do already know how *Romeo and Juliet* ends. Then, just to be safe in case Igor has any questions, I watch the entire ballet on YouTube. Most of it, anyway. It's hard, because the music keeps making my mind drift, making me think of the places Gabe's hands drifted to while we were alone in that private box. I look out my window at his and wonder if he's thinking about the same things.

If he is, he doesn't say anything about it. He doesn't call or text me, doesn't say anything Monday morning on our drive to the rink. We warm up in silence, then I stand with my hands folded behind my back and a small knot in my stomach as Igor approaches us. His eyes pierce me first, then switch to Gabe. And what's that expression on his face? Almost the beginnings of a smile? "You enjoyed tickets?" he asks.

Gabe coughs into his elbow. "Um, yes. Yes, sir."

Heat flames in my chest.

The corners of Igor's mouth twitch up the tiniest bit more. "A beautiful performance, I am sure. And now, the program, please."

Gabe takes my hand and we skate to the middle of the rink. He gives my fingers a quick squeeze. "You were nervous."

I let out my breath and a little laugh along with it. "I watched the entire ballet on YouTube on Sunday," I confess. "But I wasn't sure I'd be able to keep a straight face."

Gabe releases me and kneels on the ice. "In the end, he only cares if it makes the skating better or worse."

The music begins. I feel Gabe's hands at my waist as he lifts me for our opening triple twist. I pull tight in the air, wanting only his hands catching me again. Igor watches our long program and nods in satisfaction. "Is better each day, yes? You match mood of music nicely."

The program is getting better each day. Every time we skate it, the longing is fresh and raw again, the need growing deeper. When Gabe looks at me now, I can see he's reliving the ballet, too. He pushes the limits of every touch, his hands lower on my back, his face so close to mine on our end pose that he'd be kissing me again if he were any closer.

But he doesn't say anything about our "extra practice."

From the moment we step off the ice each day, he holds me to that pinkie-swear promise. He doesn't touch me. He doesn't talk to me. He doesn't even look at me. Evidently, practice is practice.

Wednesday after skating and ballet, I walk into the kitchen at home. Nothing's even started for dinner. I open the fridge. There's a half-full bottle of ketchup and a not-quite-empty gallon of milk. I twist the top off the milk and start to pour myself a glass, but I catch a whiff of eau de hockey. I dump it and go looking for Mom upstairs.

I hear her talking in her sewing room and head down the hall. Through the doorway, I see her on the phone. "I love you. I love you so much. And I'm thinking right now about holding you—"

My fingers fly into my ears. I'm glad Dad's missing Mom and not cuddling up to some other woman, but I don't need to hear my parents having phone sex. Even with my ears plugged, though, I hear the horrendous creak of the floorboard as I step backward. I stuff my hands in my pockets and start walking faster, but—

"Maddy? Dad's on the phone."

I gathered that much. I wipe the wince off my face before I turn around.

Mom holds her cell out to me. "Want to say hi?"

"Hi, Dad," I say without even taking the phone. "Um, I actually wanted to see if it was okay for me to go over to Kate's?"

"One sec," Mom says into the phone, then she turns her attention to me. "That's fine. Are you going to eat over there?"

I don't know, I haven't been invited, but there's nothing to eat here so I say sure. I book it downstairs, texting Kate.

Kate's dad and stepmother are out of town for her stepsister's gymnastics competition, so she's glad to hang out. She apologizes that there's only carrot sticks and tofu rolls for dinner but it doesn't bother me. It's better than ketchup. "Did you find a dress yet?" I ask her as we settle ourselves at her kitchen table.

"About that. I heard you backed out on Jonah. Don't tell me you're still thinking of pairing up with Gabe."

Not quite the response I was looking for. "You said it was a bad idea. Why do you and Chris do it, then?"

"Because he's a guy and that's mostly what they think about, that's why."

Holy toe picks. So maybe I've heard a whisper here or there at school, but I always assumed it was typical Chris running his mouth off. I can't believe she never told me. "Wait a sec, you guys actually . . . do it. *It?*"

"What did you mean?"

I have so many more questions for her now, but, "Why do you guys date, if it's such a bad idea?"

"Because we started ice dancing together and dating at the same time. It's always been that way for us. You see what it's like, though. I know what it looks like. It's personal, for good and for bad. But Chris and I, we aren't going to Worlds or anything. I don't even know if we'll be together next year. I mean, I'm looking at schools in New York. California."

That's why they're fighting so much lately. "You don't know if you'll even stay together with Chris. But you slept with him?"

"It's just sex." She doesn't look at me.

Is she sorry she did it? I would be. I always figured I'd wait. When I do lose my virginity, I want it to be with someone special. I want it to be about forever. "What's it like?"

"It hurt the first time." She draws her knees up to her chest, balancing her feet on the edge of her chair, her shins pressing against the edge of the table. "It gets better after." She smiles a teeny bit. "Chris isn't so much for practice at the rink. Other areas, he's more interested in improving his technique."

"The first time . . . did you know you were going to?"

"After our first competition, there was . . . an emotional high, you know?" She shrugs. "Or maybe you don't. You win all the time, but I hadn't been on the podium in three years. And there we were. Silver medalists. I didn't mean to. I wasn't going to. But . . . we sneaked into Chris's hotel room. We were just fooling around and it got out of hand. It's so easy, Maddy. Especially with . . ."

She looks right at me then, her smile fading out, and I know she's not talking about Chris anymore. It's so easy. Especially with Gabe.

Saturday, Igor wraps up our lesson by presenting us with a DVD of Shakespeare's tragic pair. "Ms. Rasgotra tells me your families usually dine together Saturday evenings. Perhaps you can watch this after?"

Gabe takes the DVD from Igor. "Yes, sir. No problem."

No problem? Watching this with our parents will be as much fun as trying to wash stinky hockey equipment. Because *Romeo and Juliet* only makes me think of the program, and the program only makes me think of Gabe. Thoughts I don't want to be thinking in front of our parents.

At Gabe's house that night, though, his father takes one look and laughs. He holds the DVD case out to Gabe's mother. "Jensine, take a look at this!"

She squints at the cover. "It can't be!"

Mr. Nielsen hands the movie back to Gabe. "Your mother and I watched this in our senior English class." He laughs. "Of course, it was in filmstrip form back then."

"Correction, dear. *You* watched this in our English class. *I* watched you." Mrs. Nielsen pecks her husband's cheek.

He turns to kiss her on the lips. "Thank goodness for alphabetical seating and boring movies or you never would've noticed me."

I feel my chest flutter. Because just maybe—

Mrs. Nielsen hands Gabe the bowl of popcorn. "Why don't you and Maddy take this in the family room?" She beckons to my parents. "Cyn, Will—this way to Margaritaville!"

"But, Mom—" Gabe protests.

Mrs. Nielsen's face is set. "You're not getting one, Gabe."

Mr. Nielsen claps Gabe on the back. "Only four more years," he jokes, following the others to the kitchen.

I turn and walk toward the family room with my hands

shoved into my pockets. He wasn't so disappointed to be alone with me last week. I slump onto the couch and build a wall around myself with throw pillows.

Oblivious, Gabe walks to the entertainment center and puts the disc into the player. When he turns and sees me, he laughs. "Oh, come on, Mad. Like they'd leave us alone in here if they thought that's where we *wanted* to be." He sets the popcorn on the coffee table and removes a pillow from my wall.

I force my voice to be even. "Do you want to be here?"

He pushes aside the rest of the pillows and sits beside me. "I'm here, aren't I?" He cocks an ear toward the laughter and blender noises echoing down the hall from the kitchen, then slips an arm around my shoulder.

This isn't how my plan was supposed to work out. Gabe was supposed to realize last Saturday that he couldn't wait one more second for me, confess that he wants us to be more than just practice, and profess his undying love. "And what exactly are we doing?"

Gabe looks at me. "Well, we're having an extra *practice* or I'm saving you the trouble of spilling the popcorn. You pick."

"That was an accident."

He withdraws his arm from me and shrugs. He reaches for a handful of popcorn, then drops it down my front. "That? Was on purpose."

I gape as the kernels tickle their way down the inside of my T-shirt.

He eases me backward on the couch, kneels on the floor,

and whispers, "Tell me you didn't have a good time at the ballet last week." He lifts up the bottom of my shirt and starts eating popcorn off the flat of my stomach, his lips brushing against the waistband of my jeans.

I draw in my abs, glad that I put on cute underwear this morning. "I didn't have a good time." It's true. Last week was more of a mind-blowing experience.

Gabe's fingertips travel up to my ribcage. He slides his other hand beneath me and in one fluid motion unhooks my bra. "Well, then, we definitely need the extra practice," he whispers in my ear, his hands now searching my bare skin.

It's not a move he needs more practice with but I let my body arch into his touch all the same. I know how to handle myself on the ice, but this isn't ice. This is fire. And soon, it's going to be out of control. Gabe doesn't push for anything more than my bra but it's enough for me to realize that I'm not thinking about if this is special and that right now I don't give even a single Axel about forever. When his hands are on me, I feel the same sense of exhilaration I feel just before the top of a split triple twist. I'm soaring and weightless.

And the movie ends way too soon.

Monday afternoon Igor films our program and we sit in the meeting room to review it. Watching the projector screen, my skin feels like I could power the rink's compressors just from my own electric energy. Is that really us? The pair on the tape looks like Gordeeva and Grinkov. Igor pauses the video. I rub my eyes but the couple frozen in front of me is wearing my blue practice dress and Gabe's Riverview Great Danes T-shirt. I look at Gabe. "We are—"

"So far beyond incredible." Gabe finishes my thought. Pushing the limits on what qualifies as *practice*, he gives my knee a quick squeeze under the table.

"This is year." Igor says. We snap our heads to look at him. "*This* year."

I suck in my breath. Beside me I can hear Gabe doing the same.

Gabe whispers. "We're taking the senior pair test."

Igor nods.

Gabe twirls in a circle on his chair and whoops. "We're taking the senior pair test!"

I've dreamed of this moment since I was old enough to make pretend podiums out of cardboard boxes and crawl to the top. Senior level. National television, interviews, the most coveted medals. But it's already almost September. My mind spins. The testing deadline for this year's qualifying competitions is this week. For the senior test, we need three gold-level judges. Finding such a high-level test session can take a couple months.

Gabe's read my mind again; I see his face fall. "Damn."

Igor looks at Gabe, but he doesn't scold him for swearing. "Your parents fly in judges for special session, Gabriel. You test in two days."

We both know what this means. At seventeen, Gabe and

I are very young to be senior-level pairs. But we're not too young for the Worlds age requirement. Maybe, just maybe . . .

The silence is gone in the car today. "Senior Worlds!" Gabe's eyes shine, wider than I've ever seen them.

"I know!" My seat belt is digging into my skin so tightly that I'm surprised my legs aren't losing circulation but I can't stop myself from bouncing. "I mean, I thought about it when Igor signed us up for our senior moves last fall, but I only dreamed . . ." I scream into my hands. *This* year. We could go this season.

Gabe straightens the car before he drives onto the curb. "We'll have to make top two our first year. Just the podium won't be enough this time."

"Sure," I say. "But we posted better scores than half the senior teams last year when we were juniors. And think how many times we've moved up before and still medaled. It's not impossible."

Gabe looks at me. "We can do it again."

I correct him. "We *will* do it again."

10

I burst through the kitchen door. "Mom! You'll never guess—"

Helen stands at the sink, her back to me. "She's not here," she says, the "here" coming out more like "heyuh" with her British accent. She looks over her shoulder and wipes the loose graying brown strands of hair back from her face with a soapy green glove. "She has rounds tonight, remember?"

"And Dad?"

"County called him for a consult, something about an intracerebral-hematoma-I-don't-know. He said not to wait on him for dinner."

I let my skate bag thunk on the floor.

Helen reaches for a towel. "Congratulations, by the way. I hear you and Maddy are taking your senior test?"

"How did you—" I stop. Igor said my parents were flying in judges; of course they knew about the test. I'm the last to know.

"Your mother told me." Helen answers the question I didn't finish asking. "I'm sorry I can't stay to celebrate with you, I've actually an appointment." She dries the last pan and hangs it back in its place above the island stove top, then gestures to the pot on the burner. "Dinner's ready when you're hungry."

I lift the lid and breathe in. Shrimp scampi. My favorite. A timer chimes and I turn to see Helen pull a tray of bread sticks from the wall oven. The warm air rushes over my face as the scent of garlic fills the room.

Helen sets down the tray, closes the oven, and reaches for her purse. "There's salad in the fridge. Put the food away when you're done, will you? Axel's been begging for tastes all afternoon and he'd love to get his paws into it."

As she heads out the door, Axel brushes against my leg and *meows*. I look out the window at Helen's car backing down the driveway, then pull a piece of shrimp from the pot and toss it to Axel. Before I can even pet him, he runs away with his prize. Guess I'm eating alone tonight.

I survey the counter. Helen's made an entire tray of bread sticks, a giant pot of scampi, and there's a salad in the fridge? I crack open the door and let the coolness flow over me. Sure, Helen and Mom love to make jokes about how much I eat, but there's enough food in the salad bowl alone for a platoon. I hesitate. My two weeks are long over, but I'm still very interested in practicing with Mad. Am I about to climb a slippery slope?

No. It's just dinner. We eat together every Saturday, anyway. I pull the bowl out and grab a bottle of dressing. Then I head next door.

Mrs. Spier's Taurus wagon is parked next to the porch. The car wasn't there when Mad and I came home only minutes ago, so maybe I'm in time. As I cross the yard, I see Mad's mom bent over under the hatch, wrestling with . . . a giant roll of TP? "Mrs. Spier?"

"Oh, Gabe, perfect. I need some muscle here." She stands up too fast and collides with the hatch. "Ouch!" She rubs the back of her head. "Help me out with this fabric bolt, please."

I hand her the bowl, balancing the dressing on top. The bolt is huge. With layer after layer of white fabric wrapped around a circular cardboard core, it really does look like supersized toilet paper. "What's this for?"

"A wedding gown."

The shiny fabric slides right out from my hands. "Slippery."

"Weddings often are. I've seen too many girls turn into bridezillas."

I pull the bolt from the car. "Where do you want this?"

Mrs. Spier is looking at the salad. "What's this for?"

I shift my grip on the bolt. It's not as heavy as Mad but she's thin and cooperative. The bolt is like trying to lift a hockey player wearing full gear by the waist. "Helen made way too much food and Mom and Dad are at work. I was hoping I could eat with you and Mad?"

"We haven't had you over for dinner in a long time." Smiling, she balances the bowl against her hip and touches my shoulder blade with her free hand. "Of course you're always welcome, even if you're not bringing Helen's home cooking."

I'm losing my grip on the slippery fabric again. "You want this—"

"Oh, sorry." Mrs. Spier hurries ahead of me to hold the front door. "Upstairs, in my sewing room."

I lug the bolt up the steps. From the landing at the top of the stairs, I can see Mad in her room. Her back to me, she stands at her dresser. I'm about to greet her when she drops her skirt to the floor and steps out of it. I drag my eyes away.

"Hey, Mom," Mad calls. "There's like no food in this house—"———

I set the bolt on its end in the hall. "I've been called a lot of things. Never that before, though."

"Gabe?" Mad yanks her jeans on and pokes her head into the hall, holding her unbuttoned shirt closed over her chest as she glances in both directions. She loosens her hold on her shirt and looks at me. "What are you—?" She looks at the fabric and groans. "Not again. She promised we could work on *my* dress tonight."

There's a sliver of exposed skin at her neck. All the way down to her waist. Don't look, my brain screams. This isn't practice. I lift my gaze to her face as her words register. *Her* dress? "You need a wedding dress?"

"My *skating* dress. Unless that was a proposal?"

I change the subject before I make my pothole any bigger. "I brought dinner over."

She perks up. "You're going to eat with us."

"It was you or Axel. And he only wants me for my shrimp." I start to carry the bolt the rest of the way down the hall. "Finish changing while I bring over the rest of the feast."

By the time I've transported the bread sticks and pasta, Mrs. Spier's set the kitchen table for three. She lights a pillar candle as Mad and I sit down. I wait for her to finish saying grace, then look at Mad. "Did you tell her yet?"

Mouth full of pasta, Mad shakes her head.

"Tell me what?"

"Mad and I . . ." I shift my gaze to Mad.

She swallows her food in a giant gulp. "Are taking the senior pairs test."

"Exciting. So this will be your last season as juniors?"

Mad sets her fork down. "No, Mom. We're taking the test on Wednesday."

Mrs. Spier's brow furrows. "Next week? Oh dear, I wish Igor had said something earlier. A senior test fee, I'll have to—"

Mad interrupts her. "No, *this* Wednesday. But Igor said the Nielsens paid the fees already, that you just need to sign my test forms."

"Gabe, your mom is such a sweetheart." Mrs. Spier shovels the rest of her food in her mouth, then picks up her plate. "With today's rush order, I'd better get to my sewing or I won't have any hope of getting to costumes. . . ."

I lose the rest of her mumbling as she leaves the room. I look over the candle at Mad. I'm bursting with words, but I don't know what to say. I feel as slippery and awkward as the fabric bolt I carried upstairs earlier. Wishing Igor were here to just tell me what to do, I work at my food in silence.

Mad does the same.

I empty my plate, but I'm not even tasting my meal. Mad's upset, but *she* made the proposal crack earlier. I crumple my napkin, take a breath. "Is this about—"

She sets her fork down. "No. Mom's been promising to work on my costume every night since Igor gave us the new program. Whatever. It's just a test."

My parents have crazy schedules, but at least they don't spend most their time out of town. And I have Helen when I get home. Between her dad's political career and her mom's dress business, I know Mad's alone a lot. I look at her glistening eyes and feel bad. I never noticed how much it bothers her. I stand, push my chair in. "Come on. Come with me."

Even though it's still the end of August, the cool evening air outside whispers the arrival of fall. I lead Mad toward the maple tree between our houses. Its yellow leaves ripple in the breeze as we walk under its branches. I circle my hands around Mad's waist and lift her onto the tire swing. I try to sit across from her but we've grown since the last time we were out here and our legs don't fit through the center together anymore. I stand next to the swing instead.

"I know it's stupid," Mad says, her voice almost as quiet as the rustling leaves. "That we could just wear our warm-ups if we had to. But . . . I want it to be perfect."

"It's not stupid."

She lifts her legs out of the hole and balances on the edge of the swing, then gestures for me to sit. I put my legs through. She straddles me and we fit that way. I push off from the ground and lean back in the swing, look up at the leaves, hundreds of gold medals framed by the light of the evening sun.

I feel her warm against my lap and grip the chains of the swing in my hands. "Mad, what if . . . ?" I can't finish, there're so many "what-ifs" twirling through my brain. What if we make it to Worlds? What if we win? What if Mad and I really—

Mad's face glows golden and the tiniest smile forms on her lips. "Not 'what if,' " she says. "When."

She sounds a little too sure of herself. Is she talking about Worlds or about . . . us? I put my feet down and stop the swing abruptly, trying not to notice when the change in momentum slams her body into mine, hard. I need a change of scenery and activity, pronto. I lift Mad off my lap, then step out of the swing. "Come on," I say again.

"Where are we going now?"

I smile. "I'm going to teach you how to drive."

The church parking lot is usually empty at this time of day, but as I approach the entrance I see it's overflowing with cars. Concert tonight. I make a U-turn and circle the block as I think. The arena lot would be big enough, too, but there'll be tons of cars there with hockey practice and men's league. There's only one other place I can think of.

The twisty drive up to the Point would be an awful place to practice driving, but the lot at the top is deserted. I back the car into a space at one end. Mad looks around. "This is a nice park. I've never been here before."

I cough and shift the focus back to driving. "Let's get started."

Mad taps her fingers on her thighs. "I'm not sure this is a good idea. Seriously. I think I wrecked my dad's aide's car."

I get out and open the passenger door for her. Reluctantly she switches seats with me. "Show me what your dad taught you so far."

Mad locates the clutch, brake, and gas pedals, points out the gearshift.

"Okay. Feel out where the different gears are." I put my hand on top of hers but it feels weird with my left hand so I lean toward her, resting my left hand against the edge of the driver's seat while I put my right hand on hers.

Mad finds each gear a couple times, then I guide her to put the car in first. So far so good. "Put your hands on the steering wheel now, and just keep it straight."

Her hands are shaking, trying to hold on to the wheel. Holy Batman, she's actually scared of something. "I'm going to burn the clutch out."

"No, you're not. Push the clutch all the way to the floor and hold the brake."

She does, then together we turn the key in the ignition.

"Now you're going to move your foot from the brake and push the gas pedal while you let the clutch up." The car's engine races but we don't go anywhere. I laugh. "Oops."

Mad freaks, stalling the car. "Ohmigod, what did I do?"

"I forgot to tell you to release the parking brake, that's all." I guide her hand to the brake and the fingers of my left hand brush against her thigh. *Practice*, my body says. *Not that kind*, says my brain. I move my fingers away once more. "Try again, but not quite so much gas."

Her knuckles are white on the steering wheel. This time, she lets the clutch out too quick and doesn't put enough pressure on the gas pedal. The car hops forward, jerking us against our seat belts and knocking me off balance and into her. I remove my hand from her leg again. She whispers, "I'm sorry. I can't do it, Gabe."

"Yet. How many crashes did it take before you got that Axel?"

Her face twists up into a little smile. "Guess I haven't *crashed* the car even once yet."

"Where would you be if you'd given up just because it was hard? Keep trying. It's like you need to balance the pressure. Let off the clutch at the same rate you're giving it gas. Keep them both slow at first until you get the hang of it."

"Okay." She blows out her breath. Tries again. And the car inches forward.

"That's it. You're driving."

"I'm driving. *I'm driving.*" In her excitement, she forgets about the gas and stalls the car out, but this time she gets it going again on her own.

"Go a little faster."

She does, driving a little snail trail around the parking lot. She's still in first gear, so it literally is a snail trail. After she makes the loop, I say, "Let's move to second now. Push in the clutch, slide the gearshift into the two position, and same thing with the clutch and the gas."

The transition is lurchy, but she gets through it. We keep practicing and pretty soon Mad is starting the car from first and shifting into second like she's done it all her life. We work on steering and parking. The first time, Mad manages to park the car right over the middle of one of the lines but the second time is between them, if lopsided, and the third is spot-on.

Mad puts the parking brake on and turns to look at me. "Thanks, Gabe."

"You're welcome." I squeeze her hand without even thinking about it, then let go quick and look out the windshield. The sky is tinged with red. I didn't realize how late it was getting.

"I *could* do it," Mad says. I turn to her and she locks her eyes on mine. "All I needed to do was try."

I look away again.

"I was scared, but I didn't need to be. It wasn't perfect right away. I bet I'll still make mistakes sometimes. Everybody makes mistakes sometimes."

"Yeah," I say to the floor of the car.

"Can I tell you a secret?"

"Sure."

"Do you know I'm afraid? Every time I learn a new jump. Every time. It's not about being fearless, it's about learning to face your fears."

"Mad . . ."

" 'Change is the law of life. And those who look only to the past or present are certain to miss the future.' "

"What?"

"John F. Kennedy. It's something my dad quotes. Do you think . . . you could try?"

Do, or do not. There is no try. It's a dumb Yoda quote, not a presidential one, but it's true all the same. "One thing at a time," I say. "We'd better go."

She switches places with me. We leave the park just in time to pass Chris's rust-bucket Rabbit pulling up the drive. Mad waves. "There's Chris and Kate."

I scrunch down in my seat, a stupid move because anyone would know it was me just from the car and there's no way either Chris or Kate missed Mad's goofy wave.

"They must've come to see the sunset. We could go back." Mad looks over her shoulder at the disappearing Rabbit as I turn onto the street. A little gasp of surprise, then she giggles. "Or not. So that's Miller's Point?" She punches my arm. "I can't believe you took me to the Point to practice driving."

"People change."

Mad stops laughing. "Yeah, they do. Is that a good thing?"

I don't know yet. "Those who look only to the past or present are certain to miss the future," JFK said. Is the future Mad and I might have worth risking my skating career?

11

Back at home, I try to FaceTime Dad to tell him about my driving lesson and the test but he's not available. I send him an e-mail instead, then head for Mom's sewing room. Maybe I can help her cut pieces or something so she can finish my dress.

The door is mostly closed, and there's no sound of snipping scissors or a whirring machine. Only hushed, harsh whispers. I peer through the crack and see Mom sitting at her sewing desk, her phone pressed against her ear. "What are we going to do about . . . Yes, I mean *we* . . . That's not fair."

Who is she talking to? Another bridezilla calling outside of business hours?

"She's taking the senior pair test," Mom says. One hand moves toward her face, wiping an eye? "Just like you, so determined."

Dad. I smile, then I hear Mom's next words. "I know you're not going to give up on us."

Dad? Give up? And what did she mean about "on us?"

I have to keep listening but now I know I'd better not get caught, so I step backward out of sight. And, *crrrEAK!* Stupid floor.

"Just a second," Mom says, then calls out, "Maddy, is that you?"

I peek my head around the door. "Yeah. I was just going to . . . brush my teeth."

"I've got your father on the phone. Want to tell him about the test?"

She already did, but I take the phone and tell him again.

"I'm so proud of you, Maddy," he says, but his voice sounds worn, like it would be streaked with gray if I could see it. I pass the phone back to Mom without telling him about the driving. I know it's an hour later in D.C., but it's not that late. Something's going on.

"I love you," Mom says into the phone. "We'll talk more later . . . Bye."

"Is everything okay?"

Mom leans on her desk as she stands. "Nothing for you to worry about, Maddy. Everything's going to be fine."

I hear what she doesn't say. She's worried about something and everything's not fine right now.

Between the test excitement and worrying about Dad, I hardly sleep. In the morning, only the enticing thought of playing Juliet gets me out of bed. When Gabe and I step onto the ice, though, Igor's playing our old *Incredibles* music. We rush through our warm-ups and, not even waiting for him to approach us, let the boards slam us into side-by-side stops in front of him.

Igor looks up from his rule book, cocking his head at us.

"What happened to *Romeo and Juliet*?" Gabe and I chorus.

"We save, yes? For senior debut?"

I feel Gabe relax and realize his hand's still curled around mine. He must've realized the same thing because he lets go. But no one saw, anyway. Igor's nose is back in the rule book and Chris and Kate are in the far corner, each blaming the other for causing their most recent fall.

Igor's eyes flick back between the rule book and the senior test form lying next to it on the boards. "We just do doubles instead of triples. The rest, the same."

We haven't skated the *Incredibles* program in weeks, but I remember the choreography well enough. Letting go of Juliet's emotions is more difficult. Igor yells at me. "You are superhero, Madelyn!" But something's changed since then, and I'm not as fearless as I used to be. After a couple run-throughs, though, Igor pronounces us ready.

At home after dinner, I pace the hallway outside Mom's sewing room on my tiptoes, listening to her machine whir and freezing whenever it stops. Mom doesn't call Dad, but she does call me out. "What's going on, Maddy?"

Exactly what I should ask her.

She comes out and slips her arm around my shoulders. "Nervous about the test?"

"No." It's the truth. Competitive standards for the junior level are so high above the senior test requirements that we'll pass easily. We don't even have to do any triples. "What's going on with Dad?"

Mom rumples my hair and drops her voice to sound like Dad. "Doing what's right isn't the problem. It is knowing what's right."

"Lyndon B. Johnson. But—"

She gives me a small smile. "Your father and I are having a little disagreement about what the right course of action is, that's all."

I go to my room and get in bed, leaving my door open. But Mom shuts her sewing room door and clicks the lock into place. I roll over and try to sleep. At least I'm ready for one thing.

The next afternoon, Gabe and I are warming up with our jump ropes in the lobby when the judges walk in. I break my stride and trip on my rope. Gabe stops, too, and spells a swear word at the back of the little old lady who's just hobbled by us. Super-fantastic-awesome. Frances Teatum's on our panel. Notoriously picky, she fails skaters who even breathe out of time with their music. We've only ever gotten two marks of "retry" on tests, one of them from guess who. On our junior pair test, she commented that our artistry was "severely lacking." Not good when the senior test form demands that a passing program must "superbly express the mood and rhythm of the music."

I step closer to Gabe and whisper, "At least we only need two out of three."

Gabe turns his head back to the arena entrance and turns away again just as quickly, wincing. I look over my shoulder and this time I'm the one swearing. Daniel Montgomery? Seriously? He and Frances Teatum are skates-off the most difficult judges in our region, maybe even in the whole country. If Frances Teatum will fail you for breathing out of time with your music, Daniel Montgomery will fail you for breathing at all. Our other "retry" came from him.

Gabe sinks onto one of the lobby benches. "Are you shitting me? What was Igor thinking?"

I shake my head. "I don't know."

Igor greets the judges, and Ms. Rasgotra escorts them to the hospitality room. Approaching us, Igor gestures to the south corridor. "My office. Now."

My stomach cramps as I hustle after him. Gabe and I have to pass this test today. If we don't, we'll have to wait twenty-eight days to retest and we'll miss the entry deadline for this season. I've never whined to Igor about anything before, but— "Ms. Teatum *and* Mr. Montgomery?"

Igor's eyes flash, and I shut my mouth. "You think this is plan? Wendy and Wilma Parker called last night. Sick. Stomach flu. We could get no one else to replace them. Listen now, you both. *Incredibles* program is not enough. Technically, is good. Artistically, no."

Gabe looks at Igor. "We're doing *Romeo and Juliet.*"

"You must." Igor runs through the changes we'll need to make.

"But Igor . . ." I gesture to my black-and-red spandex suit, not exactly Elizabethan apparel. Are we supposed to use our imaginary superpowers to time travel back to Shakespeare's day and pick up some new clothes?

Igor yanks his closet door open, thrusts our new costumes at us, and for a moment I forget my nerves. I run my fingers over the fabric. The last time I saw this dress, it was in pieces all over the sewing room table. Now, it's a finished work of perfection. The soft layers of chiffon showcase every imaginable shade of blue and will fly out to emphasize my speed.

"Go!" Igor snaps, crashing me back down to reality. We run. While the judges watch a novice moves test and two junior free skates on the Olympic rink, Ms. Rasgotra supervises our last-minute practice on the NHL rink.

As we cut through the lobby, I see single skater Regina sobbing over her test papers as our club mate Lucy tries to comfort her. Junior free skate fail. Not good, not good, not good. I'm breathless and jumpy when we meet Igor at the doors of the Olympic rink.

Igor puts his hands on our shoulders. "I did not mean to make you so nervous." His steel-gray eyes look deeply into first my eyes, then Gabe's. "Skate for judges as you skate for me. Enjoy each other. The rest comes."

We take our opening position, me holding a pivot as Gabe kneels just out of reach. My knees feel stiff and locked but still I fight to keep myself from shaking as our music begins. Then Gabe's hand takes mine. I focus on the warmth of it and lose myself in the music. Lose myself in Gabe as we push together to fill out the space of the larger rink. Double twist, double flips, combination spin. The elements fly by.

Throw double Salchow, star lift, death spiral. And we're done.

The arena is dead silent as we hold our final pose. Mr. Montgomery is head judge today. "Thank you," he says, without so much as a nod. I paste a smile on my face and keep my chin up as we skate off the ice. None of the judges even look up from their notes.

We haven't been asked to reskate anything, but a re-skate wouldn't help our presentation marks anyway. I sit on a bench in the lobby with Gabe, close my eyes, and wring my hands. Did I remember to do double toe loops instead of triples in our jump combination?

Gabe takes my hands in his to stop me. He doesn't let go. And I know he's praying, too. There's nothing else we can do anymore.

We were the last test of the day, and it shouldn't be long. All the same, it seems an entire Olympic cycle has passed before I hear the soft tap of Frances Teatum's cane on the lobby's foam tiles. I open my eyes and snatch my hands from Gabe's. The last thing I need is a scolding on public displays of affection. The wiry eighty-year-old taps her way across the lobby and stops in front of our bench. Super. I brace myself for the forthcoming lecture.

Ms. Teatum, however, remains silent. She shifts her weight and switches her cane to her left hand, then extends her right hand to me. I scramble to my feet and shake her hand. Gabe does the same. Ms. Teatum raps her cane against the bench. "I'll expect to see you on the television at Worlds now, mind you."

As she disappears back into the judges' room, Igor bursts out of the front office. He grips our test papers in one hand and I can't read his expression. I take the photocopies he hands me, my own hands shaking as my eyes dart to the middle of the paper, looking for the pass/retry box next to the total marks.

Pass.

Pass.

We only need two, but I look at the third anyway. Another pass.

"It was unanimous," I say to Gabe, still in shock. I flip back through the papers, checking the marks this time. "Mr. Montgomery even scored us above the passing average!"

Gabe grabs me in a bear hug and swings me in a circle.

Just then Chris walks into the arena. He checks out our papers. "Congrats, guys." Then he looks at Gabe. "Ready to *mount* that podium?"

I cross my arms at Chris as Gabe shushes him. "Could you at least *attempt* to censor your mouth?"

But the sex joke must've gone over our coach's head because Igor puts his hands on our backs. "Everything is going to plan."

I'm adding our test papers to my scrapbook when I hear knocking on my door frame. Mom walks over to my desk and glances at the picture of Gabe and I striking a superhero pose in our *Incredibles* outfits on the bottom of the podium at last year's Junior Grand Prix Final. "I loved that program," she says.

"Me, too." After all, who wouldn't like to be a superhero? I'd love to have the superhero ability to read minds. I'd use it on Gabe. So he's game enough to make out during Igor's homework assignments, and I've noticed his car has been at home on Friday nights as well. But he never talks to me about it. About us. He never says *anything* about us. We're flutzing, like cheating a lutz jump by changing edge just before takeoff. It might seem like we have a relationship, but when the moment of truth arrives? Flip.

"Of course, the new program is, well, *incredible* in its own way." Mom puts her arm around my shoulder.

"I love my new dress. Thank you."

"You're welcome."

I don't have to be a mind reader to know what Mom's thinking. *I know the difference between pretend and reality.* But the reality here is that I'm skating on thin ice. Gabe and I can't hold this pattern forever. Sooner or later something's going to break.

I close my scrapbook and slide it away. It's a dangerous question, but I'm desperate to talk to someone, anyone. And maybe I can worm something out about her and Dad. "How did you know Daddy was *the one*?"

Her eyes narrow. "Why the sudden interest?"

"This guy from school, my chem partner, actually . . . he asked me to the fall formal but I turned him down. I mean, I just don't think I'm interested in him like that."

"I wasn't interested in your father, either, at first. I didn't want to be a politician's wife. Your dad had to convince me." She's quiet for a minute. Is she sorry he convinced her?

Dad will be home tomorrow, then he and Mom can smooth over their whole phone fight. "We should do something as a family while he's home this weekend, not just Saturday with the Nielsens."

Mom looks away. "He's not coming home this weekend."

"Why not?"

She still doesn't look at me. "He's got . . . a lot going on right now, that's all."

That doesn't include me and Mom?

12

Gabe

When Igor hands me a DVD of *Samson and Delilah* after Saturday's practice, I've never been so excited to not watch a movie in my life. My parents and Mad's mom take a pass on the 1949 flick. Mad and I do, too, acting out our own seduction scenes instead. With September bringing our new short program to music from the opera of *Samson and Delilah*, practice is getting better and better. After a week of playing at strong man and temptress, I rub my hands in anticipation as Igor wraps up our lesson the following Saturday. What will this week's homework be?

The buzzer sounds. The Zamboni gates swing open. But no assignment comes. "Dismissed," Igor says, and turns his back to us.

I speed to the dance room. Maybe Ms. Rasgotra's got something for us. But all I get in ballet class is a smack on the back of my head for not keeping my eyes forward during my arabesque and a shove on the shoulder for not sinking low enough on my grand pliés. We line up in the corner for pirouettes and I spot the door, hoping to see Igor walking through it each time I whip my head around. No such luck.

* * *

In the dining room at Mad's that night, I sit across the table from her. We chew our food in silence, except for "Please pass the bread" and "Would you like more salad?" Oblivious, Mom and Mrs. Spier listen as Dad educates them on recent advances with brain cancer treatment plans. En-ter-tain-ing. Maybe we can discuss STDs over dessert?

During games, I slaughter everyone at Yahtzee, setting a new family game night record for most bonus points. Dad smiles at me. "Somebody's getting lucky tonight."

Or not.

"Sides," Ms. Rasgotra says in Pilates class Monday night. "Mermaid stretch. Inhale."

"Girly move," Chris exhales next to me. "Know what it always makes me think of, though? Where's a mermaid's—"

"Other side," Ms. Rasgotra announces.

Chris grins at me as we flip over. "So. You and Mad, at the Point?"

I'd hoped he'd forgotten by now. The flush spreads all the way to my ears. My face must be as red as the Viper. Luckily Chris can't see it with my back to him. We transition to planks. "Driving lessons. That's all."

He snorts. "You wouldn't even let me drive the Viper."

"You never asked."

I keep my head forward but in my peripheral vision I see

him turn his face toward me. His eyes bug out. "You'd let me drive your car? Seriously?"

Ms. Rasgotra strolls between us and twists Chris's head back for him. "No talking in class. *Seriously.*"

Despite what everyone thinks, I don't give a pelvic curl about my car. I wait for Ms. Rasgotra to move out of hearing range. "Sure."

"Today? After class?"

"Tonight. I've got to drop Mad off."

That night, as Chris zooms my car down the highway, testing zero to sixty for himself, I sit back in the passenger seat. He's so tripped, I think I made his week. It gets me thinking. Maybe I should be more appreciative of what I've got. Mad's mine every practice. It should be enough.

It's not. Saturday, I feel like I'm watching a recording of myself from last week. The only thing different is that instead of playing games for families night, I'm stuck watching Mad from one end of the love seat while everyone else watches the movie. When ballet class ends again the following week without an appearance from Igor, I head down the south corridor.

Igor's in his office, the doorway open as is his strict policy. He sits at his desk, scanning the pages of the notebook lying in front of him.

I stand in the doorway. He doesn't notice. I cough.

"Yes, come in," he says without looking up. His pencil scratches notes across the page.

I slide into the seat across from his desk.

After a moment of nothing but scratching, Igor looks at me. "Yes, what?"

"Do you want me and Mad to, um, work on anything this weekend?"

Igor looks at his notes again. "If you desire. You know what needs to be done."

"Yes, sir." I resist the urge to whoop, fist pump, and victory dance. I slip out of the office, looking at the empty hinges and wondering how long it'll be before Igor notices that Chris has removed his door. Again.

Not looking where I'm going, I run right into Mad. Shit, triple shit. Did she hear me?

"Hey, there you are," Mad says. "Can you get me your car keys, please? I need something from my backpack."

I let my breath out. I'm clear.

"Gabe. Kate's having a girl emergency. Keys. Please."

TMI, but at least Mad didn't overhear too much information. I go get my keys.

It's our turn to host families night. After dinner, Mom stands up to clear the table. Helen does dishes, laundry, and floors, but she doesn't do weekends. I stand up, too, and put my hands on Mom's shoulders to stop her. "I'll clean up tonight."

She's surprised but doesn't protest. "Thank you, Gabe."

Out of Mom's line of sight, I look at Mad, then nod in the direction of the kitchen.

Mad cocks her head at me. "What—"

I put my finger to my lips, then point at her, me, and the kitchen.

13

"Um, what a good idea," I say, figuring out Gabe's game of gestures. "I'll help." In the kitchen, I check out the towering piles of dirty dishes. Gabe never does chores. The smile crooks the corners of my mouth. He wants to be alone with me, big-time.

Sure enough, Gabe turns on the tap and dumps a few dishes under the running water but leaves the rest as he hoists me onto the counter, where my precarious position on the edge of the sink makes me have to lean against him to keep my balance. He stands between my legs and slips his arms around my waist.

I lean away as much as I can without falling. "I don't remember Igor giving us any extra assignments this week."

Now Gabe is leaning into me. "I talked to Igor."

So I heard. I slip back a little farther, my rear now hanging into the sink.

Gabe's voice is low in my ear. "He said to work on stuff this weekend *if we so desire.*"

I squirm. *You know what needs to be done.* But I'm pretty sure Igor didn't tell Gabe to make out with me this weekend and I don't want tonight to be about "extra practice." It's time for Gabe to jump. Then I feel an odd, warm sensation on the back of my jeans. I push against Gabe. "I'm getting all wet!"

He kisses my ear. "That's how it's supposed to be."

This time I shove him. "No, the sink!"

No longer held up by my behind, the KitchenAid bowl tips, cascading water onto Gabe's socks. He jumps back in surprise, then slaps off the tap.

My jeans are soaked. "What am I supposed to do about this?"

He ignores the water on the floor and steps toward me again, copping a feel of my wet seat. "Hmm." His hands move to my waistband. "Yeah, you're going to have to take your pants off."

I swat him away. "Fine, but I'll do that at home. You can take care of these dishes."

In my room, I scowl at my nearly empty dresser drawers. Mom was too busy to do laundry this week, and honestly, with as much homework as I had, I was, too. But now I don't have a single pair of clean jeans left and my custom-clothing-designer mom is going to notice if I show up back at the Nielsens wearing a skirt or aqua leggings. I rifle through my hamper, but with my skating tights thrown in there, everything stinks. I sigh, pull on the denim skirt, and hope it's enough.

Back at Gabe's, there's a mountain of wet towels leaning against one cabinet but the dishes are almost under control. Gabe checks out my new outfit. "Nice." He puts a slightly damp hand against my thigh just under the edge of my skirt and nods his head back toward the counter. "I don't suppose you want to?"

I roll my eyes at him. "What are we going to do when our parents notice I've changed clothes?"

He shrugs. "Tell them the truth?"

"Which is?" That he's madly in love with me. Come on, Gabe, jump.

"That I spilled water on you. You think they're not going to believe that?"

He has a point. It's not like he's used to doing chores. I sigh and help him finish the dishes.

Just like I thought, though, when we walk into the dining room, Mom and Gabe's parents hush up. I keep my mouth shut. Gabe can explain this one to my mother.

Gabe looks at me. Suddenly it seems he's not so keen on his half-true story.

Then Mr. Nielsen clears his throat. "Gabe, why don't you and Maddy go pick out a game?"

As we walk through the dining room, everyone is silent. Totally not-even-breathing silent. I look back over my shoulder, and all three adults are watching us.

Kneeling on the floor in front of the family room cabinets with Gabe, I turn to him. "Was that creepy or what?"

He's already looking over the game boxes. "Was what creepy?"

"They're watching us."

"No. If they're worried about us, why send us in here alone?"

I think for a moment, but he's right. It doesn't make sense. And Mom didn't say anything about my quote-unquote costume change.

"What do you want to play?"

I study our choices. Yahtzee? Scrabble? Taboo? No, definitely not that one today. No way do I want to face the chance of describing words like lingerie or naked. Wait. I stare at the box. "Taboo." Gabe reaches to pull the game out and I stop him. "No, I meant our parents. They're talking about something they don't want us to hear."

Gabe grimaces. "Probably some medical case we don't want to hear about anyway."

With the excitement of passing our test I had forgotten, but now my mother's words on the phone scream in my brain. *I know you won't give up on us.*

"How about—" Gabe's finger brushes against my cheek and that's when I realize it's wet. "Sorry, Mad. I was an ass about the sink. I didn't realize you were so sliced up about it."

"It's okay," I say, like saying it will make it true. "Let's play Scrabble."

As Gabe unfolds the board, I pull my letters from the bag and line them up in alphabetical order. Two A's, an I, two F's, R, and S. FAIRS, I spell on the end of my tray. I look at my remaining two letters. A. F. Slowly, I move them together. I shudder. This is the fourth weekend in a row that Dad hasn't come home. He's never stayed away so long before, and even FDR and JFK had AFFAIRS.

That night, I can't sleep. Gabe still hasn't taken any steps to define our relationship, but he wants me now, enough to set us up for time together. He's never been allowed to skip families night to go out and his car's still staying home on Friday nights, too. But it's ice-crystal clear he wants more, and if I don't give it to him, will he go somewhere else? Go to someone else again?

I get out of bed and walk over to my window. His house is dark except for a soft light from his room. On a whim, I pull my flashlight out from the bottom of my desk drawer. Gabe and I haven't done this since middle school, but I switch the lights out in my room and signal him all the same. Nothing. I signal again, but he must be busy.

I'm putting my flashlight away when I see the lights go out in Gabe's room. His answer comes slowly, like he's rusty and has to use his cheat sheet. It's okay, I'm a little rusty, too, and it gives me time to decipher his message. "WHAT'S UP?"

Where to start? My parents' troubles are their own business, I guess. But Gabe and I? I breathe, then jump. "I WANT YOU."

"I WANT YOU, TOO."

The rest of Gabe's house is still dark. I take a deeper breath. I turn the lights back on in my room and draw the curtains open. Standing in front of my window, I grab the bottom of my tank top.

14

Gabe

Holy Batman and Robin. I resist the urge to press my face to the glass, even though Mad won't see me do it with the lights off in my room. Is she really—?

She is. She wiggles her tank top over her head. *Damn.*

She drops her pajama shorts to the ground.

I get it now, why bug zappers work. No way is this a good idea, but here I am, flying closer and closer to the light.

She turns her back to me. Peeking over her shoulder, she slides her other arm up her back and unfastens her bra.

I press my face to the glass. What am I getting myself into?

She shimmies out of her panties.

And I know exactly what I'm getting myself into. I'm getting myself into Mad.

She walks out of sight and the lights click back off in her room. "SWEET DREAMS," she signals.

I lie down on my bed, but I don't sleep. I can't stop thinking about tonight's . . . practice.

I head down to the basement for some practice of a more

traditional variety. I sit on the bench but I don't touch the weights. I don't want to think about the traditional kind of practice. I want to think about Mad's pants. On the floor. Along with the rest of her clothes. I'm not *thinking*, that's what.

Off the ice, I've gotten myself onto an even more slippery surface. I've got the itch, and forget about my long-gone two weeks. I move the weight pin farther down, then get to work. I do a bazillion reps, but I can't push away the idea growing in my brain.

Me and Mad. I have to try it.

15

When I wake up the next morning, I've got a ball of ice in my stomach. What was I thinking last night? I rub my hands together to warm them, then press them against my cramping abdomen. Just because Mom and Dad are having distance issues doesn't mean I should throw myself at Gabe like . . . ugh!

I want to pull my covers over my head and stay in bed. Then I remember it's Sunday, so I do just that. Maybe Gabe was too tired to even remember what happened. I lie in bed for an hour before Mom comes stumbling in, her eyes puffy and her hair so far beyond a wreck that it's a freeway pileup. "I'm exhausted, Mad. You mind if we skip church today?"

This would never glide if Dad were home, but guess what? He's not.

Mom and I finally rouse ourselves and have brunch together at one o'clock. After sleeping in, we both look better but I don't feel better. I don't see or talk to Gabe all afternoon or evening and I'm starting to think maybe he was too tired to remember. Or he's embarrassed about it, too, and we'll both pretend this never happened. But just after I turn my lights out to go to bed, I see the flashes at his window. "EARLY PRACTICE TOMORROW. BE AT CAR 4:30."

"WHY?"

"FIELD TRIP."

In the car the next morning, my stomach winds and twists with the road. The headlights show off only a thick fog but I've been down this curvy drive recently enough to know where we're going. The question is, is it someplace I want to go?

Miller's Point is as deserted as it was on the day of my driving lesson but I'm not going to be in the driver's seat this time. Gabe pulls up to the guardrail at the edge of the overlook. We should be able to see the lights of the lower bank, but with the heavy fog it looks like there's nothing beyond the steep cliff. When Gabe cuts the headlights, the blackness swallows everything.

It's eerily quiet. The nocturnal animals have worn themselves out and the rest of the world isn't awake yet. Gabe sets the alarm on his phone, the tapping of his fingers against the screen sounding impossibly loud. He reaches across the gearshift for me, puts his fingers in my hair. "We can't stay very long. I have no idea what the sheriff's patrol schedule is at this time."

I let him kiss me, but his words have started a nagging thought in my brain. A thought that grows larger as I count ex-whatevers. Gabe's been here often enough to memorize the police routes? Is that what our extra practices are to him, just another fling? I pull away. "Not here."

He stares out the window into the pitch-black emptiness. "It feels sleazy to you. I didn't mean it to be like that."

What did he mean it to be like? And what was I expecting, exactly? People don't come to Miller's Point for the view, not the view of the river anyway.

He reaches for the parking brake. "Sorry. We'll go."

I don't want to stay here but I don't want to go, either. "It's just . . . you've been here a lot."

"I don't think about you that way, you know." He finds my hand and laces his fingers with mine. "It's different some-how. With you. It's not just about getting off."

Driving. Triple Axels. Those were nothing. I've never been as scared in my whole life as I am right now. My voice not even a whisper, I ask, "What do you think about me?"

The first bird's chirp signals the beginning of morning and his hand squeezes mine. "You're the only girl who was ever worth getting up early for."

It's a start. A shaky first-time-on-the-ice step, but a start. I squeeze his hand back.

We're at the rink practicing our star lift when Gabe says to me, "You're going to have to help me."

"I'm locking my arms. What else do you want me to do?"

"Not with the lift." As I dismount, I see Gabe's ears starting to turn red. "With . . . you and me. You're going to have to tell me, when it's too much."

"Okay." I smile. Another step. A couple more, and we'll be gliding right along.

After practice, I twirl into the locker room like I'm still in the lift, soaring in the air with Gabe holding me. Then I hear my club mates' voices and come crashing down.

"You think he really likes her?" Lucy asks.

"Gabe? *Two Weeks?*" Regina snort laughs. "It's Igor's choreography, that's all."

Jealous much? All the same, I slam the locker room door so Lucy and Regina will know someone's coming in and shut up. And I don't say anything to them about me and Gabe.

16

Gabe

After the impromptu performance Mad and I put on, Miss Xander rushed us through *Romeo and Juliet*. But by the end of September, we've been studying *Macbeth* for weeks. I think even Mad is sick of it.

"Which shows me many more; and some I see, that two-fold balls and treble scepters carry," Miss Xander reads. She tries to ignore Chris's snort at her use of the word balls, but he's not the only one snickering. She sighs and looks up from her book. "Shakespeare meant the golden orbs monarchs carried at their coronations. James was twice crowned, both in Scotland and England, hence two-fold, or two *orbs*."

"Then why didn't he just say so?" Chris calls out.

Miss Xander sighs again. "To say golden orbs wouldn't have fit with the meter, Christopher. That's part of the beauty of Shakespeare's work."

"To just say 'orbs' would," Chris mutters.

Miss Xander's already continuing, this time reading from her notes. "Now, if you look at the next line, you'll see it might seem to be missing a syllable in the third foot, but take note of the preceding ejacu—" She slumps her shoulders and finishes the word in a whisper, "—lation."

She's only drawn more attention to her poor word choice and Kurt and the hockey team are almost rolling on the floor, they're laughing so hard. Chris doesn't even make fun of her this time. "How does she *do* this to herself?" he whispers to me.

Her face purple, Miss Xander nevertheless picks up the play again and pushes onward. She gets quite a way through it, until "he wants the natural touch—" Her words are drowned out in another outburst of laughter.

She slaps her book down on the table. This time, even she's had enough. Her own outburst gives her enough quiet to get started, and she rips into us. "How do you even expect to understand when you don't pay attention? Lady Macbeth is about to contrast her husband's behavior with that of a wren. He's run away, but even a wren would stay to protect its family. Your immature behavior is making you miss the entire metaphor!"

Mad eases her hand in the air. "Maybe it would help if we thought of some comparisons first with more modern stuff?" She's the teacher's-pet type, but after her little show with me, Miss Xander is suspicious of all of us, even Mad. "It would be, like, self-directed learning?"

The teacher talk piques Miss Xander's interest. "Well," she says. She looks around the room and evidently decides it can't get any worse than it already is. "I suppose we could try it." She picks up a marker and moves to the board. "Tell me some modern things that are important to you."

People start to call things out and Miss Xander looks for a minute as though she wishes she'd asked us to raise our hands, but she goes with the sudden flow of participation. She jots down our ideas, her handwriting getting messier and messier as she scrambles to keep up. Money, cell phones, cars, video games, the list goes on, even including Taco Bell and Flamin' Hot Cheetos.

She stands back, massaging her right wrist. Her face is still flushed, but this time I think her smile might be real. "Okay. Now Shakespeare's plays, like all great works of fiction, have central themes." Noticing she's losing us again already, she rushes on. "Big ideas, things we can resonate with in our own lives. Things that apply to everyone."

She makes a new column on the board: love, fear, order, guilt, truth, courage, loyalty. She taps the marker against her list. "Take one of these big ideas." She points to our list. "How is it like or unlike one of these modern-day things?"

Chris inches his hand up. Miss Xander winces, but no one else is playing, not even Mad. "Christopher?"

"So love is like Taco Bell, it's delicious but it can make you want to crap?"

Miss Xander nods, her thoughts an open book. Are we genuinely interested or trying to trip her again? "Yeah. Um, yes. Sort of like that. I mean, that's technically correct."

Piper raises her hand. "Could we maybe write our ideas down?"

"Yes," Miss Xander says quickly. She hands Piper a stack of lined paper. "Excellent idea, let's do that."

I look away as Piper passes me my paper. After she's moved

on, I look at the empty sheet. Beside me, Chris's pen speeds eighty miles an hour but I don't have any ideas. I steal a glance. Yeah, not copying that. I look back at the board. Money is on top of the first list, and love on top of the second. How is money like love? I look across the room at Mad. Love is like money, I write, because it's fun to have. No. I scratch it out and stare over at the window.

A few tables up, I see Piper giggling with her seat mate as they slide their paper back and forth. Piper folds it in half, then turns around and drops it on the desk of the girl behind her, who opens it and laughs. The note makes its way around the room. Since I broke it off with Piper last year—all right, since *Mad* broke things off with Piper for me—I've tried to stay clear of her, but everyone's giggling so much I'm curious.

When it comes to the girl in front of me, though, she tosses it across the aisle instead of back. The paper's made its way to Kurt when the bell rings. He reads it, but he doesn't giggle. He laughs. Mean. The classroom's emptying out, but I stall gathering my stuff. I've got to see what that note says.

Kurt waits for me to walk up to him. Laughing again, he holds the note away from me and checks my shoulder when I try to reach for it. The note falls to the floor but Kurt doesn't pick it up. He looks me in the eye. "The truth is like hockey-stick checking. Hurts like hell. Take a look. See what everyone really thinks of you."

He leaves. I pick the note up off the floor. Open it.

G.N.'s love is like a cell phone call, you never know when he's going to drop you.

G.N.'s love is like Hot Cheetos, you want him but he's going to burn you.

G.N.'s love is like a sports car, it's the ride of your life but it always runs out of gas.

I walk to the trash and rip up the note.

"What's eating you?" Mad says to me on the car ride home from practice that afternoon.

Me, I think, feeling the Hot Cheetos afterburn. I ripped up the paper. I couldn't rip up the words. At least she didn't see any of it. "Just thinking about my birthday." It's this Saturday, October 5.

"The big one-eight. Worried about becoming a man?" Her finger sneaks along the edge of my thigh. "Anything in particular you want?"

Before, I would've taken her up on where her finger is tracing. Now? I can't drop Mad. Don't want to burn her. And if I run out of gas this time, I'm going to be stranded. What the hell do I think I'm doing? I don't even know what love is. I joke instead. "How about a gold medal at Sectionals?"

Mad looks at me. She's not joking. "I'm on it."

We don't do much for my birthday, just dinner with Mad and her mom. My parents wanted to throw a gala event, but I talked them out of it. I've got a big enough slice of cake trying to figure out what's going on with me and Mad without having to do it in front of our friends. With our parents around, she's as careful as me about keeping *us* wrapped up.

"Make a wish," Mad says to me in the darkened dining room. I look at her face, lit only by the glow of my eighteen candles. I don't wish for Mad. I wish for us. For me. People change, and I'm going to. This time, with Mad, I want to do things right. This time? I think I want to find out what love really is.

17

We get Monday off school for a teacher in-service day and Mom and I go out to the courthouse so I can take my written driving test. An hour later, I have my instruction permit.

It's way easier driving my mom's automatic, even if we're on the road now instead of in a parking lot. Easier for me, anyway. Mom is looking more than a little car sick. "Slow down. Careful!"

She means about my driving, but I can't help thinking about me and Gabe. This morning after practice, he asked me if it was okay if we don't tell anyone about us yet. Mom interrupted before he could say why and—

"Look out!" Mom shouts.

I pull over to the curb and park. We've both had enough for the day.

* * *

After our afternoon ice session, Gabe and I walk out to his car together. As we approach the Viper, he tosses me the keys. "Want to drive?"

It's sweet of him, but I toss the keys back. "No, but thanks." I'm still nerved from my drive with Mom earlier and I wouldn't be comfortable taking Gabe's car on the highway when I haven't been past second gear. "I think I need a little more practice."

"I could help you with that." Gabe opens the passenger door for me. Once I'm settled, he gets in on the driver's side. "Want to go somewhere and practice more?"

No looks. No chest-staring, no sneaked peeks at my lap. It takes me a second to figure out he means to practice *driving*. But I don't really want to do that right now, either.

The cornfields, now spotted with ghoulish signs for haunted corn mazes, zip by as Gabe drives. So smooth, so confident in the way he handles the car. So smooth in so many other ways. "Gabe, why do we need to be a secret?"

"Well . . . it'd be fun for awhile, wouldn't it? You know, like a real-life Romeo and Juliet?"

"*Romeo and Juliet* is a tragedy," I point out. "They commit suicide. Super fun."

Gabe glances over at me. "Okay, and . . . well." He looks back out the windshield. "Other reasons, too."

"Such as?"

"Can't you just trust me on this one?"

"You have to trust me, too."

He's quiet for a long time. Finally, he says, "Fine. I admit it. Your dad scares the shit out of me. All his SEAL glory stories."

I do get the vibe that Dad would go more for the Jonah type as his first choice for my boyfriend. A four point when it comes to grades, no priors when it comes to girls. All the same, it's a flimsy excuse, especially when Dad hasn't even been coming home. The secret issue makes me nervous, but the driving isn't the only place where I haven't been past second gear. Maybe I wouldn't mind a little time to figure this relationship stuff out in private myself. Maybe it kind of *is* like practice. Get it under control before you put it out there for everyone to see.

Back at home, Gabe gets my bag out of the trunk for me. He clears his throat. "Open invite, if you want help."

"With the driving."

"Yeah."

"Or if I want to drive?"

"That, too." He's still standing there, holding my bag.

I like Gabe driving, I realize. I always have. It was probably part of the reason I had such a hard time learning to do it myself. My heart wasn't in it. The thought of maybe losing Gabe driving me around made me uncomfortable. Gabe's uncomfortable right now about something, I realize.

"Do you want to, maybe, go somewhere? Together?" he asks.

"For practice?"

Gabe reddens. "Something more than that."

His words make me smile. Something more than that.

Like a secret date? "Any time. Open invitation." My smile melts. "But where—?"

Sometimes we can be creepy good at reading each other's minds. In perfect-pair unison, we say, "The Halloween dance." We can go in disguise.

I don't miss Dad this weekend. I tell Mom that Gabe and I have a group project to work on for English and we meet at his house while his dad heads off for eighteen holes of Saturday afternoon golf and his mom volunteers at the women's clinic across the river in Palisades. In the study, I sit on Gabe's lap on the desk chair, feeling excited that Gabe's into doing a couples costume. I click through pictures online.

"This one." Gabe points to a shot of a couple dressed up like a bar of soap and a shower scrubby.

The girl's scrubby costume is super cute, yards of tulle bunched up around her with a big loop of white cord sticking out. It shows off her shoulders and legs. My own shoulders are sculpted from skating and I'd look way hot wearing it, but, "I thought we needed costumes where no one could see our faces."

"Your face," Gabe says. "No one's going to be surprised to see me at the dance with some girl."

All of a sudden, Gabe's lap is uncomfortable. "Some girl."

"Jeez, Mad. I didn't mean it like that."

"So what are we going to do? Put tulle all over my face, too?"

"No, I'll be the scrubby. You'll be the soap."

The soap. The soap costume is just a box covered in white paper with the word SOAP written on it in big letters.

"Come on, Mad. It'll be fun."

Us being secretly disguised had potential for fun. Just me being the secret is a whole different program.

"Last year, I went with Piper as surf and turf. It was hilarious. I wore my swimsuit and carried a surfboard and—"

"Piper got to be turf." Which is really the same as . . . dirt. " I thought I was the only girl you'd wear matching outfits with."

"It was just a costume." Gabe flushes. "Sorry. I won't talk about . . . if you don't want me to."

Whether he talks about them or not, they'll always be there. Always be part of who Gabe . . . was? Is? I'm not sure which is worse, knowing or not knowing, but I'm sure I don't want to look at costumes anymore today.

I slide off Gabe's lap, stand, and look at him, all melting milk chocolate eyes. He does look sorry, and he did sound really excited, for whatever reason, about dressing up like a shower scrub—

I can't help it, I burst out laughing. "It *is* a great costume for you. You want to go to the dance as a *scrub*."

He smiles. "And you want to go with me."

I *do* want to go to the dance with Gabe. "All right."

There's a definite rush in sneaking around to get costumes together the next weekend. Since Gabe won't come into the fabric store with me, I get back at him by buying hot pink tulle for his costume. We spray paint my box brilliant white and I write "soap" on it in fancy script. Gabe gets the genius idea to cut out different-size packing bubbles and glue them on to look like foam. When we've finished, he stands looking at it. "It needs something more."

"It's a cardboard box." What more can we do?

"Bling."

"What?"

"It needs some bling, like those sparkle things your mom puts on your dresses."

"Swarovski crystals."

"Yeah."

Swarovskis are expensive but I find some rhinestones in the old arts and crafts box we played with as kids. Gabe's right, though. That little extra sparkle makes the pretend bubbles pop. I'm going to be one classy bar of soap. "Thanks, Gabe."

Gabe slips an arm around my waist. "I couldn't be the soap, anyway. Not with you."

"Why's that?"

"You make me think dirty thoughts." He kisses the side of my neck and then before I know what he's doing, he nips me quick, the teeniest touch of teeth.

I giggle and whirl away from him but, God, we haven't really fooled around for a while and I just want to be caught again until—

"Maddy?"

I stop quick and Gabe does, too. I don't want to get caught by Mom. He steps away from me just as Mom walks into the garage. "What's this?"

Gabe's face is totally straight. "Our English project."

Mom examines the sparkles on the box. "Really?"

"Yeah. Since we studied *Romeo and Juliet*, we get extra credit for Halloween by dressing up as a classic pairing and bringing in a picture."

Mom buys it, blade, boot, and lace. "How fun. Shall I take your picture for you?"

We put the costumes on right over our clothes. Gabe was right. Mom can't even take the picture for a couple minutes, she's laughing too hard to hold the camera steady once she realizes that scrubby costume belongs to Gabe.

That night at dinner, she shows the Nielsens. Gabe's mom holds her sides, her own laughter bubbling out anyway. "This is a riot. It's a shame these are just for the picture."

Smooth as ice, Gabe looks over at me. "Well, we could go to the Halloween dance next Saturday. Just as friends. Want to, Mad?"

He is a crazy-good liar. I shrug and play along. "Sounds like a plan."

I've heard the Riverview formals are held off campus, but the Halloween dance must not rank so high. The gym is dressed up a bit. There's black crepe streamers twisted everywhere and fake cobwebs in the corners and a bunch of kids doing a monster mosh pit in the middle of the floor. But the real attraction here is the costumes. Of course there's the usual vampires, slutty witches, and gory zombies. Kurt looks totally lame wearing his hockey jersey but Jonah is rocking it by just pairing a beret with his street clothes.

There's some other cute couple costumes, too. Chris and Kate have dressed up like a mummy and Cleopatra. With Kate's dark wig, I almost don't recognize them until I see some of Chris's orange hair sticking out from under his wrappings. Gabe's cousin Sara is hanging off Andy's arm, a Mounds bar to his Almond Joy. Another twosome is dressed as playing cards, a pair of aces, and a girl dressed as an outlet and a guy dressed as a plug keep making the teacher chaperons grimace as they suggestively model their "connection" for everyone without technically breaking any school rules.

Gabe and I start to walk toward the snack table but we don't even make it there before we've stolen all the attention from the Electric Company. I stay quiet in the box so no one knows who I am, not hard to do with "Somebody's Watching Me" blaring, even easier to do once I realize that nobody's watching me, that everyone's exclaiming over Gabe.

Kurt and a couple of the hockey guys start in on Gabe about his costume at first, but after a bunch of girls crowd around, putting their hands on Gabe's bare shoulders or, worse, on his leg like they're going to reach up his shower scrubby skirt, the players knock it off fast. Like a rooster in a tutu, Gabe struts in the spotlight. Anita walks up to him in a skimpy red mini-dress that has HOT written across her chest and SAUCE across her stomach.

With the white tights, shirt, and gloves I'm wearing under the box to complete my costume, I'm getting hot, especially around my face. I step away toward the snack table, even though I can't drink any punch or eat any treats with my face covered, and I'm not hungry, anyway. I wish I didn't know what Gabe's done with Anita.

"It's such a mess when I get saucy," Anita coos behind me. "Want to scrub me up?"

"Sorry," I hear Gabe say. "But I'm here with someone and it isn't hygienic to share shower scrubbies."

All night, Gabe only dances with me. As well as I can dance inside a box, that is. People chat him up every time we take a break. I've always known Gabe was popular, but I've never seen him like this, not really. Sure, I've seen his fan club at school, but only flashes rushing through the halls. Here, he's like . . . my dad. Drawing people to him in that charismatic way of a well-liked politician. And as lost as I am in the box, I'm a little proud of Gabe. A little scared, too, because there's this whole other part of Gabe's life that I never knew about, and because I also know a thing or two about beloved politicians, and maybe a thing or two about . . . my dad, who now hasn't been home for two months.

On the car ride home, I finally get up my nerve and ask Gabe. "Tell me again. Why do we need to be a secret?"

"Well . . . you never peek at your presents."

And he does, but he *is* a politician changing topic like that and, "What does that have to do with anything?"

"Why don't you peek?"

"Because waiting is half the fun."

"Exactly," he says.

"But *you* always peek."

"People change. I told you, Mad. It's different this time. With . . . us."

Us. The word melts my edges a little, but there's something more. Maybe this isn't really about secrets. Maybe it's about something painfully obvious. "You were a show-off, at the dance."

Gabe's quiet a minute. "Yeah. That bother you?"

"Yes."

"Sorry, but . . ." Gabe sighs. "Not really. Usually I show you off. I like a turn once in a while."

"Show me off? You hid me under a box."

"For one dance. What do I do for hours a day? Every day? All the time we're on the ice, Mad, that's all I do. Nobody looks at the pair guy, except to wonder if he's straight or gay. All I'm there for is to make you look beautiful. At least you make it easy to do."

I thought I knew everything about Gabe. Maybe I don't. "I'm sorry."

"Me, too," Gabe says.

Mom's waiting up when I get home. "How was the dance?"

I hesitate. It's misleading, maybe, but it's true. "I think it would've been more fun to go with a boyfriend."

But she wasn't waiting up to ask me about the dance. "Good news," she says. "Your dad's coming home tomorrow."

Dad's flight is due in at 9:12 A.M. but Saturday morning means I have practice and ballet. When we're finally done, I rush into the house but . . . no Dad. There's a note on the kitchen island: *Went to lunch meeting. Sandwich in the fridge for you, see you soon. Love, Mom and Dad.*

I sigh. I eat the sandwich from the fridge. It's even chicken salad on whole wheat, my favorite, but it's not what I'm hungry for right now.

Eating takes five minutes. I get a glass of milk and drink that, too, but now what? I'm actually caught up on my homework. I try to read a book, but I can't focus. I'm too tightly wound. Then I think of it.

I get out my violin. I don't usually practice outside of orchestra class, in fact I wouldn't even have it at home if it weren't Saturday. Mr. Rico doesn't let us leave them in our lockers over the weekend, so he can at least pretend that the B-orchestra students practice.

I'm never going to be a concert violinist, and our orchestra grades are based on attendance and music theory tests, not our seat ranks, so I haven't got a lot of motivation to move up from last chair. Plus, Kate's second to last chair, so as long as we don't challenge anyone we can sit together. But there's something about getting my strings in tune that makes me feel like the rest of me's better tuned as well.

I take my time tuning, still feeling jittery. Then I start with the Air movement from Handel's *Water Music*, just because we're playing it in class right now so it's easy enough. Forcing myself to focus and control the bow helps, but I need a slower piece. As long as I'm playing wedding music, I play my favorite piece next, Pachelbel's Canon in D.

The slow, long notes at the beginning mellow me out, but

when I get to the faster parts I trip up again. I lower my violin. I'm not a very good violinist, but I know why. I don't practice. I don't work at it.

Wedding music usually makes me think of Gabe but right now I'm thinking more about my parents. Well, about both Gabe and my parents, actually. Relationships take practice. Hard work. It's not like my parents have never fought before. I remember talking with Gabe in the car last night. Maybe his answers weren't what I expected or even wanted, but it felt better to talk it through.

Practice makes perfect, right? I pick my violin back up and work on the hard parts again.

By the time Mom and Dad get home, it's not perfect but it's sounding way better. They walk into the living room but I don't stop. I finish.

"Beautiful." Mom claps.

I drop my violin and rush for Dad. He circles his arms around me. "Maddy, I've missed you so much."

"Me, too, Dad."

Mom says, "I had all of lunch with you, Will. Why don't you two go to the hiking park? You can take a walk." She looks at Dad. "Talk."

There's something I don't like about that look. I duck past them both, quick. "I'll get my shoes."

The hiking park is only a couple of miles from our house, but Dad insists on driving. "I thought you were a SEAL," I say as we head for the trails. "Not a wimp."

Dad laughs, but he says, "Some of us aren't in as good shape as we used to be."

"Maybe you need to exercise more."

"There's a lot of things I need to do more."

We pass the wedding arch in the clearing at the foot of the trails. "Like come home," I say.

"Yes."

Off to the side, just off the trail, there's a man with a little girl. Their backs to us, they squat side by side at the base of a huge old tree. "A fairy house," the little girl squeals, pointing among the gnarled roots.

I smile as we walk past. The sun is warm on my face, fall lighting a fire around us. It's too warm for the end of October but it makes a perfect daddy-daughter day. I sling my arm around Dad. "I love you."

Dad's arm squeezes my waist, tight. "I love you, too. Always."

There's something almost too fierce about the way he says it and I think about Mom. *Talk.* There's a bench up ahead where the trail curls to overlook the pond. "Let's stop up there."

We sit. Somewhere behind us a squirrel rustles the leaves. I twist around. It's two squirrels, actually, chasing each other. One chatters at the other. Fighting.

"Gorgeous," Dad says.

I turn back around. The leaves of the trees flame, gold turning to crimson as the branches kiss the brilliant blue of the sky, all of it mirrored in the pond below. It *is* gorgeous. Then a breeze bites at the back of my neck, the sudden gust

♥ 138 ♥

rippling the reflection. Distorting a picture of perfection that was never real anyway.

Which picture is my parents? Is our family as strongly rooted as I thought we were or just a surface image? I have to ask him. Right now, before I lose my nerve. So I talk to Dad the way we talk best. "Truth will ultimately prevail where there is pains to bring it to light." It's his favorite quote of all, the foundation of his Honest Bill nickname.

"George Washington," Dad says quietly.

The breeze ripples my voice now. "I want to know the truth."

He sighs. "Maddy . . ."

It's not the most graceful setup, but I blurt it out anyway. "Tell me, right to my face, that you're not seeing another woman."

"I'm not." The lines ease from his face. "I'm not seeing another woman. Your mother is more than enough woman for me."

Honest Bill has spoken. But, "Then why haven't you been coming home?"

"There's been a lot of extra work trying to balance my senatorial responsibilities with preparing for campaigning," he says. "Could be worse. Could be a representative doing nothing but campaigning."

What Dad loves best about the Senate is the six-year term. Just as much campaigning, but more time to get things done in between. Less talking, more doing.

Dad and I don't talk much more. We don't hike much longer, either. We do something better. We go home and, together with Mom, we make lasagna for families night.

Playing Trivial Pursuit around the table later with Gabe and his parents, I struggle to hide my laughter as Gabe changes every question he reads to somehow make it skating related. Our parents don't even notice, they're all smiling so wide they could be filming a Crest commercial. Under the table, Gabe's foot finds mine. I look at my parents beside me, just as oblivious to Gabe's footsie maneuver as they are to his adapted questions. One secret I was imagining, and the other is okay for now.

The next morning I wake up on skating time. We don't have practice on Sunday but I get up early anyway, figuring I'll surprise Mom and Dad and make breakfast. I head downstairs. Heart-shaped pancakes, I decide. I'll serve them breakfast in bed.

I stop as I walk past the living room. Dad's sleeping on the couch. I tiptoe over to him. His left arm droops toward the floor and one of his FDR biographies rests open over his face, still clutched in his right hand. He just fell asleep reading down here, I tell myself.

My vision ripples away the image of his pajamas. Dad's never lied to me, not ever, but this time his talk doesn't match what he's doing.

18

With Sectionals rapidly approaching, about all Mad and I get to do for the next couple of weeks is eat, sleep, and skate. I'm hoping we can at least hang together on the plane, but our flights to Sectionals are booked solid.

On the first flight I'm squished between the window and a fat lady with awful gas. Behind me is a woman with a screaming baby. When her toddler starts kicking my seat, I give up on my *Hamlet* homework. I try thinking happy thoughts about me and Mad instead, but that gets me thinking about wanting to do the right thing. Ay, there's the rub. By the time we land in Chicago, I'm desperate to get off.

I plop into a seat next to Mad as we wait in the airport lounge for our next flight. We're not even in Lansing yet and she's fidgeting up a blizzard. Why? Sure, it's our first senior-level competition, but only four pairs are entered. There are so few senior pairs in the U.S. that even if we finish dead last, we're going to Nationals. Chris and Kate, in junior ice dance, only have to *not* be last and they'll qualify, too.

Besides, Mad relishes competitions. She never gets nervous or tight. "Hey, you're stealing my signature move." She looks at me odd and I point to her pencil. "Competition nerves?"

Mad stops tapping her book with her eraser. "Sorry. It's just . . ."

Suddenly, I've got the nervous twitches, too. My toes dance inside my shoes. Please, no more discussions about us. I know Mad's not thrilled with the plan to keep our relationship secret for a while, but—

"It's . . . my dad."

I stop my toe ballet. "Your dad?"

"It's the first time he's missed a major competition and . . . I'm afraid."

"That you're not going to skate well when he's not watching? We do it every day at practice. Your mom's coming, anyway."

"That's what I'm afraid of," Mad says. "She's coming and he's not. Something's not right with them, Gabe. I'm worried he might be . . . having an affair."

Straightlaced Senator Spier? *Honest Bill?* "Did you ask your parents about it?"

"I asked him."

"What'd he say?"

"That Mom's enough woman for him. But last time he came home he slept on the couch."

I don't know what to say. I give Mad's hand a quick squeeze but I drop her hand and our conversation as I see four other skaters from our club heading our way. "We'll talk more later?"

Mad nods.

Eight-year-old Hailey approaches me. She holds out a pack of cards. "I'll kick your ass at War."

"Don't say ass," I tell her.

She grins at me. "Why not? You just did."

"Deal 'em out," Mad says to Hailey. "Show him what you've got."

I sit down on the floor with Hailey, get my skating pants handed to me on a plate, and then it's time to board our next plane.

Eight of Igor's students are competing at Sectionals this year, and we've all got rooms in the host hotel. The two singles skaters and Hailey and her juvenile dance partner are all younger and staying with their mothers, which leaves Mad to room with Kate and me with Chris.

Chris drops his duffel bag on the floor of our room and heads out right away. I unpack my stuff and think about how many Saturday dinners the Senator's missed this fall. The hushed conversations between Mad's mom and my own parents. Could it be true? I still don't know what to say but I feel like I should do something to try and comfort Mad, so I head for the girls' room.

When I knock at the door, Chris answers wearing nothing but a towel and still dripping. He yanks me inside. "Jeez, you're going to get us busted."

Is he for real? "The night before a competition and you're screwing around?"

He cocks his head at me. "We were holding hands under the sheets and got sweaty. Idiot."

"You know Igor wouldn't like—"

"Like Igor likes anything I do."

"What about Kate?"

Chris crosses his arms over his chest. "Is it so hard to imagine that maybe *she* likes it? That maybe you're not the only one who knows how to get a girl off?"

Why have I got my tights so twisted over this? It isn't going to screw up *my* performance tomorrow. I'm not the one who might regret ignoring Igor's orders. But, "What if she gets—"

"Then I'll dump her and get a new partner." Chris rolls his eyes at me, then jerks his head toward the strip of condoms on the nightstand. "That would be what birth control is for."

I know Chris is careful. Hell, I'm his hook-up. Mom's office always has free samples. None of this is news to me, so what's got me so wound?

I'm *jealous*, that's what I am. Chris is getting a party and, even if I don't want to cop to it, I want one, too. I try to shake the feeling off. Remind myself that I don't want the Axel-crash relationship that comes with that kind of party. I want to do things right. "Where's Mad?"

"In the shower with Kate."

Sarcastic or not, that wasn't funny. I take a swing at him.

Chris steps back. "Can't you take a joke? She's not here, so chill-ax. Like she even looks at anybody but you. I swear, you really are an idiot."

"Where is she?"

"She went to the arena about half an hour ago to see the senior ladies practice sessions." He gestures to the door. "Now, if you don't mind . . ."

I leave without answering. Choosing a walk instead of the

hotel shuttle, I let the crisp mid-November air cool my temper. Inside the arena, Mad's in the stands of the main rink, jotting observations of the senior ladies in her notebook. "Anybody good yet?"

She shrugs and smiles. "Not much for triples. I could take them so far."

I slip into the seat next to her and we watch the second practice group take the ice. Mad would be at the top of this pack, if she were a singles skater. She's just as fast, if not faster, and just as flexible. I see skater after skater blow their easier triples, some of them even their double Axels. *Mad could be a national champion. Without me.* Before, those thoughts made me proud of Mad. Now? They're another reminder that I can't run out of gas this time.

After the second session, Mad's ready to head back but I wonder if Chris has cleared out yet. We haven't even been gone an hour. Thoughts of my own, probably empty, room trace through my brain, but Igor's instructions were clear. Today we rest. "Want to get something to eat?"

Mad wrinkles her nose. "No, thanks. You know I'll be sick if I eat concession food the day before we compete."

"Not here. There's a sandwich shop outside the arena, across the street."

Her nose un-wrinkles and she looks at me with wide eyes. "Sure."

As she turns to grab her bag, I let my grimace twist my face. Side-by-side shit. What am I doing? Last time Mad and I hung out in public didn't go so hot. This time I won't be hiding her under a box but I'm not sure if that's going to be better or worse.

I can't walk around holding her hand off ice. Even if we're not at home, there are too many people here who know us.

Mad's cool, though. We walk side by side but we don't touch. Just friends, getting lunch. She cracks me up sharing figure skater pick-up lines she read on the Internet: *Is that a skate guard in your pocket or are you just happy to see me?* At the sandwich shop, she lets a harried woman trying to corral three kids cut ahead of us in line.

We sit by the window with our sandwiches. I look across the table at Mad. Funny Mad. Kind Mad. I spend more of my waking hours with her than with any other person but we're always going to skating. Or from skating. Or actually skating. Or lately, fooling around half under the guise of improving our skating. How well do we really know each other?

She finishes chewing. "Bunga for your thoughts?"

"Just thinking about . . . you. About . . . us."

"Is that so?" She waggles her eyebrows at me. "Skate guard in your pocket?"

As always, but there's more to it than that. "How much do you know about me?"

Mad graces me with that sweet smile of hers. "Enough to write quite a sordid biography. Where do you want me to start?" Her smile stretches to a Cheshire cat grin. "How about with your superstition about wearing the same socks the entire week before a competition?" She reads the look I shoot her and laughs. "You're right, you never told me, but guess what? After that long, you can smell them. Especially when they've been in your skates. Igor thinks my incredible arch in the death spiral is due to his awesome coaching ability, when in reality I'm just trying to get my head farther away from your stinky feet."

I laugh, but she's started me thinking about something else. Superstitions help keep me from stressing. Competitions don't stress Mad, but—

"Sorry, it was a joke."

"No, it was funny. True, too. You just got me thinking about your dad."

Her eyebrows seesaw, one dropping down and the other vaulting skyward. "Stinky socks makes you think about my dad?"

"No. Yes. Look, the socks are my superstition because competitions are stressful. Not for you, maybe, but for most of us. Your dad's reelection is coming up soon, isn't it? And think how much worse it is for the defending champions, everyone waiting to see if you'll get knocked down. He's probably just stressed and not sleeping well. Remember how crabby my folks were during their residencies, back when we were in grade school?"

"You worried they were getting divorced," Mad says.

"You said I could come live with you if they did. That you'd share your room with me. That offer still stand?"

"Dad did say he had a lot of extra work with the campaigning." She smiles at me. Not a ha-ha smile, a "thanks, Gabe," smile.

"You're welcome." I'm not going to screw up this time. Maybe Mad could write a book about me, but I want to learn more about her. I reach for her notebook. "I know this is your top-secret spy notebook, but is it okay if I take some paper out of it?" She nods and I tear out two blank sheets. "I challenge you to a favorites game. We'll each write down our favorite things and see how many the other can guess."

"All right. What are the categories? Books, movies, foods, colors?"

"Pick whatever you want, just frame the question around it when you ask."

For a few minutes, there's only the scratching of pens against paper as we write. Once we get to the questions, I'm surprised by how much I know and don't know at the same time. Foods, movies, and games are pretty easy from Saturday nights. It doesn't surprise me that Mad knows those things about me, too. But her favorite class at school is English? "With Xander? It's not because I'm in it, is it?"

Mad tilts her head at me. "Don't be too full of yourself. I'm just disappointed that Mrs. Mason picked this year to have a baby. I heard she was really good, and Miss Xander . . ." She straightens her body. "Anyway—"

I think of how many times Chris and I have disrupted class just to get out of work. "We ruin it for you, don't we? I won't any-more."

Mad shrugs. "I still get to read a lot, and I like that best. But—" She stops talking and looks at me. "Thank you." She looks down at her paper. "Favorite color?"

I picture her skate guards. "Blue." I grin as she nods. No way she'll guess mine. Everyone thinks it's red, because of the Viper. "Mine?"

Mad's look glints with triumph. "Black."

"How'd you know?"

She giggles. "Hello, who had to listen to your sob story? Boo hoo, my parents bought me the wrong color sports car for my birthday. Poor me, I wanted the Batmobile and all I got was this lousy Viper." She punches my arm across the table. "I got new skates and a couple practice dresses for my sixteenth, which shouldn't even count as presents because I needed them anyway. You're so spoiled sometimes. Was there ever something you really wanted that you didn't get?"

I don't know yet. I punch her gently back. "Duh. I didn't get the damn Batmobile." Okay, I'm going to have to go for something difficult. We've both dreamed of headlining an ice show for a career. But . . . "What would I do if I couldn't skate?"

Mad pauses. "I . . . don't know. You got me."

"I'd go to school to study architecture." I spin my paper so she can see I actually wrote it down.

"I didn't do an answer for that question."

"I know." I take my paper back. "You've never thought about what you'd do if you couldn't skate."

She looks at me. I'm right. And as I stare back into her eyes, I see the rest of her answer. She'd rather die.

We watch Chris and Kate skate the next morning. They drew fifth for their adaptation of the Cha Cha Congelado. I always thought the compulsory dances were boring and I don't find the short dances that replaced them any more interesting. As I wait to watch our friends, I let my mind wander. To the shower. With Mad.

"There they are." Mad grabs my arm and startles me out of my daydream.

"Uh-huh." I take the warmth of her touch back into the steaming water.

"They look nervous." Mad grips my arm harder. "They look really nervous."

Reluctantly leaving my fantasy for the moment, I sigh. "Not all of us are lucky enough to belong to your 'no fear' club, Mad." But I lean forward and peer at Chris and Kate anyway. They're waiting on the other side of the arena with Igor. Chris paces and Kate keeps adjusting the skirt of her dress. Weird. Chris and Kate usually do all right when they're on, and they were definitely on yesterday.

The announcer calls their names and they take the ice with locked knees that don't loosen even as their music begins. Their skating's technically correct but looks stiff and forced, and their twitches even follow them into the kiss and cry where they await their scores. Depending on the scores, people usually use the space to kiss or cry. Chris and Kate do neither. He snaps his skate guards on and off and she twists the arm of a teddy bear. They end up fourth, and they leave the area still twitchy. Wonder if Chris regrets screwing around instead of visualizing program run-throughs yesterday? There's a reason for Igor's competition behavior rules. But I've got other things to think about as Mad and I leave the stands to begin preparing for our own short program.

I've seen Mad's Delilah costume before. Igor always insists on a full dress rehearsal a couple of weeks before the competition in order to avoid any celebrity-blooper-worthy mishaps, but today as we warm up I've got time to appreciate it. Her short, transparent skirt doesn't leave much to the imagination, and when she dismounts from our lift, her body upside down with her hands on my thighs, I've got a hell of a view.

Mad grins at me, her face red from the blood rush. "See something you like? Watch out, Samson, you know what I can do." Using her fingers as scissors, she cuts the air.

I shake my head. "No way. I already let you cut my hair once, and look where that got me."

I don't belong to Mad's no-fear club either, but this time Mad and I are a sure bet for final rounds in two days and for Nationals, even if we miss every element. So for once, I'm completely relaxed as we take the ice.

The short program has strict requirements, and we open with a forward inside death spiral followed by a split triple twist. I chase Mad down the ice through our step sequence, feeling her just within my grasp and out of reach at the same time. Side-by-side triple toe loops, then a throw triple flip are next. Then comes our one-handed platter lift, which changes to the star position for the dismount. We finish with our combination pair spin. The music ends, and we smile and bow to the crowd.

In the kiss and cry, I listen to our scores. "For technical elements, thirty-two point five seven." Holy shit, Batman. I stop breathing. "For program components, 28.38. Combined score, 60.95." We didn't just qualify. We're in first place. I thump my chest to start my heart beating again. Mad and I might really be ready for Worlds.

*   *   *

The next day, I walk to the girls' room. So maybe I'm thinking about more than Worlds. So maybe this technically isn't part of the plan. So hell. Like Mad said, we're not Chris and Kate. No matter how tomorrow goes down, we're moving on to Nationals and I'm in a celebratory mood. We broke sixty points on the short program.

Mad answers and Kate's nowhere to be seen. Perfect. "Hey, Mad. Do you—"

A heavy hand clamps down on my shoulder and I turn to see Igor. His eyes flick from me to Mad and back again. "Christopher and Katelyn—have you seen them?"

"No." I'd bet my skates on their location, but I haven't *seen* them.

"We skate tomorrow. We are resting, today, yes? Mental focus, visualizing?" Igor's eyes chastise me.

Guess I'm going to be stuck visualizing my shower with Mad again. "Yeah. Um, yes, sir. I was just going to ask Mad if she wanted to catch some of the lower level pairs."

"Sure," Mad says. "Let me get my coat."

With Igor watching our backs, we head for the west rink.

19

Gabe and I settle ourselves about halfway down in the stands. *We are resting today, yes?* Igor looked at Gabe when he asked that. Just Gabe. He doesn't know about me and Gabe. What does he think Gabe's going to do?

I glance over at Gabe. He's looking me over and I smile. I know what he wanted to do, and it has nothing to do with the juvenile pairs warming up on the ice below. Above us, the heat lamps are out and I'm freezing. I wouldn't mind Gabe warming me up right now. I pull my jacket tighter around me and shiver.

"Want me to get you some tea?" Gabe asks.

I nod. As he leaves, taking the stairs two at a time, my phone buzzes in my pocket. I pull it out and open the text. Harold Ziegler, Dad's publicity manager, sent me a link from today's local paper, a photographer's shot of me and Gabe at the sandwich shop yesterday. Coupled with a photo from our short program and headlined: MORE TO THIS PAIR THAN MEETS THE

EYE? Uh-oh. Harold's message asks, Something going on that I should know about?

Is something going on? Yes, but I don't know exactly what. The ice-cold truth is that apart from secrecy, Gabe hasn't committed to squat. What is *"us,"* exactly? Are we secretly dating? We've only been on two sort-of dates, to the Halloween dance and to the sandwich shop yesterday. Right now it feels like we're friends with secret benefits, and no way I'm telling Harold that.

I text Harold back: just lunch with my best friend. I stare at the sent message on my phone. Gabe has always been my best friend, even more than Kate. I thought so, at least. But I think about our question game at the sandwich shop. I never knew he even liked architecture. How much do I really know about him? I think about the dance, Gabe in the spotlight, surrounded by friends and admirers. Am I even Gabe's best friend?

My phone screen fades to black. I should probably show Gabe the picture but I don't want to. He's not going to like it. I put my phone in my jacket pocket and stare out at the ice as the announcer calls the names of the first pair to skate. There's no need to put Gabe in a bad mood before we skate tomorrow. The photo can wait until after our long program.

A steamy go-cup appears right in front of my face. "Black, one sugar," Gabe says.

I take it, then I feel the soft brush of fleece against my cheeks. Gabe's bought me a blanket from the vendor stands, blue microfleece with figure skates printed all over it. He tucks it around my shoulders. "Do you like it? I know you admired the pink one yesterday but when I saw this one underneath I thought maybe it was better."

It is. Cocooned, I let the cup warm my hands. Gabe has a lot of friends, but I don't think he knows how they take their tea or just the way to drape their favorite-color blanket around them. I am Gabe's best friend. We have more to figure out, but Igor was right. Today is a day for rest. We can talk tomorrow.

The junior free dances are up later, so Gabe and I hang around to cheer on Chris and Kate. We shout and stomp our feet in the stands when their names are announced for the warm-up.

If they can just hold on to fourth, we'll all go to Nationals together, but it doesn't look good. They look beyond nervous, yesterday's twitches not even making the podium when compared to today, and Igor looks like he's about to have a medal-worthy outburst. After a shaky warm-up, they leave until their turn to skate. "What's that all about?"

Gabe shrugs. "Chris was pissy yesterday. Probably they got into it again."

The first two couples in their group aren't that great, shallow edges and sloppy timing. I relax a little. Chris and Kate only need to be fourth.

It's the same stiff knees from their short dance but it's better than the bumbled twizzles and lack of emotion we saw from the last team. They'll make it, might even get third. I breathe a sigh of relief—too early. Just that fast, Chris catches his toe pick on a turn and wipes out completely, falling sideways like a timbered tree. He's up just as fast, but the damage is done. The fall will be a mandatory deduction, and they'll get a lower grade of execution on their entire step sequence.

"Shit," Gabe says beside me.

Chris and Kate slap on smiles for their bows. In the kiss and cry, Kate cries this time, and Chris looks like he'd like to. Before the announcer even reads their scores, I know. "It's over."

Gabe sneaks his pinkie under the edge of my blanket and finds mine. "Pinkie swear me that we're not going to fight before tomorrow."

Yeah, that photo can definitely wait.

And it really is better that way, skating-wise. The next day, I wear my longing on the sleeves of my beautiful chiffon dress. I let all the desire and uncertainty of my relationship with Gabe show from my face to the tips of my fingers. I breathe the music as I soar above the ice. Our lifts are perfect, light and easy. Our throws are higher than ever. Each element of our program is strong, secure. Solid skating and raw emotion: a perfect pairing.

As I lie in Gabe's arms at our end pose, the arena is completely hushed. Then comes a roar like I've never heard before. The crowd is beyond wild, feet stamping on the bleachers, people screaming our names. Gabe lifts me to my feet and I can see that the audience is on theirs as well. We have a standing ovation.

20

Gabe

We bow to the judges and to the crowd, flowers and stuffed animals raining down on us. Picking our way through the obstacle course now covering the ice, we head for the kiss and cry. I look at Mad's baby blues and I know right then I can't even sit next to her. There's no way I'll be able to stop myself, and this is the kiss and cry, not the make-out and cry.

Brrawk! Brawk-brawk! My own mind calls me chicken. And I am. I duck my fried face to my chest and sit on the far end of the bench, forcing Igor to sit between us.

Caught in my own shamed thoughts, I don't even hear the marks. An elbow pokes my side. "Gabriel." Igor elbows me again, harder this time. "First place. Smile."

First place. We've earned the Midwestern Sectional championship title in our senior debut. We're not just going to Nationals, we're going as one of the teams to beat. I got that birthday present I asked Mad for. But somehow I don't feel like a winner.

Igor pats my shoulder. "Accomplished mission, yes?"

I look at Mad. The fake smile on her face matches mine. Skating mission accomplished. Relationship mission? Total tank.

We're headed for the locker rooms when the shit really splatters. The attack comes out of nowhere, a mob of microphones and cameras. This many reporters? At Sectionals? Igor must've sent press releases out in advance. A tall, thin woman shoves her mike in my face. "Tell us how you feel about your performance, Gabriel!"

Another reporter goes for Mad. "Are you excited about Nationals?"

The dark coats and press badges push in on us from all sides, making me claustrophobic.

"You've never missed the podium, but do you think you can pull off a medal at your first senior nationals?"

"Do your parents pressure you to skate?"

"What do you think your chances are at making the World team?"

Mad and I haven't even had a chance to answer any of the questions when the big hit comes. "Can you describe your relationship with each other?"

The buzzing stops. Everyone wants the answer to that one. I glance at Mad. Forget looking like a deer caught in the headlights, she's a frozen dead opossum. "Mad and I ... have been ... skating together ... for years." I stretch each word out to give myself more time to think, sure that the footage of this interview will make me look mentally challenged. "I couldn't . . . imagine my life without her. She's . . ."

She's holding her breath. If I don't think of something soon, her skin is going to match that indigo dress. But nobody knows about us. Not our friends, not our parents. I can't holler into a microphone that she's my girlfriend. I can't. I don't even know how to have a girlfriend.

Mad's dad is such a smooth talker. What would the Senator say? No comment. No way I can say that; everyone will be pissed at me then. Desperate, I run through phrases in my head. She's my gold medal girl. True but corny. Mrs. Incredible to my Mr. Incredible. Worse yet, Juliet to my Romeo. Yeah, a Shakespearean tragedy, just like this interview's about to become.

Wait. Shakespeare. "I don't think William Shakespeare himself had enough words to describe what she means to me."

Mad inhales and smiles as the microphone is thrust into her face. "Ditto."

The cameras flash and like magic Igor breaks through the reporters. That was the perfect quote our coach wanted the media to have. He pushes the crowd aside. "Please excuse. We have medal ceremony to attend."

After the ceremony we take our bags of tossies, all the stuffed animals and flowers, and deliver them to the children's center at Lansing's Sparrow Hospital before heading off to dinner with my parents and Mad's mom. Between my quote and the kids' smiles, Mad and I are smiling again, for real this time.

Back at the hotel that night, I swipe my key card across the door. Inside, Chris is sprawled across his bed, staring up toward the ceiling. I close the door, glance around the room. No Kate, and no shower running either. "Wow, I get to stay in my own room? To what do I owe this high honor?"

"Stuff it." Chris rolls to his stomach and buries his face in his pillow.

No surprise that they're fighting again. "What started it this time?"

He ignores me.

I look for the TV remote. Tonight's going to be fun. "This is because you didn't place."

His head stays in the pillow but his right arm lifts from the mattress. He gives me the finger.

I sit on my own bed. Turn on the TV. Surf. Nothing good. The last channel is a fund-raising commercial for Sparrow's Children's Center. All those sick kids, and Chris is sulking over a bad skate. I click the TV back off. "You know, if you spent more time practicing—"

"Like you, golden boy?" Chris sits up. "This is a big game of 'Igor Says' and if I follow the directions I'll win?"

"My parents pay Igor for a reason. He knows what he's doing."

"Do *you* know what you're doing?"

I look Chris in the eye. "Yeah."

Chris looks away. "Maybe there's more to it than winning. You wouldn't know, though, would you? The gold. The girl. Any gold, any girl, doesn't matter. You always get it all. Spoiled rotten rich shit."

We might both be figure skaters, but there's a face-off coming. "Say that again."

He doesn't. Instead, he lies back down, facing away from me. "Go ahead. Hit me."

I still want to sock him, but I punch down my pillow instead. I arrange my blankets just so, but the room feels like a furnace, Chris's anger burning just below the smooth exterior. I kick off my comforter. Still can't sleep. Finally, I grab my pillow and the spare blanket and leave.

21

Maddy

I lean into the pile of pillows on my hotel bed and unwrap the ribbon from around my gold medal. The shiny surface dances with light from the nightstand lamp. I flip it over and trace my finger along the engraving. *Madelyn Spier, Riverview FSC, 1st place.* I clasp my hands over the perfect circle, feeling its smooth edges against my palms, and hear the cheers of the crowd once more.

The hotel room door bangs open and I stuff the medal into the pocket of my robe.

"It's okay, Maddy." Kate flips her key card onto the dresser. She plops onto her own bed and hugs her pillow to her chest. "You guys were great. You deserved to win."

I remove the medal from my pocket but I wind its ribbon around it again and put it back in my suitcase. "Are *you* okay?"

Kate rolls to her back and looks up at the ceiling. "First alternate. Doesn't really have the same ring as first place." Her eyes blink rapidly.

I pull back my own covers and slide into my bed. "Next year?"

Kate curls into a fetal position. "I don't really want to talk about it, Maddy."

There won't be a next year, I realize. Not if Kate goes away for college. There won't be any more competitions together at all. This is our last time as—

Tap, tap. I roll and cock my ear toward the door. Is someone knocking? *Tap, tap.* A bit louder this time. "Were you expecting somebody?"

Groaning, Kate rolls off her bed and shuffles for the door. "It's probably Chris." She opens the door and shades her eyes against the bright light from the hall. "I know this weekend didn't turn out the way we expected but I—" She steps back. "Gabe?"

I sit back up in bed.

Gabe hesitates just inside the door, a pillow clutched in one hand and a blanket tucked under his arm. "Can I sleep in here? Please? Just on the floor?"

I look at him, then at Kate, then back at him. I start to open my mouth, but—

"The floor won't be necessary," Kate says. "You can sleep in my bed."

I close my mouth.

Gabe looks from Kate to me and back to Kate again. "The floor's good, really."

Kate grabs her pillow and smacks Gabe across the stomach with it. "I'm not sleeping in it with you." She tosses her pillow onto my bed. "Maddy and I will share."

Gabe crawls into Kate's bed. "Thanks."

Kate climbs in bed with me, whispering. "I'm sorry. You don't mind, do you? I just can't deal with Chris tonight."

I don't mind, not really. But as Kate tosses and turns and pulls the blankets off me yet again, I find myself wishing that, last time as roomies or not, I'd just opened my mouth earlier and said that Gabe could sleep in my bed. With me.

The next morning, we're in the hotel breakfast room. Kate works a crossword while Gabe and I eat. Chris walks over with his tray and sits down with us. He mumbles a "sorry" to Gabe but he and Kate don't talk. As I look at them I'm not sure if that's a good or bad thing. Finally, Kate says, "I'm so stuck on this one."

"Let me see?" Chris reaches for the paper. "Seven letters, starts with M?" Then he starts shaking. He snatches Kate's pencil and pushes so hard as he writes the answer that he breaks the tip twice. He shoves the puzzle back at her, grabs his tray, and leaves.

"This is ridiculous." Gabe stands. "I'm going—"

"Don't." Kate sighs, looking at the puzzle. "I started it, I'll go." She flips the paper over, shoves it at me this time. "Here. You don't have a copy for your scrapbook yet, do you?"

Gabe looks at the paper. "Hey, is that—"

"Yeah," Kate says. "Didn't Maddy show you?"

I look down, too. It's the picture of Gabe and me at the sandwich shop.

Kate leaves but Gabe stands there, stiff as ice. "You knew."

"Yes."

"You didn't think I'd want to know?"

"I didn't want to upset you before we skated. *You* made me pinkie swear. It's just a photo, anyway, just friends having lunch. Are we not even allowed to be friends in public?"

"Just a photo. Just some reporters. I told you I wasn't ready to go public."

I cross my arms against his words, look him in the eyes. "I knew about the picture, not the reporters. And you could've just said 'no comment.'"

"Is that what you want?"

"It sounds like that's what *you* want."

"It's not that easy, Mad. Excuse me if I'd like to start with a smaller audience than the entire country. Our parents don't even know."

"You really think they're going to be upset about it?"

"Yeah."

So maybe Dad nerves Gabe out a little, but, "Really?"

"My parents forbid me from going out with you."

"No way." Gabe's mom loves me. She even bought me my first pair of skates.

"It's not you. They're just afraid I'll screw up. They said to think of it like our partnership's a business deal or something."

I scrunch my nose. "That makes it sound like you're buying me."

He sets the paper down so our picture is hidden against the table and looks away, his voice soft. "I need us to be a secret still, Mad. Please. If they ask, can you tell them it's nothing?"

We're nothing. My heart screams no, but I whisper, "All right."

As Gabe walks away, I look back at the paper. At Chris's seven dark letters. MISTAKE.

No one asks me anything more about the photo, not even Harold, so I'm spared uttering the cold, hard truth. Igor has me stay late for extra harness practice, sparing me awkward nothingness with Gabe in the car. The days sludge by.

Kate and Chris are giving me a ride home when I realize suddenly that there's no school tomorrow. It's Thanksgiving break. Dad's coming home again today and he's probably already there. When Chris drops me off at the sidewalk, I run up the steps to our front door.

At the last second, I decide a surprise would be better and I slip the door open and step inside. As soon as I do, I realize it wouldn't have mattered if I'd stomped my way in.

"This whole thing is nonsense," Mom argues from the kitchen. The pots rattle in the sink, louder than they should for normal dish washing. "You need to—"

"You know I can't do that," Dad answers.

"Can't? Or won't?" The kitchen is quiet. Too quiet. "When are you going to tell Maddy?"

"I'm not."

"That's honest, Honest Bill."

"Damned if you do and damned if you don't," Dad mutters.

"Don't you dare quote Eleanor Roosevelt at me." The ice

in Mom's voice goes slushy. "I won't be your Eleanor, Will. I can't."

"A secret is different than a lie. She's got enough stress right now. So maybe our dreams have hit a road bump. Her train is now, Cyn. I'm not going to derail it."

"Our dreams. *Our* dreams?" Mom's voice shakes. "This was never my dream."

"I have a headache," Dad snaps. "I'm going outside for some fresh air."

I step out of the way just in time to avoid being hit by the swinging kitchen door. Pressed against the wall, the door hides me for a split second but then swings back again. Dad doesn't even notice, he's so focused. On leaving.

22

Thanksgiving doesn't feel very thankful. Things have been off with Mad and me since Sectionals. She apologized about the picture and I said I forgave her but we've been tiptoeing around each other in a 24/7 ballet pas de deux. The air outside's turned frosty and when the Spiers come over for dinner, Jack Frost swirls inside our house. As my dad carves the turkey, Mad's parents pick at each other like they're Chris and Kate. The ill mood is contagious, and my parents start acting all somber. The only thing I'm thankful for is that in a couple of hours the whole thing will be over.

Dad has so much to drink he accidentally pours me a glass of wine. I leave it on the table. "Let's get out of here," I whisper to Mad.

She gives me a wary look. "We're not volunteering to do the dishes again, are we?"

"No." Even though at the rate things are going, I'll be doing KP after the Spiers go home or Helen will be doing it tomorrow.

I think our parents are all about to pass out right on the table. They don't even seem to notice that we leave the room.

We sit on the couch in the family room, not touching, and stare at the gray skies outside. "I'm sorry your parents are fighting," I say. I hear Mad sniffle beside me and feel even shittier. I was trying to make her feel better, not worse.

Mad chokes out crying breaths but then I realize she's trying to talk. "Sometimes I think . . . my whole life is a lie."

"What?"

"My parents. Us."

She apologized to me about the photo. I realize now that I never apologized to her. I was angry about the ambush, but she didn't know that was coming, either. "A secret is different than a lie."

Now she's full-out crying. "That's what my dad said. A secret is different than a lie."

"What?"

It takes her a minute to get it together enough to talk. "They had a huge fight yesterday. Dad quoted Eleanor Roosevelt at Mom."

Eleanor Roosevelt was a pretty accomplished woman, wasn't she? Didn't she even do the President's job when he was sick? Maybe I shouldn't zone out so much in history. "What's wrong with Eleanor Roosevelt?"

"FDR was with his *mistress* when he died."

No shit. Ouch. I put my arm around Mad. "Whatever happens, I want to be here for you, okay? This . . . *us* . . . isn't a lie."

Mad pulls away from me. "Then why does it have to be a secret?"

"My parents—"

"No. Even if they didn't like it at first, they'd get over it."

She's right. We're not star-crossed lovers from feuding families. My parents like *Mad*. But there's more to it. "And . . . me." The real reason my parents don't want me to go out with Mad. "I've never done this before. All I've done is screw around. I'm losing my relationship virginity to you. I need to take it slow."

She leans into me.

"Sorry I got mad about the photo."

Her arm circles my waist. I don't need to say anything more. "Okay."

We sit and hold each other while the gray fades to starless black, but our own storm clouds have lifted. Things might not be okay with Mad's parents, but with Mad and me, the universe is back in orbit.

The next day, we get a little bit more practice in with school closed. After, Igor calls me aside. "Christmas ice show," he says.

Ugh, the fruitcake of my holiday season. With a cheese-ball theme to go along with it. We've performed *The Nutcracker, The Snow Queen, How the Grinch Stole Christmas*, even the Nativity story. Kate and Chris were cast as Mary and Joseph and by some divine miracle managed not to fight for the entire twelve days of rehearsals. But what's left for this year? Charlie Brown? I ask warily, "What's the story?"

"No story this year," Igor says. "Medley of holiday songs. I like you to pick own music. With Madelyn, please."

A mash-up of Christmas tunes and an excuse to hang out? Sounds like a plan to me.

Mad's face lights up like it's Christmas already when I tell her the news in the car. Back home, she runs inside her house quick. I snag a couple mugs of cocoa and a plate of cookies from Helen. Then I start a fire in the family room. When I turn back around, Mad's skipping toward me with her arms full of CDs. A couple of the cases start to slip off the top of her pile. I catch them just in time. "Wouldn't it be easier to just look on iTunes?"

Mad decorates the coffee table with stacks of CDs. "It would be much easier. That's the point." She turns back to me. Puts her arms around my neck and gives me a deep, long kiss. Pulling back, she grins. "I want this to take a *long* time."

After that kiss, so do I. I drag an old portable CD player out of the cabinet. All right, after a little more kissing I drag out the CD player. Set it up on the end table. Mad plays the first candidate. The music is slow, soft and gentle. A woman begins to sing. I try not to fidget. "Um, what's this one?"

"'The Prayer'? It's a duet between—"

"It's Celine Dion, isn't it?"

"Yeah." Mad frowns. "No go?"

"Kind of a matter of principle."

"I get it." She tosses the CD into the newly created "no" pile. "Your turn."

I put on an Elvis album and press play. The King wails about Santa Claus. We look at each other and bust our guts laughing.

"Definitely not." I rifle through a couple cases, then sit back against the couch. "It should be something fun. I like our programs this season but they're kind of somber. Not funny fun, though. We should do a song that's . . ."

Mad smiles. "Flirty fun."

I move closer to her so our thighs brush against each other. "Yeah."

She leans into my arm, then runs a finger from the inside of my knee up my leg.

I'm not thinking about picking music anymore.

Mad pecks my cheek. "I know just the song." She slips "All I Want for Christmas" into the player, gets up, and dances.

I lean back into the couch, put my hands behind my head, and let my eyes run up and down her body. "I like it. Bet I'd like it even better if we were in my room and you were in your underwear. Seriously, though?" I sit back up. "You don't need me to do that song. It'd be a great solo, but we should do something that needs both of us for the performance."

Mad stops dancing. She looks at me. "Both of us," she says slowly. She pauses. "Gabe . . . maybe you should be the star this time."

"What?"

"You said, at Halloween, that you're always showing me off. It's true. We can't do anything about that for competitions, but a show is just entertainment. What if we switched roles?"

She'd be the pair guy and I'd be the girl. I've seen it done before as a spoof. She could never lift me but she could fake throwing me and we could probably manage a pivot spiral. It'd be beyond funny but . . . there *is* something different about being with Mad. "Thanks, but I want to show you off."

Though I don't take her up on her offer, the melty-marshmallow gesture warms me more than cocoa. Suddenly, I just want to hold her. I switch the player to the radio's Christmas station. I pull Mad onto my lap. "Let's just listen awhile. Maybe we'll hear something." We nestle together to Kenny G's rendition of "Let It Snow." The first snowflakes of the year fight to stick to the ground outside.

"This is nice," Mad says. "Not for skating, but for other things." She rubs her stockinged feet against my leg, and glances toward the hall. "Is Helen going to check on us?"

I tighten my arm around her. "She's listening to NPR while she bakes. We're good." I'm cool with the cuddling but if Mad wants more than that I'm not about to say no. I move to kiss her again, and then we both hear it. Perfect from the first swingy notes. "Baby, It's Cold Outside."

"This is it." Mad turns the volume up.

I grab my phone and download the song. I set it to repeat and we play at walking through steps and elements.

The music lets us recycle our footwork and some other favorite moves from our old *Incredibles* routine. More teasing than skating, the program glides together easily. We're ready to try it on the ice that afternoon.

Igor's pleased when we demonstrate. "It shows well."

Chris and Kate, along with one of their learn-to-skate students, make a program out of "I Saw Mommy Kissing Santa Claus." Good choice, I think, when I see their number in the show lineup. If they get in another fight before Christmas, they can always switch Chris's role to that of the jealous husband.

They don't fight. Chris brings Kate a sprig of mistletoe. In secret, I give one to Mad, too. It's going to be a holly-jolly Christmas.

Riverview isn't exactly a headliner on the entertainment list, but we usually have a good turnout for the show. This year, though, Igor raises ticket prices and the house sells out. Ms. Rasgotra makes an announcement prohibiting flash photography during the performances, but when Mad and I are up, everyone ignores it. Our first-place finish at Sectionals has the media hyped about the youngest senior pair skaters the U.S. has seen in years.

Our *Romeo and Juliet* program is longing. This show program? Is flirty fun. *Foreplay* fun. Never mind all those lines about how she "really can't stay. . . ." From our first steps on the ice, even before we set up our opening pose, Mad spends the entire program convincing me otherwise. No jumps this time, no throws. All lifts, a death spiral, a pair spin with Mad doing a standing split, her right foot on my shoulder. Our bodies in constant contact with each other. The way we're touching each other on ice, hands everywhere, we'd be kicked out of a Riverview Prep dance.

As a choreographic surprise for the last element, I get my own ten seconds of fame. We do a reverse pivot spiral, Mad setting the pivot this time while she reels me in around her. The music crests and I twirl Mad into our end pose. Just as the last note sounds, I drop her back into a dip. Millimeters from mine, her lips do look delicious, just like in the song.

And I kiss her.

That wasn't part of the choreography.

Anyone who blinked would've missed it, I pull back that fast. But the cameras are everywhere, the stands a fireworks finale of flashes. Each one illuminating my lapse in judgment. I stand and twirl Mad again, setting up for our bows. I can't look at her. Side-by-side quadruple shit.

23

Gabe just kissed me. On the ice, under the spotlights, in front of *everyone*. As he pulls me up out of the dip and twirls me for our bows, I can't believe my smile doesn't split my face right open. It's the best Christmas present I could've asked for, and it's not even Christmas yet.

We were the last number, and I don't even remember skating the finale. All I can think of is the candlelight skate. Every year after the show, Ms. Rasgotra decks the boards around the Olympic rink with artificial tea light candles and Igor sets the spotlights to swirl soft snowflake patterns across the ice. Skating in the dark has its own allure, even if we only skate laps and simple dance patterns. I can't wait to waltz with Gabe.

Gabe runs off to the restroom as soon as the finale's over. By the time he gets back, the first song is already done. Impatiently, I reach for his hand.

He steps sideways, slipping his fingers away. He looks around.

"What?" I ask, but I see them, too. The photographers raise their cameras as they step toward us.

"I'm going to ask Kate to dance. Let's not give them too much to speculate on, okay?"

Too much to speculate on? He just kissed me in front of all of them not ten minutes ago. Too shocked to say anything, I watch Gabe walk over to Kate, and escort her to the ice.

"Wanna dance?" Chris asks from beside me. He's still dressed in his Santa Claus suit, bouncing belly and all, but that doesn't improve my Christmas spirit.

"What did you think of the new ending?" I ask Chris as we step onto the ice.

"What new ending?"

"For our 'Baby, It's Cold Outside' number."

"You guys changed it?" he asks. "I thought the reverse pivot was cool."

He doesn't even know, I realize. He and the rest of our club were waiting behind the backdrop to skate the finale. Igor and Ms. Rasgotra wouldn't have seen, either, trying to corral the learn-to-skate kids. And everyone in the stands would just think it was part of the choreography. I put in a couple of laps and excuse myself to sign some autographs, leaving Chris to the long line of children now waiting their turn to skate with Santa.

I've signed one autograph book, three pairs of skates, and a couple dozen programs when my crowd disperses. Chris's skate-with-Santa line doesn't seem to be any shorter, and with the parents slipping him bills for hamming it up for their kids, he seems in no hurry to have his own partner back. Likewise, Gabe is still dancing with Kate. I could go out and skate by myself but I don't want to. Wistfully, I watch Gabe lead Kate in the European Waltz as "Silver Bells" plays, the way he matches his steps to hers as they navigate through the skating parents taking laps and the solo dancers. That should've been my waltz, but anyone watching would mistake Gabe for Kate's dance partner. The song finally ends, and they cut through the crowd and step off the ice.

I walk toward them but they don't look for me. Side by side and chatting with each other, they head for the meeting room snack tables. I sink onto a bench. Somewhere, over the chatter, a kid starts wailing. Alone in the crowds of people, I lean back against the wall and close my eyes.

I don't know how long I sit there before Gabe comes looking for me. "Mad? You asleep?"

"No." I open my eyes. Most of the crowds have gone and the few people who remain are packing up their things.

"Last dance." Gabe shrugs in the direction of the ice. "You want to?"

I take the hand he offers and follow him.

"Have Yourself a Merry Little Christmas" plays softly over the speakers. Gabe nods his head to the music to check the meter. "Fourteenstep?"

The ice is rough under my skates, rutted from the many skaters before us. Half of the tea lights have lost their battery power, and my legs are stiff from sitting. It's an easy dance, one Gabe and I passed ages ago, but I feel mechanical skating it. I keep time with Gabe and the music, but my robotic movements don't match his smooth rhythm. It's not what I wanted.

Gabe drives me home afterward. I stare out the window at the colorful displays of Christmas lights twinkling from almost every yard. But there isn't any magic to them now. They shine too brightly on what I'd rather not see. So he's sweet to me when we're alone, but only when we're alone. This is real, he told me. But the reality? He hasn't taken a single stroke toward ending our secret status. Off the ice, he only wants me when nobody's watching.

Gabe pulls into his garage. The second the brake is on, he's reaching for me.

"Don't touch me."

He stops. "What's wrong?"

"Seriously? *Seriously?* You kiss me and then it's like you're pretending you don't even know me?"

He sighs. "I freaked, okay? It was so easy to just kiss you. Just slipped out like it was nothing. When I kiss you, I want it to mean something."

"Kissing me felt like nothing."

"No, that's not what I meant. See? I suck at this. I can't even talk to you." He drops his head to his hands and pulls at his curls, breathing the longest, loudest breath I've ever heard him breathe. When he talks again, his voice totters like a beginning Snowplow Sam skater. "It's like in skating, you know how Igor won't let us put something in a program until we can do it at least eighty percent of the time? I'm nowhere near eighty percent at this. Hell, I'm nowhere near eight percent."

"You kiss me all the time when we're alone."

"It's not the kissing that's the problem. I'm good at kissing."

He's so good at kissing. As angry as I am at him, I still want him to kiss me. It makes me even madder. "What's the problem, then?"

"Being in a relationship, okay? I know how to be a couple on the ice. I don't know how to be one off the ice. I've never been good at that. Never been able to make it work."

I've seen this program before, and the originality is definitely lacking. "Maybe this isn't just about you. Maybe it's about us. Don't you trust me?"

"I do. I do trust you. I just want some time to figure things out."

The first time we went skating, Gabe didn't even want to go. He had a great time once we got started, but I had to pull him onto the ice. And now I push. "Fine, you figure it out. But until you do, don't look at me. If we don't have ice under our feet, we're not touching each other. Until you're ready for this secret to be over, we're secretly over."

24

Christmas break means extra practices, but I don't mind. During practice, with Igor barking commands at me, I know what to do. Off ice? Baby, it's been cold since the show. I've mucked everything up. I slide two more five-pound plates onto the weight bar, then lie back down on the bench.

With Chris spotting me, I adjust my grip and push up. One. Two. Three—

"You doing New Year's Eve again this year?"

I wobble and almost drop the weights. My arms collapse and it's all I can do to keep the bar off my chest. My face stretches from the effort. "Chris!"

He finally helps me lift the weight back onto the rack.

I sit and rub my groaning pecs. "Jeez. Don't ask me shit in the middle of a set."

He only lifts his eyebrows. "But you are, right? 'Cause everyone's already planning on it."

I've got a more pressing problem than New Year's Eve. "What'd you get Kate for Christmas?"

"Nothing."

"Man, that's not cool. Seriously, what?"

"Seriously, nothing. Yet. There's still three more shopping days left."

I try not to sound too exasperated. "So what are you planning on getting?"

"Why do you want to know?"

"Uh, research."

Chris waggles his eyebrows at me. "Well, since she sat on Santa's lap already and told me what she wants, maybe I'll just give her that." He raises his voice to mimic a girl and thrusts his hips back and forth. "Give it to me, baby, uh-huh, uh-huh—"

I clap my hands over my eyes as the hockey team struts into the weight room behind Chris's back.

"Come on, that was funny," Chris says.

I drop my hands and nod over his shoulder.

He turns. Looks. "Oh."

Kurt stops, and the swarm of players stops with him. The air is suddenly ice thick. The rest of the players look at Kurt. "Sorry, ladies," he says. "Didn't mean to interrupt your *gay* little holiday party."

The snarky remark is on the tip of my tongue, but I think about Mad, thinking her whole life is a lie. I look at Mike, standing behind Kurt.

Mike won't look at me. I know his secret.

I'd never tell Kurt that *Mike* is gay, but I'm sick of secrets. Really sick of secrets. I sling my arm around Chris's shoulder. "No worries, the more the merrier."

Chris shoves me off. "Sicko, you're taking it too far." He squares his shoulders and looks at Kurt. "You weren't interrupting anything. Just my impression of—"

"Drop it," I warn.

"*Anita*," he finishes.

At the mention of his ex-girlfriend, Kurt's face grows redder than the brick wall behind him and he looks like he'd like nothing better than to smash both Chris and me up against that wall. Right now. The mutters of "Who's Anita?" from the freshmen behind him, though, keep his arms crossed over his chest as we walk past.

I head for the locker room, but this isn't over yet.

After my shower, I manage to catch Kate coming out of the girls' locker room. "Hey, Kate. What do you want for Christmas?"

Kate stops short. She lets go of the handle of her skate bag and it clatters upright on the floor. "Ohmigod, did Chris ask you to ask me that?"

"Um . . ."

Dancing around on her toes, Kate's apparently mistaken my hesitancy to mean that yes, Chris did ask me and I just wasn't supposed to tell. "It would be so cool if he would make me something. You know, something he put some effort into instead of last-minute shopping."

Okey-dokey, now I'm gouging a hole deep enough to trip both myself and Chris. I put my hand gently on her shoulder to stop her twirling. Watching her is making me light-headed. "He's not really the crafty type, is he?"

"Well, even something like a special playlist. You know, something that said he was thinking about *us*."

"Super. Thanks." I escape before I get myself in even more trouble and go back to the locker room. "Hey, Chris."

"What?"

"I just overheard Kate talking about how super romantic playlists are. You should make her one for Christmas."

Chris perks at the idea. "Sweet meat. That would even be cheap."

"You're welcome," I tell him. One problem solved.

At home during families dinner that night, I ponder my newest dilemma. I can't make Mad a playlist. We've spent years listening to music together at the rink or in the car and she's already borrowed all of my music that she likes. The traditional romantic gifts: flowers, chocolates, stuffed animals, jewelry? Out. Our families will celebrate Christmas together the way we always do and I can't give her something lovey-dovey in front of our parents when I'm not even supposed to be dating her. And my usual gift-card routine would get me negative points this year. I decide to sleep on it.

Sunday afternoon I head for the mall. Guess everyone else missed Chris's reminder that there are still three whole shopping days left because the place is worse than Cappi's on a Friday night. I check out the mannequins at Victoria's Secret.

As much as I enjoy seeing Mad's underwear, that's a definite no. There's tons of clothing stores, but Mom probably got her clothes.

I walk into Barnes & Noble and look for skating books in the sports section. Not much selection. A game? Too friendly. A journal? Does she even keep one? I could get her a new secret spy notebook but I know what she writes in there. I don't want her taking notes on the single skaters to see how she measures up. I want her to be with me.

I leave the store and scowl my way past Santa's village. In the food court, I buy a giant cinnamon roll. I break off pieces and chew them as I chew up various ideas. Shoes? No. A purse? She already has one. I need a spectacular gift, something that will show Mad how sorry I am. Too bad the only thing I seem to be worse at than relationships is shopping.

The carousel music is giving me a headache. I chow the rest of my snack as I book it out of the mall.

There's a mega craft store on the corner across the street. "Something he made," Kate said. I'm not the crafty type, either, but how hard can it be?

Inside, more Christmas decorations than I saw in the entire mall are somehow squeezed into the front quarter of the store. The center aisles overflow with winter floral arrangements and wedding paraphernalia. What do people even do with all this? It must be obvious I don't belong here, because a sales clerk zooms up to me. "Welcome to Jo-Michael's," she chirps. "Can I help you?"

Please. "I need a present."

"Do you want to make a present or give craft supplies as a present?"

I look around helplessly. "Give craft supplies?"

"What kind of supplies are you interested in?"

"I don't know. I need something for my . . ." Just say it, I tell myself. Let a little secret out. The clerk doesn't even know me.

"Girlfriend?"

I scrunch down. "For my partner."

The sales clerk's mouth makes a small "o."

I resist rolling my eyes. "My *skating* partner."

"What does she like?"

Um, skating? Me, maybe? *And her scrapbook, the story of us.* That's it. "Scrap-booking. You have stuff for that, right?"

They do. A whole aisle of albums, another of paper, two aisles of stickers, and one dedicated to special machines for cutting out fancy shapes and letters. As far as I know, Mad only keeps a skating scrapbook. I scour all five aisles and manage to find some paper that looks like the surface of a frozen pond, some skating stickers, and a stamp of pair skaters. I don't know if her scrapbook's the 12×12 kind or the 8×11 kind, so I get both.

At home, I dress the present up, skipping my usual gift-bag routine and raiding Mom's specialty wrapping stash. Helen has to help me fix my poorly wrapped corners. I sit on my bed with the present on my lap and curl the ribbons one at a time on the blade of the scissors the way she showed me. Each curl only twists my stomach more. Mad's going to want something that shows she's my girlfriend. But it was never about two weeks. It's always been about the G word.

Finally the present is ready. I clutch it to my chest. It's pretty on the outside, but I know the promise it holds isn't enough. I stare out my window. The maple tree's decked with snow. In the afternoon sun, melting clumps fall from the branches. I shudder.

I set the package on my desk and pick up my keys.

25

On Christmas Eve, I help the Nielsens unload their arms full of presents in our living room, trying to feel out my own gifts as I do. The offering from Mr. and Mrs. Nielsen is squishy, probably clothes. And, wait. Gabe's gift to me is in an actual box this year? He's glammed it up, red ribbon curls spilling over the top of the silver wrapping paper. Wide and flat, it thunks softly as I tip it. Some sort of book? It's too light, and there's the slightest plastic sound. Definitely not a gift card. I set the gifts under the tree and smile. I've put Gabe and I on ice since the show, but it's been harder than I thought it would be. As I look into his big, brown puppy eyes, making up's pretty high on my wish list and it looks like maybe I'm getting at least one thing that I want.

But even more than I can't wait to open Gabe's gift, I can't wait until *he* opens his gift from me. All through dinner I fever with the anticipation. I don't even taste the cranberry sauce I eat. The tradition is that we don't open presents until after dinner and games. I lose and don't even know how badly. When it's finally time for presents, I hand Gabe his from me first. He's a ripper; it'll be over fast.

But he doesn't rip. Is he really changing? He slits the tape one piece at a time, carefully folds the paper back, and takes the lid off the box so slowly I think I might scream. Then the grin wraps around his face like a string of lights around a tree as he reaches into the box and holds up the Batmobile ornament. "You remembered. This is awesome, Mad. Where'd you find this?"

I blush with pleasure. "On eBay." I reach over and press a button on the top of the ornament. A snippet of the Batman theme song plays.

Gabe laughs. "This is going on the tree as soon as we get home."

The adults' gifts to each other are the usual boring ties and wine. Dad gets a book from the Nielsens. I lean over and peer at the title. *JFK's Secret Doctor.* "Sounds scandalous."

"Lots of great presidents had health issues," Dad snaps. "It's nothing to joke about."

I sit back as Mom chides, "Will."

Dad sighs and rubs his forehead. "I'm sorry, Maddy."

"It's okay." But it's not. This is the first time Dad's been home since Thanksgiving, he didn't make the holiday ice show this year either, and all I really want for Christmas is for things to be normal again.

Mrs. Nielsen quickly hands me her gift. I'm right, she bought me clothes. They're nice, a red cashmere sweater and a cute pair of gray slacks, and I thank her sincerely, but they don't take away the sting.

At least I still have Gabe's gift left. I rip the wrapping from it.

Scrapbook paper. I flip through the contents. And stickers. In the bottom, a rubber stamp.

Mom peers over my shoulder. "You don't have that stamp yet, do you?"

I pick it up. It's pair skaters. He tried. "I don't. Thanks, Gabe."

Gabe's face falls.

I force a small smile. "I like it, I do." But I know he knows that I don't.

Dad downs another glass of wine, starts up with some nostalgic crap about Christmas being the time to appreciate what we have.

Gabe excuses himself to the bathroom, but he bypasses the half bath and goes upstairs.

I'm just as glad. I need some space.

After the Nielsens leave, I sit in the window seat in Dad's office and look out at the stars. It's my Christmas tradition, to sit there until I hear sleigh bells. This year I'll wait all night, because Dad won't be sneaking outside to ring them. He's passed out already, sleeping on the couch again.

I don't know what I expected Gabe to give me. He didn't even want to dance with me at the candlelight skate, not like he was going to dazzle me with diamonds or offer me his heart on bended knee. Why even bother with relationships if you'll just be disappointed? Everything's wrong; it's not even snowing.

I pull my legs up against my chest and stare at the wood grain of the paneling, feeling the weight of all Dad's presidential biographies lining the shelves, smothering me. Eventually my back gets stiff enough that I decide to just go to bed.

In my room, I let myself drop backward onto my comforter. My head hits my pillow and I wince. Something with sharp corners, probably a book, is underneath it. I pull it out but it isn't a book. It's a box, about the size of a book. Covered in glittery paper, with my name scrawled across the top in black Sharpie marker.

I rip through the wrapping and lift the lid of the box. There's a frame inside, one of those collapsible kinds that opens for display. I open it and set it on my nightstand. It holds two pictures, both of me and Gabe as kids. The left side shows our first time on the ice. I was four and he was five. We're wearing clashing puffy jackets and snow pants, scarves and helmets, and all you can see of our bodies is our laughing, smiling faces as we march along mitten in mitten. The right side is us up in the maple tree, back before the accident, when we were still allowed to climb it. It's a pretty frame and they're cute photos but I already had copies of both of them. I pick up the empty box to move it from my bed and that's when I notice it isn't empty. Inside the bottom of the white box is a folded sheet of white printer paper. I unfold the note.

Mad,

Remember how chickenshit I was our first time? Wouldn't even take one step without you. And the tree? You know how I feel about you.

I'm so afraid of falling I can't even say it out loud yet but I'm writing it here. I want you to be my girlfriend. If you'll come back and hold my hand, I'm ready for one baby step at a time.

Yours, Gabe

I blink at the words. Gabe's girlfriend. Maybe I can't have everything back to normal for Christmas but, in the final rankings, Gabe defining our relationship takes second by a mere hundredth of a point. It's still a secret, but it's a start.

Still clutching the note, I get out of bed. I pick up my flashlight and walk to the window. It's starting to snow. I signal Gabe. I LOVE IT.

There's no answer from Gabe's dark window. I start to flash again, then I hear the bells. I look out my window at the lawn. Gabe's standing in the side yard, ringing sleigh bells.

I smile down at him. I want to be there for you, he said. He's being there. So maybe he needs some basic-skills work with relationships. Nothing says "I love you" like breaking your arm to stop someone else's fall and I've waited thirteen years already, haven't I?

Christmas morning is a bright new dawn, sunlight sparkling off the blanket of white that fell overnight. I slip downstairs, not wanting to break the peace of the morning. As I pass the living room, I stop. Dad's on the couch again. But this time, so is Mom. I don't even want my cup of tea anymore, don't care about opening any more presents. I tiptoe into the living room and curl up in an arm chair next to the couch.

26

Gabe

The day after Christmas, I catch a movie matinée with Chris between practices. As I wait in the theater lobby for him to get a pop refill, I bask in the sunlight pouring through the two-story, floor-to-ceiling windows. I scored top presentation marks from Mad for my surprises and morning practice went great. Better yet, when I walked in the house after practice my parents told me they changed their minds about the hospital benefit ball. Not only are they going, they're taking Mad's parents along. I texted Mad right away. We have a date for New Year's Eve.

I pull out my phone and tap open the app store. What was that app the Jo-Michael's lady recommended again? Pinterest? I download it, search for romance ideas. Roses frozen in ice cubes? I'm going to knock Mad's skates off.

Chris returns from the concession line. I shove my phone in my pocket before he can see.

We stroll through the lobby to the exit. The bright sunshine streaming through the glass is deceiving, and I open the lobby doors to a blast of bitter wind. I pull my hood up and run for the car with Chris right behind me.

"So." Chris takes a long slurp of his Mountain Dew, tries to fit his oversize cup in the Viper's cup holder, then settles it between his legs instead. "About that party . . ."

Time to take care of this. I flip Chris my phone before starting the car. "Call my mom and put it on speaker for me. I'll ask." No way Mom's going to let me have a party while she and Dad are out. Let her tell Chris no for me.

Chris busts out laughing. "What's this?"

Shit, the rose-cubes. I grab for my phone.

Chris yanks it out of reach, almost spilling his Dew. He scrolls through the page. Whistles. "God, what a sacrilege of an F-150." He flashes me a look of a truck with a gauzy white canopy draped over the pink down comforter in its bed. "Since when are you Mr. Romantic, Two Weeks?"

I ignore him, put the car in reverse. "You better call. Mom's got rounds soon."

Chris finds the number in my contact list, calls, and holds the phone out toward me as I drive down the road.

"Hey, Mom," I say when she picks up. "Can I have a New Year's Eve party?"

"We'll be out," she says. I open my mouth to say "too bad" to Chris. Mom cuts me off before the words can escape. "But ask Helen."

I swerve back into my own lane. "What?"

"Ask Helen. If she doesn't mind supervising, you can have a few friends over like last year."

"Um, okay. Thanks," I mumble, feeling my perfect plans begin to crack up.

Chris ends the call and pumps his fist in the air. "Yes!"

"Yeah, but it's New Year's Eve, remember? Helen's probably busy." *Please, let her be busy.* "I'll ask her when I get home." In case by some miracle of Satan she happens to have nothing to do on the biggest holiday of the year. I put my hand out for my phone.

Chris holds it out of reach and begins scrolling through my contacts again.

"Gabe?" Helen, on speaker. And with Chris right in the car with me, I'm not wiggling out of this.

"Um, are you busy on New Year's Eve?" *Please say yes, please say yes,* I chant to myself.

"Yes."

YES! I glance at Chris and shrug my "I told you so."

"Why?" Helen asks.

"Nothing. I was just wondering if you by any chance wanted to supervise a bunch of loud, obnoxious teenagers. Obviously, though, if you've got plans . . ."

Helen laughs over the speaker. "Gabe, those *are* my plans."

Feeling as though I've run out of gas, I ease the car to the curb. I reach for my phone again and Chris passes it over this time but I can already hear Helen confirming my worst nightmare loud and clear.

"Your mom already talked to me. She thought you might want to throw a party again this year. Believe it or not, I was once a loud and obnoxious teenager meself. Let's just be keeping the guest list to a dozen or less, all right?"

A dozen or less. How about one? But Chris is raising the roof next to me. Like it or not, I'm throwing a party.

I break the news to Mad at afternoon practice. "So for New Year's, you mind if I invite a few friends to join us? Chris and Kate? My friend, Andy, and my cousins? Maybe Jonah?"

She doesn't mind. In fact, she sounds . . . even more excited? "You mean it?"

That's when I figure it out. She thinks I want to tell them about us at the party. Ready or not, I'm about to have to take that first baby step. Let the countdown to my nightmare begin—time for everyone to watch me drop the ball.

The closer it gets to December 31, the more Grinchy I feel about New Year's. I must find a way to stop it from coming. We play Jenga for families night and I can't pull out one piece all evening without knocking the whole tower over. I'm not even ready to tell Chris about me and Mad, let alone a whole group of friends. But I never was good at planning things out. I've always relied on Igor for that one.

The day before New Year's Eve, still lost on ideas, I come home from afternoon practice and find Mom making crab dip in the kitchen. "Mom? Where's Helen?"

Mom opens a package of cream cheese and dumps it into the bowl on the island with a loud plop. She wipes the white specks from her cheeks, blinking in surprise, then bends over the recipe card once more. "She wasn't feeling well. She went home to rest so she'll be better in time for your party tomorrow."

There *is* a God. I stick my head into the pantry like I'm

looking for a snack so Mom won't see the hallelujah on my face. "I can cancel it. Everyone will understand."

"I don't think that will be necessary, Gabe, but it's very mature of you. Put your stuff away and come help me finish getting the party refreshments together, though."

"Shit."

"Gabriel Thomas!"

Triple shit. I didn't mean to say that out loud. I poke my head out of the pantry. "Sorry, Mom. I just . . . stubbed my toe." With a real grimace on my face, I fake hobble out to help with the crab dip. But when we're done, I go get some roses. Just in case.

The next morning, Helen isn't feeling any better. I don't usually have time to eat anything fancy for breakfast and love school holidays when morning practice is a much more tolerable nine o'clock and Helen whips up omelettes or Belgian waffles. Today, though, I happily pour my own Cheerios.

Helen's a no-show for lunch, too. When I come home from afternoon practice, I scan the driveway. Her Jetta wagon is MIA. I dance into the house. And almost run into Mom bustling around the kitchen, her evening gown swirling around her ankles as she frantically checks over the supplies for my party. "Don't put the food out until at least 8:30, and make sure you put out ice with it. I don't want anyone getting food poisoning."

My mouth drops open. I close it, then rub my ears, sure I've misheard.

"And don't forget to lock Axel up. I didn't make crab dip for the cat."

"You're still letting me have the party?"

Mom picks up her purse. "I'm trusting you to be responsible, so yes." She grabs her wrap from Dad, fluffs it around her shoulders, and pecks my cheek.

And they're gone.

But nobody else needs to know they said I could still have the party. I text Chris. Helen's sick, no supervision for party.

Chris texts back. K, I'll pass it on.

I text Mad. Party's off, Helen's sick. Come over & review tape?

Her reply doesn't come for an agonizing ten minutes. K.

27

Maddy

I stare at the message on my phone until the phone fades to black, putting itself to sleep. It's not really "K." I set my phone on the bathroom counter and look first at the curling iron and then at myself in the mirror. I don't feel like finishing my replication of my ballet night updo anymore but even if no one else is going to be there I'm not going over to Gabe's with only half my hair done.

I twist the next section around the iron, but I bring it too close and clip the edge of my ear with the hot metal rod. "Ouch!" I jerk the iron away. I was so psyched about this party. Just a few friends from the rink and from school. No reporters. I thought Gabe was ready for that first baby step. It was only going to be eight of us; his parents would still let him have everyone over even without Helen. He never wanted to have everyone else over; Chris must've weaseled him into hosting a party like he did last year.

Screw the hairdo. Review tape? Honestly, why can't he

just be . . . honest? He wanted me back because he was missing fooling around.

I reach for the water spritzer, spray down my hair, and comb it out straight again. I touch up my lip gloss, then shove the rest of my make-up back in the drawer.

In my room, I look at the sparkly top I bought for the party because I knew Gabe would like it. I put it back in the closet and don't even change my T-shirt.

I flop on my bed. Eight o'clock comes and goes and I stay flopped. Do I even want to go? At 8:15, my phone buzzes. Gabe's texting me again. Coming?

Not bothering to reply to his message, I shrug on my coat and boots and trudge through the slush in the driveway.

I almost open the door into Gabe, he's waiting right behind it. He doesn't even wait for me to take my coat off. He pulls me nose to nose while my boots drip puddles on the floor. "Hey, girlfriend."

His grin says he's pretty proud of himself, but I'm not smiling. Same old move, that when no one else is around I can be his girlfriend. "Hey." I let him pull me closer until my lips almost brush against his, then I pull back. I kick my boots off. I'm still wiggling one arm out of my coat when Gabe takes me by the hand and pulls me toward the family room. "Um, do I even get to take my coat—"

I stop as we enter the room. A fire burns low in the hearth and soft candlelight glows from the end tables. Two crystal wine glasses glimmer on the coffee table, reflecting the light of the candles. Between them a bottle of sparkling white grape juice chills in a bucket of ice and beside them sits a plate of chocolate-covered strawberries. It's a good surprise, one he's obviously put some effort into. But we need to talk. I take a breath. "I thought we were going to review tape."

Gabe puts his hands on my shoulders and turns my body to face his. "I have a confession to make. I'm really glad Helen's sick. Because, Mad? There's only one person that I want to kiss at midnight and I wanted to spend New Year's with you. Just you."

"Then next time why don't you just ask if I want to come over and make out?"

He eases my coat from my shoulders and clicks the TV on with the remote. "Because, yeah, I wouldn't say no to making out, but I want to watch tape tonight, too."

I look at the TV. There we are, eight and nine years old as a pre-juvenile pair. Lake Placid, the first time we ever landed a throw Axel in competition.

Gabe blushes. "I made a tape of our greatest hits. Do you like it?"

Yeah, I do. I smile. We've got all night, we can make our New Year's relationship resolution later.

Gabe takes my hand and leads me around to the couch, where I notice there's something different about the ice cubes. I pluck one from the bucket. It's a little melty, exposing the edge of the rose frozen inside it. "Aw, Gabe."

He smiles, then pops the cork on the grape juice, pours, and hands me a glass. "To us."

I clink my glass against his and we settle ourselves on the couch. I nestle into his arm and we sip from our glasses and feed each other strawberries. Gabe seems content just to sit and cuddle. Maybe he did want to hang out more than anything else.

But I'm wanting something more. With chocolate still melting on my tongue, I set my glass on the table, ease Gabe's from his hand, and set it beside mine. I put my face next to his. "You know, we don't have to wait until midnight."

We tumble backward on the couch. Gabe's hands slip under my shirt and I sit up. He pulls his hands back. "Sorry. I thought you meant—"

I put my finger to his lips to shush him. "I did. But I just realized . . ." I pull my shirt over my head and toss it to the floor. "We have the house all to ourselves for hours." Gabe's staring at me and I'm enjoying every second. I unfasten my bra and toss it after my shirt. "Nobody is going to interrupt us."

"Mad." Gabe's eyes are glued to me.

The doorbell rings.

I grab my shirt and bra from the floor. "I thought the party was canceled." My fingers fumble with the hooks as I try to refasten my bra.

Gabe groans and heads for the front door. "It was." But before he's even left the room, we hear the front door open and slam, followed by feet stamping on the mat.

"Gabe?" Chris's voice from the entryway.

Clicking heels on the wooden floor in the hall. Kate's voice follows, growing louder. "You want coats in the family room closet like last time?"

My shirt isn't lying right. I tug at it, smooth it down. As Gabe disappears in the direction of the foyer, I run my fingers through my hair to un-muss it. I drop my hands to my sides in the nick of time. "Hi, Kate."

"Maddy," Kate says slowly, her eyes looking from my chest to the frozen roses and back again. "You and Gabe having a little, um, pre-party?"

The front of my neck itches. I cross my arms over my chest to keep from scratching. So I wanted people to know about me and Gabe, but not exactly like this. "We were watching old tape." I nod at the images of our novice years thankfully still flashing across the screen, then turn away from Kate and pick up the remote. I click over to a television station. When I turn back, she's still looking at me. I cross my arms over my chest again.

She steps over to me, puts her hands on my arms, and pulls them from my chest. "Sure, sweetie. That's why your shirt's on backwards."

I look down at my front and feel like dying. Quickly, I spin my top around to fix it. My face flames.

"Romeo and Juliet." The sarcasm gone from her voice this time, Kate looks right into my eyes. "Remember how it ends."

28

Gabe

In the foyer, I yank Chris aside. "I texted you the party was off."

Chris looks confused. "You texted there wasn't going to be any adult supervision. Everybody's coming now."

I look out the foyer window. Andy's on his way up the walk, with Jonah and my cousins Sara and Louisa behind him, and more cars are parking on the street in front of my house.

Quadruple shit.

"Come on, Gabe. None of us are going to cause trouble."

Unless they figure out I only wanted to party with Mad. As my friends ditch their boots in the foyer, I hustle back toward the family room. I grab Mad's glass from the coffee table with one hand and her arm with the other. I pull her toward the kitchen. "Misunderstanding, the party's back on. Can you please start putting food out? I'll explain later."

I run back and grab the rose cubes and strawberries. And the doorbell rings.

I ditch them in the trash on the way to answer it again. "Anita."

She grins at me. "Hi, handsome."

I didn't invite Anita. Who invited Anita? I'm getting a bad gut feeling. "This is a private party."

"Just my kind of event." Anita pushes past me, brushing intentionally close as she comes through the doorway. And now cars are filling the street. Kids from school trample their way through the snow in the yard up to the door.

Then I see Kurt headed up the walk, a brown paper bag in each hand. Several of the players trailing him carry six-packs and not the root beer variety. I stand across the doorway. "No way. Take it back to the car."

Every muscle in my body is tight. I've taken Kurt in a fight before, but the whole A team is a different story. Fortunately, the players gripe but concede. When they return empty-handed, I let them in.

The flood of guests isn't slowing down. Every few minutes, the doorbell rings again. I put Chris in charge of the door and head to the kitchen. Mom made a lot of food, but I'm way over my guest list of eight. Supplies are running low, and the punch bowl is already empty. I grab bottles of soda and juice from the fridge.

"Lame. There's not even any punch?"

I turn to see Kurt. I huff my hair out of my face. "Don't see you doing anything to help."

Kurt elbows me away from the fridge and opens the freezer. He reaches for the bags of ice, turns, and starts dumping ice cubes into the punch bowl.

A New Year's miracle, but I'll take it. "Thanks." I start screwing tops off the bottles. Just that quick, it's like old times again. Me right wing to his center. Passing the puck, getting the job done.

An insanely loud cheer from down the hall startles me and I spill pop down my front. "Dammit."

"Go! Go! Go!" come the shouts.

Kurt takes the ginger ale from me. Another round of cheering rings out and he tips his head in the direction of the doorway. "I got this. You cover that." As I hurry out of the kitchen, he hollers after me, "Order some pizza, too!"

I check out the family room. Okay. Just a bunch of guys watching a football game on TV. So much for having the couch all to myself and Mad. I feel someone at my shoulder and turn. Mad stands with her hands behind her back, frowning at me.

"Mad, I'm sorry. Thanks for helping with the food. Shit, the pizza." I whip out my phone and look up the number for Vitale's. "Yeah, I need some pizzas for a party . . . Delivered . . . Um, maybe twenty?"

Mad's still standing there.

I cup my hand over the receiver. "Did you want something?"

"I'm ready for you to explain."

Now? Can't she see I'm on the phone? I turn away from her. "Just make half supreme and the rest pepperoni . . . no wait, two plain cheese . . . eighty-one Cedarview Street . . . thirty minutes? . . . yeah, thanks." I slide my phone in my pocket and turn back around.

Mad's voice is even but forced. "You said you'd explain later. It's later."

I sigh. "I texted Chris that Helen was sick so there was no supervision for the party. I assumed he'd know that meant it was canceled. Bad assumption, obviously."

She brings her hands out from behind her back. She's holding her wine glass from earlier. "Why'd you hide my glass?"

Good question. One that needs a damn good answer . . . that I don't have. "Um . . ."

"You said you were ready."

A lie. I have a sneaky suspicion that I'll never be ready. Not about to tell her that now, though. "Come on, Mad. Coming out to the whole school is a hell of a jump."

"You didn't even want our best friends seeing us together. When are you going to take that first step? How long are we going to be a secret, Gabe?"

I shift my weight from one foot to the other. Another question I don't know the answer to. I change edge. "Why'd you put your shirt back on so fast?"

Mad crosses her arms in front of her, the stem of her glass clenched in one hand. "Let me think about that one. What would everyone think if they came in the house and saw me half-naked?"

"That we hooked up. Mad, you know what they say about me. What would everyone think if they knew you and I had been curled up on the couch with two wine glasses and a plate of chocolate-covered strawberries? What would they think about *you*?"

Her face softens. "That I slept with you."

"I've done a lot of things I'm ashamed of. You're not one of them but I don't want people joking about how I parked my pink Porsche in your garage. I don't want to listen to bets on how long we're going to last. I don't want everyone talking about it so much that our parents find out."

"What do you want?"

"I'm sorry, Mad, I know this isn't what you want to talk about. But honestly? Right now I could use some help making sure this party doesn't get out of control. Are you up to that?"

"Are you still going to kiss me at midnight?"

Guess I already kissed her in front of everyone in English and at the show anyway. "If you still want me to."

"Okay." She turns and walks away.

I'm not sure if it's really okay, but I have bigger issues at the moment. I check out the living room. Lisette and Piper are having a pillow fight. I catch Mom's favorite lamp just in time. I set it back on the end table, look up, and get smacked across the face by two couch cushions. So maybe I deserve it since I've been to the Point with both of them, but— I throw my hands up as they take aim again. "What do I have to do to get you to stop?"

Piper and Lisette hold their cushions ready to attack. Piper looks at Lisette. Lisette looks at Piper. They both look at me. "Kiss me at midnight," they chorus.

I turn for the door, the thwacking pillows chasing me out of the room. Down the hall, I smell smoke coming from the den. I have to make two people I don't even recognize put out their cigarettes. How far has word about this party spread? I put on some music and hope maybe people will dance. On the way out, I bump into Alyson. I run off before she can even open her mouth. If I'm going to keep my promise to Mad, we'll have to hide at midnight. This party is turning into the freaking Ex-Games. Worst. New Year's. Ever.

I peek in the dining room. Mad has about a dozen people crowded around the table playing Apples to Apples. Why didn't I think of putting games out? Go, Mad.

I lean against the door frame and watch her laughing as she deals out cards. Could she be right? Am I making too much about us? What would it hurt if people knew? I could out our relationship right now, just walk over and slip my arm around her. Kiss her cheek. We wouldn't have to hide at midnight. We wouldn't have to hide anymore.

"Excuse me." Kurt's behind me, his hands full of red plastic Solo cups.

I let him through before he sloshes punch all over the floor, then step toward Mad.

"Hey, Gabe," Chris yells from the foyer. "Did you order two hundred bucks' worth of pizza?"

An hour later, the pizza's gone. Chris took Kate home when she complained she didn't feel good but everyone else is still here. After Mom's favorite lamp narrowly escapes disaster once again, I make a sweep of the house, moving anything breakable as far out of the way as I can. And if I have to tell one more person to save the smoking for outside I'm going to— Dammit, I don't know what I'm going to do.

I sink onto the bottom step of the stairs, not even caring when a giggling tangle of arms and legs squeezes past me. My skull throbs from the loud music. I can't believe none of the neighbors have called the cops yet. I drop my head between my knees. It's New Year's Eve. Probably no one else is home.

I feel the light touch against my back. Mad? I lift my head and suppress a groan. "Anita."

She holds two brown paper sacks in one hand. With the other

hand she grabs hold of my arm, jerking my shoulder as she pulls me off the step. She swings her arm around me and steers me toward the living room. "Come on, we're starting a game of seven minutes in heaven. And for hosting this fine event, I think you should go first." She whispers in my ear. "I'll join you."

I duck out from under her arm. "No, thanks."

Anita shrugs. "Whatever . . ." She looks down my front, than back up at me. She flips her long blond hair over one shoulder. "Let me know if you change your mind?"

"I won't."

She isn't listening to me, she's rustling the bags. She opens the first bag and pulls a name from it. "Then first up is Maddy, with . . ."

I grab the slip of paper from her. Why the hell is Mad playing this game? My eyes dart from the paper in my hands to Mad to Anita to . . . the bags. Two tall brown bags. Liquor bags. Where did those come from?

Anita reaches into the other bag, opens a second slip. "Kurt!"

The name slams into my stomach like a punch to the gut. No wonder Kurt didn't press me about the alcohol, he must've stuck the bottles under his coat at the car. No wonder Kurt was so *helpful* in the kitchen. Red plastic cups scream at me from the end tables, the coffee table, and even the edges of the shelves.

Kurt offers his arm to Mad. She giggles and takes it.

Hell, no. I march across the room. Nose to nose with Kurt, I say, "Change of plans. I'm playing."

Kurt leers at me. "No, thanks. I don't swing that way." He sidesteps me with Mad still on his arm.

Mad totters from the movement. She's blitzed. I grab Kurt's arm. "You're not going anywhere with her."

The room goes dropped-call silent.

Kurt looks at me. "You going to stop me?"

Damn straight. I lock eyes with him, forming the fingers of my free hand into a fist.

"Kurt?" Almost a squeak of a voice. Kurt's new girlfriend, the girl everyone calls Mouse, stands in the doorway. "What are you doing?"

"Nothing, baby," Kurt says. "Just helping her up." His eyes stay locked on mine but he releases his hold on Mad.

Mad stumbles toward me and I catch her.

Anita clears her throat and coughs loudly. "Well, this has been quite entertaining, but other people are waiting. So let's get a move on, you two." She shoves me and Mad into the coat closet and shuts the door.

I trip over the vacuum cleaner and hit my head on some empty wooden coat hangers. The clattering brings a muffled roar of laughter from the other side of the door.

Mad giggles and slides her hands under my shirt.

I wanted to be alone with Mad, but not like this. Not in a closet with half our senior class listening outside the door. I take her hands off me. I bend toward her and I can smell the alcohol on her breath. "Mad, you've been drinking," I whisper.

Mad presses herself against me again and hiccups. "Jus' the punch."

I hold her tight. "How many glasses did you drink?"

"I dunno." She reaches for my pants this time. "Les not talk ri' now."

Igor's going to kill me. If my parents or the Spiers don't get to me first. The closet has two doors; it opens through into the kitchen. I feel against Mad's leg and give silent thanks for the outline of the house key in her pocket. I let us through the closet.

"Gabe," Mad whines. "Where are we—?"

I put my finger to her lips. "We're going somewhere more private."

Mad giggles again. "Like your be'room?"

I scoop her up. "How about *your* bedroom?"

Mad clings to me. "You wanna take me to bed."

"Uh-huh." I slip out the kitchen door with her and hurry across the yard. I fish the key out of her pocket, unlock the door, and carry her upstairs.

Mad flops her body back against her comforter. She laughs and laughs. "Are you even gonna take my socks off?"

Nope. I shake out the throw blanket at the end of her bed and tuck her under it.

Mad pulls me under the blanket as well.

Not like this. Not. Like. This. I ease away from her.

Mad hiccups again. "Where're you going?"

I kiss her forehead. "I'll be right back. I'm just going to . . . use the bathroom." At my own house.

Back in my kitchen, I dump the little bit that's left of the punch down the sink. The counter's littered with empty pizza boxes and my foot's sticking to something on the floor. I've got to break this party up—how?

I consider my options. Do nothing and things will be out of control fast. My parents won't be home for at least another two hours. By then the mess will be so colossal that I'll probably be grounded for life. I could call the police myself. And be the brunt of every joke at school for the rest of my Riverview Prep career. I lean back against the counter and groan. I need some way to get people out of the house. Could I find the breaker, shut off the electricity? No, people will just want to light candles and I've got enough of a fire on my hands already.

Wait a sec. Fire.

I go into the family room, slip one of the extinguished candles I put out for Mad earlier behind my back and sneak upstairs and down the dark upper hallway. I open the door to my bedroom.

"Oh, yeah . . ."

I switch on my light. Startled, Andy and Sara look up and squint. "Oh, no," I tell them, watching my cousin rummage through my sheets and retrieve a push-up bra. I stand just outside the doorway until they leave, then go in and close the door. I light the candle, stand on my desk chair, and hold it under the smoke detector. I blow it out so that the smoke goes right to the detector.

Nothing happens. I try again, but the wick burns too clean. I need something else to burn. I grab a scrap of paper from my trash can, swap it for the candle in the votive holder, and set it on fire. Soon enough, *BEEP! BEEP! BEEP!* I repeat the process a couple times, let the last one burn out, and then I slip out of my room. People are covering their ears and pouring out of the house onto the lawn. I follow.

"Can't you shut it off?"

"No," I lie. "I tried the hush button already. There must be a spider or something stuck in there. And shit, the alarm is linked to my parents' security system. I'm going to be so busted." I grab my hair and scrunch my face as though I've got an Academy Award on the line. "Who wants to help clean up?"

"My uncle's on duty tonight. I'm out of here," Kurt says.

The hockey team follows, as do quite a few others.

I restrain myself from doing a victory dance. Instead, I start running around the yard picking up trash. Heck, I'm going to have to clean anyway. Now almost everyone is leaving, the alarms still beeping inside the house. Jonah, my cousins, and Andy grab some trash. "Thanks, guys."

And, wait. Over by the bushes, almost lost within them, is a lone hockey player. Mike's helping, too. I work my way over to him. "You don't have to stay," I tell him quietly. What I said to Kurt, I was standing up for myself just as much as for Mike.

Mike shrugs and keeps picking up. "You won't tell them."

With the six of us working, we have the yard looking decent in a matter of minutes. The alarms are still going. Andy looks at the house, then at me. He pulls at his collar. "Um, want some help inside?"

Do I ever. Inside, I hand him the roll of garbage bags. Sara and Louisa tackle the kitchen counters. Jonah vacuums, Mike mops, and I straighten. The alarms subside eventually and I think everyone's on to my security-system stunt but nobody says anything. By eleven forty-five the place isn't pristine but it's passable. "You guys want to watch the ball drop still?"

Andy and Sara cuddle up together on the couch. Jonah grabs

a wing chair, looking cornered when Louisa perches on one of its arms, and Mike leans against the other. I tune the TV to Times Square, but then I sneak out. I've got a promise to keep.

At Mad's, I pull a chair beside her bed. She's curled up on one side, totally out. I watch her blanket rise and fall with her breathing. When the numbers on her alarm clock click over to midnight, I brush her hair back from her face and kiss her forehead. Happy New Year.

We don't have practice until noon the next day, but when eleven fifteen comes and goes and Mad still isn't at the car, I have to do something I've never had to do before. I trot across the driveway and knock on the Spiers' side door.

Senator Spier answers in his bathrobe, a plate of eggs in one hand. "Gabe? Shouldn't you and Maddy be at practice?"

"Yeah, but I'm looking for Mad." I stare at the Senator's hair. It's looking really long on one side and his part is in a funny spot but it couldn't be—

The Senator puts one hand against his hair and it slips back into perfection.

It *is*. Honest Bill isn't honest about one thing, anyway. He clears his throat and I force my eyes from his toupee, remembering why I came over. Mad. "Have you seen her?"

"When she didn't come down for breakfast, we thought you'd already left."

My stomach wrenches. Oh, God. Mad's always the first one

ready for practice in the morning. She wouldn't miss skating unless she was . . . oh, God.

The Senator turns and calls for her but I'm already dashing up the steps three at a time. Those drinking charts my parents are always shoving in my face. How much is too much? I don't have any idea how strong Kurt's punch was but Mad doesn't even tip the scale up to the hundred mark. And I left her alone, passed out. I—

She stumbles out of her bedroom, her hair in a disheveled ponytail and her eyes squinting in the bright light of the hall-way. "I'm coming," she says weakly.

I don't care if the Senator's watching. I grab her in a tight hug. "You're okay."

She groans. "Don't. Squeeze."

I let her go. "Feeling sick?"

She holds on to the wall. "My head feels like it's going to explode and I already ralphed twice."

Does she even know she's hungover? No way I'm telling her. Some things are better kept secret. "You should rest today."

"Please don't talk so loudly." Mad eases herself down one step at a time. "You know what Igor says about that."

I do. We always practice, even when we're sick, in case we ever need to compete that way. But Mad doesn't have some little cold virus. She's going to get hurt.

She lets me pull over once on the way to the arena so she can puke in the bushes but she won't let me take her back home. At the rink, I have to lace up her skates because she can't stand to bend over.

We can't skate like this. I leave Mad hanging on to the boards and skate out to where Igor stands at center ice, tapping his watch with a gloved finger. "I need a minute. Please."

Igor holds his watch in front of my face. "You have already taken ten."

"I screwed up."

"Yes." Igor huffs. "And?"

"Mad's hungover. It's my fault."

Igor says nothing.

"I'm—"

Igor holds up a hand to shush me. "Nationals. We leave in *six* days. Drinking is not part of plan. I give instruction, you follow."

"I'm sorry."

He watches Mad loosen herself from the boards and totter out onto the ice as though she's a new beginning skater. He sighs. "Is holiday, we skip this one time. Go. Take care of your partner."

29

The day after New Year's, I've finally stopped tossing chocolate-covered strawberries. I give Gabe an extension on his baby steps since even the thought of the party makes me ill. Puking all over his car has to be worth at least a couple weeks of grace, and we really need to focus on Nationals anyway. I remember Chris's toe-pick trip at Sectionals. We can talk after Nationals.

But as I cross off the days on my calendar counting toward the big red circle around January 6, the day Gabe and I leave for Boston, my nausea grows again. I look down at the scores I printed from the Internet, the results of the Eastern and Pacific Coast winners that we'll be competing against as Midwest champions. Gabe and I could have three major errors and still make the top six, but thanks to an awful track record in international pair competitions, the U.S. can only send two pairs to Worlds. When I put the sectional scores in order, even with our personal best performance at Mids, Gabe and I are number . . . three. Plus I don't have any scores from last year's winners; Evans and Martin have a bye to the Nationals as the defending champions. Last time we saw Evans and Martin was at champs camp, where they were our instructors.

With each red X, my stomach flurries grow a little larger. We can't get fourth place and still go to Worlds. By the time we get off the plane in Boston, I have a raging snowstorm in my belly.

Gabe and I are Igor's only students to qualify for the championships, leaving us without roommates. Igor sandwiches his room between ours but we wouldn't mess around here anyway. There's too much at stake.

Igor does have a three-hour coaches' meeting, though, and the opportunity is too good to pass up. I head for Gabe's room. He meets me in the hall, headed toward mine. "I have a surprise for you," we say together.

I laugh. "Mine first."

"Mine's important," Gabe says.

"Well, mine's scheduled," I answer. "We have to be there at two. Come on."

We take the subway to the Boston Public Library. The architectural tour, led by a volunteer guide, only lasts an hour. It's worth every minute, the excitement on Gabe's face. The triple-arched main entrance over the McKim Building is his favorite. "Check out those lanterns," he says. He drools over the staircase and the courtyard, too. There's a couple of older gentlemen along for the tour, obviously just as geeked as Gabe. It turns out one of them works for an architectural firm in Wichita, and when the tour is over, Gabe is in his glory chatting them up.

When we're done, we walk to Gabe's surprise for me, which turns out to be a stroll through the Public Garden to watch the skaters at the Frog Pond. I know we can't skate on it; we don't have our skates with us and even incognito we'd attract too much attention from the very first strokes, but it's beautiful. A pair of little kids is toddling along together among the crowd of skaters. Gabe grins. "Where's your spy notebook, Mad? Those might be our competitors someday."

He reaches for my hand. And doesn't let go. We're bundled up in our winter jackets, hoods hiding our hair and sunglasses hiding our faces, but we walk the rest of the garden as a pair. It's the teeniest baby step ever, I'm not even sure it moves us forward, but at least Gabe's trying to pick his feet up now.

Our little excursions clear my nausea for a day, but it's only temporary. By the time our parents check in on the day of the short program, my nerves reemerge like butterflies breaking out of their chrysalises.

We draw first in the skating order, again. At least it'll be over quickly. As I wait for our names to be called, I bounce on the balls of my feet. The stands are packed. I pick out our parents, Mom and Dad holding hands in the stands even, but it doesn't reassure me. Then I see the cameras. I stop bouncing and sway. Gabe and I. Are going to be. On. National. Television. Forget butterflies, my stomach feels like I swallowed a bird. I glance at Gabe. "We're going to—" I stop. Gabe has his warm-up jacket wrapped around his head like a turban. "What are you doing?"

He grins at me. "Hiding my hair from you, Delilah. I let you cut it once already, and I saw how that turned out."

I grin back, and the bird in my stomach takes flight.

Our rendition of *Samson and Delilah* brings the crowd to their feet. Waiting in the kiss and cry, I clutch one of the stuffed animals an enthusiastic fan tossed on the ice after our performance without even seeing what it is. I long for Gabe's hand instead, but the cameras are everywhere and Igor's sitting between us, anyway. I try to focus on Igor's words as he compliments parts of our program but I can't. I don't care what he's saying, it's the judges' opinions that matter now.

"And now," the announcer booms, "there will be a slight delay as—"

Slight delay, my skates. I resist the urge to pull tufts of fur out of the stuffed whatever and remember my manners. It was someone's gift to me, after all. I look at the tag hanging from the neck of the plush golden Lab, then wave at the camera. "Thank you, Jen!"

Finally, "The scores for our first team, Madelyn Spier and Gabriel Nielsen of the Riverview Skating Club. The technical elements score is 32.07. The program components score is 35.82. No deductions, for a total score of 67.89."

I shriek and hug Gabe, sandwiching a startled Igor in the middle. It's a new personal best, as well as the first time we've scored higher for artistry than for technical merit. Igor leans out of our way and Gabe gives me a quick squeeze in return, pecks my cheek even. We can get away with that now that the scores are out. People do all kinds of crazy things when the scores are good.

Skating first means our marks have to stand, but it also means we can see all our competitors' performances. I sit with Gabe in the stands. He sneaks his hand under my stadium blanket and takes my fingers in his. The rest of the pairs in our warm-up group look like they're showing up just so they can add national level experience to their future coaching résumés. None of them even try triple throws or jumps. The group that follows isn't much better. Our scores hold, time after time.

But it's the last four pairs I'm really worried about. I watch them warm up. Here come the triples. I keep an especially close eye on Evans and Martin setting up their throw twist, because I've heard a rumor that—

"Holy shit," Gabe breathes beside me, and I feel my stomach plunge. It's no rumor, Evans and Martin just pulled off a quad twist. I squeeze Gabe's hand under the blanket.

The warm-up ends and the first of the last four teams takes the ice. Lance Parker substitutes double jumps for the triple-toe loops in his combination, and that team's out. Three. Gorgeous side-by-side death drops, a level three lift, and then Christina Robinson touches down her hand on the landing of her throw. We've beaten the Robinson siblings. Two. Jing-Mei Pao has a scary-looking dismount from her star lift and kisses the boards on the landing of one of her jumps. Pao and Dunway drop to fourth. One pair left.

Jessica Evans and Gregory Martin nail their side-by-side jumps. I watch their pair spin in dismay. That'll be ruled a level four, and they're going to get positive grades of execution on top of that. I shouldn't want my competitors to mess up, but

I want this win so much. They set up their twist, and I hold my breath. I'm now squeezing Gabe's hand so hard that I'm probably cutting off his circulation. Evans soars into the air. One-two-three . . . I breathe as Martin catches her. Only three.

Gabe wiggles his fingers loose and massages his hands together. His eyes are fixed on the Jumbotron. "Still rock solid, even without the quad."

Evans and Martin take their bows and skate off the ice. I grip the edge of my bleacher seat so hard I break a fingernail. In the kiss and cry, magnified on the Jumbotron, Evans and Martin laugh and talk to each other, wave and blow kisses for the TV cameras. I think of what Gabe didn't say but what I know we're both thinking about. Their setup was perfect. That triple twist wasn't a mistake, they downgraded the move on purpose. They didn't think they needed the quad to beat us. I scrunch in my seat.

"And now," booms the announcer. "Program component scores for Jessica Evans and Gregory Martin, last year's national champions from the Four Seasons Figure Skating Club."

Like I needed that reminder. I move my fingers to my mouth and bite off the broken nail.

"For technical elements, 34.59."

Over two points more. I bite off another nail.

"For program components, 33.18."

Over two points *less*. I suck in a breath so deep I think I'm taking in all the air in the arena.

"No deductions."

My heart thuds in my chest as I try to do the math in my

head. So I'm usually good at math and it should be a simple addition problem but . . . ohmigod. I look at Gabe. His smile is ready to explode. "With a combined total of 67.87, Evans and Martin are in second place. And this concludes the pairs short programs. Standings heading into Saturday's long program: in first place, with 67.89 points, Madelyn Spier and Gabriel Nielsen . . ."

I scream.

At the restaurant for dinner that night, my cheeks hurt from smiling so much. Mom and Dad are still getting along, and Gabe and I? Gabe and I. Are. Number. *ONE*. Dad slings his arm around me at the table. "The primary results are in, and what a victory. Two hundredths of a point. I hope for their sake that Evans and Martin never have to run against you two for political office."

The *primary* results. I've gotten ahead of myself, it's only the short, after all. We still have to skate our long program to take the national title. The waitress sets my salad down in front of me, but I can't even lift my fork to take a bite.

Dad massages my shoulder and looks at me and Gabe. His eyes are wet and I've never seen him smile so big, not even for his cameras. " 'This generation of Americans has a rendez-vous with destiny.' "

"FDR's nomination acceptance speech, 1936," I say. The ache in my stomach expands, the contagious exhilaration now making me feel ill. We're not even at Worlds yet. Two hundredths of a point. What makes me think we can do this?

On my other side, Gabe puts his hand on my knee under the table. He bends slightly toward me and whispers. "Time to eat, Mad."

I can't even move my mouth to answer him.

He chuckles. "Welcome to the world of competition nerves that the rest of us live in all the time. Seriously, though? It's a long time until Saturday afternoon. One step at a time. Pick up your fork." He takes my right hand in his, pulls it from my lap, and closes my fingers over my fork.

I hold the fork in my hand but my wrist is still resting on the table.

"Mmm, delicious," Gabe says more loudly. He pops a bite of his pasta into his mouth. "This is so good. Mad, you should try this."

And before I know what's happening, my fork is gone from my hand and in my mouth, along with a bite of Gabe's pasta. The shock of it startles me, and I chew and then swallow. "Thank you."

"No problem."

But I still have a problem. Gabe reassures me that the nerves get better with time, but we only have a couple of days until our long program and the snowball in my stomach only grows more tightly packed as the minutes tick away. By Saturday, it's a giant ball of ice. Our first place finish in the short means that under the television rule we'll skate in the final group and I can feel the stiffness creeping over me before we even board the shuttle to the arena.

A group of shrieking fans waits outside the rink, with several girls in front holding signs reading "Marry me, Gabriel Nielsen!" I scowl. The girls press in on us as we walk past, then I hear one of them yelp. My skate bag might have rolled over her toes and, honestly, I'm not sorry.

As we enter the elevator for the ride down to the locker rooms, my stomach tumbles triple loops and my muscles are so tight I can hardly walk. The doors open and I stumble out.

Gabe puts his arm out to catch me. "You all right?"

I shake my head. "I've never been this nervous. I don't know what to do, Gabe. I can't skate like this. We're here, I can see it, and I'm choking." I rub at my muscles. "I never choke! I never get tight!"

In the arena above us, the crowd cheers, then gasps. I wobble. We've come so far. If I lose it this afternoon—"

Gabe reaches into the pocket of his warm-up jacket. "Don't listen to that, Mad." He pulls his empty hand back out of his pocket, releases his grip on me, then pats the front of his jacket with both hands. "Shit, I don't have it."

I feel like I'm about to faint.

Gabe catches me again. "Okay, no iPod. Time for plan B. Breathe." He shakes me slightly. "Bend your knees."

"I can't!"

He grabs my hands in his. "Look at me. This is a normal feeling. Trust me, I get it all the time. It's just your body's fight-or-flight instinct, because you care a lot about what happens here. But I learned to deal with it, and so can you. Now take a breath with me."

I breathe.

"Another." He looks deep in my eyes. "Let it out slowly. What do you need to do tonight?"

"Not lose it." The panicky feeling rises again.

"No. You know you can't think about what not to do. Tell me specifically what you're going to do, first element to last."

I list our elements.

"*Can* you do those things?"

"Yes."

"Will you do them tonight?"

"Yes." I try to sound confident for his sake, but my knees are still locked.

Gabe glances around. The corridor's already deserted, but he pulls me around the corner into a hallway stub reserved for janitors' closets. "Good," he says, "but we wouldn't want to miss the most important point."

"Which is?"

"This isn't about the audience or the judges, remember? Igor said this is about us. Just us. Out there, we don't have to hide. Out there, I get to shout to all those girls with the signs that I'm taken. And I, for one, plan on making the most of those four and a half minutes where I can show how I really feel about you."

His lips brush against mine and as I lift my face to him he deepens the kiss slowly, like we have all the time in the world for this, and I know we don't but, right now, in this moment, in this kiss, I feel like we do. I relax in his arms and kiss him back. "Okay."

He releases me and digs our jump ropes out of our skate

bags. "Pretend we're at home. We're going to do our warm-up routine, then we're going to get on the ice and enjoy each other, the way we always do."

It works. From our first steps on the ice, the program is both smooth and easy, desperate and soulful, the same as our rare private times. When Gabe takes me in his arms, I'm with him on the couch at home. When he lifts me, I'm with him at the ballet. When we finish, I'm ready for Miller's Point. The program vaults us to first place.

We drew the third position in the final group, so only one couple remains to take the ice. And despite having had to take the ice to the sound of our thunderous applause, Evans and Martin are again in top form. In the athlete's lounge, I pace as I watch our competitors hit element after element. Gabe puts his arm out to stop me. "Mad," he whispers.

I stop pacing just before I hit his arm. Then on the screen in front of me, I see it. Split and one-two-three-four. Quadruple twist. I can hear the applause from the crowd all the way out here. "It's over," I whisper, blinking back the tears.

"No. We still have a date with destiny."

"Rendezvous," I correct him, feeling my chin tremble.

"Whatever. That's not the point." Gabe traces the outside corner of my eye. "Evans and Martin can skate circles around us tonight."

"Can? They *are.*"

"It doesn't matter, Mad. Even if they beat us, we'll still have the silver medal."

Two pairs. The U.S. can send two pairs. "We're going," I whisper.

Gabe traces the outside corner of my other eye. "We're going."

"Not so quick." Igor's voice behind me. Gabe steps back and I turn to look at Igor. "We do not count ducks before hatch, no?"

"But we've got second place," Gabe says.

"The federation decides, not the championships."

Our parents appear behind Igor. "What's going on?" Dad asks.

Mrs. Nielsen puts her arm around Gabe. "It isn't official yet, who will make the World team."

Mom looks confused. "They might not go?"

"Gabe and Maddy don't have any international experience at the senior level," Mrs. Nielsen explains to her. "Evans and Martin are a sure bet for the first World slot with their track record but it's possible the federation might choose a different team, a better-known team, for the second slot. The Robinsons took third and they went to Worlds last year."

"We need some publicity," Dad says.

"It would not hurt," Igor replies.

Dad pulls out his phone. "I'm on it."

30

No snowsuit this time but once again, I'm marching along mitten-in-mitten with my partner. *Click* go the cameras, but we're not four and five years old anymore, and forget the first time on the ice euphoria. We're not on the ice and this is *not* fun.

"You both look a little stiff," says Harold, some publicity guy Mad's dad called in. "Try to relax."

Relax. Sure. No sweat. Except for the faucets my armpits and hands have become. Now I'm *pretending* that I'm pretending to be with Mad? This is so screwed up.

We're walking along the Charles River. A gust of wind bites my face and I feel Mad's shiver all the way through her mittens. I stop and take my hat off, pulling it down over her ears. *Click. Click-click.*

"That's better," Harold says. "But smile."

"Don't we have enough with the Children's Hospital shots?" I ask.

Harold ignores me and points to a bench up ahead. "Stop there, let's try some seated poses."

I feel like a total poser. I *am* trying, but with both sets of parents watching us all I can think of is the Senator's words to me and Mad last night. *How badly do you want to win?*

Dad's: *Money can't buy a gold medal, but it can get you damn close.*

And Mom's: *It's part of the game.*

Even the Children's Hospital this morning felt like too much. Mad and I always take our tossies to a children's ward, but making a publicity stunt out of it? What's all this going to cost us? How much are we willing to pay? How far is too far? I'm losing sight of all reality. And the scariest thought: After all the work I've put in, the years of plans, is the medal even what I really want anymore?

The photo shoot on the bench isn't going any better.

Mad's teeth chatter behind her smile. I pull her onto my lap and put my arms around her.

"That's a little too much," says the Senator.

That's too much? If he finds out what I've really done with his daughter, the next media sensation will be my body floating in the Charles.

Mad slides off my lap. "M-m-maybe we could try someplace indoors?"

"The Hub?" suggests the Senator. "I hear it's a romantic spot."

Mad's mom, the only one who didn't say anything last night, makes narrow stink eyes at him.

We try lunch at the Hub next. Towering over the city, I can't help but feel how high this raises the stakes. A secret is different than a lie, I told Mad. I think I lied.

I look out over the rooftops. In the whole of Boston, even

with our little covert excursions, there's only one place that's really felt safe to hold Mad with everyone watching. If we're going to get anything usable, we need to be . . . "On the ice."

Harold, our parents, and the camera crew look at me. "What? We already have access to shots of you on ice," Harold says.

At the arena, but, "The outdoor rink, at the Public Garden."

Mad gets it. She looks at me. "We can re-create that photo."

We rent the Frog Pond at midnight. Twinkling lights deck the trees around us, the glow of the city beyond them. Mad and I don't skate mitten-in-mitten, but we get close. I put my arm around her shoulder, she puts hers around my waist. She leans into me.

At center ice, I skid us to a stop. "Mad, I wish . . ." I wish so many things. I wish we hadn't rented the Frog Pond for private use. I wish everyone else was here, skating around with us. I wish I could have those four and a half minutes with her all the time. I turn to face her, take both her hands and pull them to my chest. I lean forward so my forehead rests against hers. "I—"

The flash is blinding. "That's it!" Harold calls out.

The next morning, Evans and Martin's quad is old news. Mad shows me Harold's clippings from the papers, his links to the Internet articles. Everything headlines us. With the then-and-now shots and our charitable-citizen behavior, Mad and I have become America's sweethearts.

The phone call comes that afternoon. We're in. Mad and I are going to China.

Back at home Monday morning, our parents let us miss another day of school to recover. We don't get to skip practice. Igor puts us right back to work. After a double program run-through, I gulp for air. Mad pants beside me. We head for the boards. "Two laps first," Igor calls out.

I groan but I turn around. Mad and I might be America's sweethearts, but we haven't won Igor's heart yet. We finish our laps and collapse onto the boards. I splash my water on my face. God, that feels good.

Igor narrows his eyes at me. I twist the cap back on my bottle.

He studies me and Mad with his chin resting between his thumb and pointer finger. "The artistry is perfect. But . . ." He pauses. Shakes his head. "Is not enough. There is no respect for American pairs, this you know, yes?"

I nod.

"Silver medal is triumph for us. *No . . . one . . . else . . . cares.* You must be better. We are needing . . ." Evans and Martin flash in my mind. One-two-three-four. And I know Igor's going to say—"The quad."

Mad draws in her breath. "The throw quadruple Salchow."

"No." I look at Mad, staring at me in shock, then back at Igor. "No. It's too dangerous." Of all the pairs elements, throws are my least favorite. I hate the horrendous falls Mad takes each time we learn a new one. It's one thing seeing her fall jumping on her own. When I'm throwing her? It's a whole different deal.

"It's not," she says, waiting for me to look at her. "Gabe, lately you're throwing me so much higher on the triple. I just need to pull in a little tighter. I can do this. *We* can do this. We're so close already."

"The twist," I say. I'd so much rather *I* catch Mad instead of the ice. "Why can't we—"

"No twist," Igor says. "For that, we are not ready."

"But—"

He puts his hand up to quiet me. "Tomorrow. We begin when you are fresh."

After our lesson, Igor sends us to practice our lifts. "It's too risky," I say to Mad as we skate back crossovers around the end of the rink in preparation. I take hold of her hands and press her above my head, transition my hands to her hips as she turns onto first her stomach and then her side. My feet turn Mohawks beneath me. I flip her upside down for the dismount.

Mad kicks her legs over cartwheel style and we glide backward together, her arm behind me with her hand resting against my shoulder blade. "You're not the one who might fall," she points out.

I turn away from her as we step forward. I'm already falling. Not on the ice, but I can feel myself slipping, my grip becoming looser each moment that Mad and I spend together. I'm not sure exactly when it happened, maybe during the absurdity of pretending to pretend, maybe before. But can I fall without hurting her? "We don't have time," I say, my back still to her. Worlds are in March, only two months away. "If you get hurt . . ." *If I hurt you . . .* "It's over for both of us."

I skate away and she chases after, following our program choreography. "Why are you so afraid?"

She's always been too fearless for her own good, on the ice as well as now, about our relationship. "Remember the tree, Mad? Sometimes you can push too far. Sometimes it's not good to be so fearless." We turn in sync with each other, and I cross behind her.

She doesn't look back. "Sometimes you're not fearless enough. This goal isn't one we can reach by holding back." She steps forward to face me, ready for our spiral sequence. "You have to let go," she whispers. "Fighting a fall only hurts worse. Just let go."

But I can't. I still can't tell her out loud how I feel about her, can't let myself free fall. The sense of dread curdles in my stomach, the same way it did the day Mad climbed too high up our tree. On the ice or off, we're headed for a major crash.

31

I'm wiping the snow from my blades when I get that creepy back-of-the-neck itch. I look over my shoulder. No one. And Gabe's already walking through the lobby doors, headed for the locker rooms. I turn back around and reach for my guards and water bottle on the barrier. As I stand, a hand touches my back and I feel breath on my neck. It has to be— "Chris! You creep-zoid!" I whirl around. "Knock it—"

Igor stands directly behind me. I must've stepped backward when I grabbed my stuff. If he hadn't put his hand up, I would've bumped right into him. My cheeks flush. "Sorry."

"A word in my office please, Madelyn."

About what? I try to read his face, but I can't detect any hint of emotion. Igor looks cool, confident. Like Gabe calls him, KGB. His usual self. I follow him down the south corridor. In his office, I take a seat opposite his desk and wait.

Igor pulls his own chair up to his desk, scraping the floor. He folds his hands on his desktop. "Gabriel is nervous. It cannot become a problem."

"You want me to do something about it." I'm learning a number of ways to mellow Gabe out, but somehow I don't think Igor means any of those.

"You did not tell him, yes?"

Igor said to keep the extra practices secret. Our surprise for Gabe. "I'll tell him tonight."

"No. This is plan. Tomorrow we warm up. One triple throw, then the quad." Igor's dark gray eyes lock on me, as though he's acquiring a target. "You must not tell Gabriel."

"You want him to think we're doing another triple."

"It is only way. This is our plan. You understand?"

"Yes."

Igor's chair rakes against the cement floor once more and he stands. I do the same. The meeting's over.

Gabe doesn't ask me why I'm late to the car. All the same, the secret burns within me. It's strange, both to keep something like that from him and how easy it is to do. Sure, Igor and I have been hiding the night practices with the harness for months, but I always knew we'd tell Gabe eventually. It was like planning a surprise birthday party for someone. This, though, is different. We're not going to surprise him, we're going to trick him.

Gabe's quiet, too. I glance at him. He's checking his rear-view mirror, which Mom tells me I need to do more often, but it seems like Gabe's checking it a lot. "What's going on?"

"Don't look now, but I think we're being followed."

I peek in the side mirror. There's a black sedan behind

♥ 238 ♥

us. It's not overly close to the Viper and we're on a two-lane country road surrounded by cornfields. Anybody else on the road would have to be following us. "Really?"

"It followed us out of the arena parking lot. You don't recognize them, do you?"

"You told me not to look." But I twist around anyway. "No, I don't."

When we get into town, Gabe pulls into McDonald's. The sedan gets stuck at the light.

Gabe inches forward in the drive-thru lane, watching the sedan, but when the light changes it drives on by.

"What'll it be today?" the cashier crackles through the speaker.

"Um, nothing, thanks." Reddening, Gabe gets out of the drive-thru and heads for home.

I cover my giggle until it subsides. "See? You were worried about nothing." Just like the quad.

"The quad isn't nothing," he says, as though he's read my mind.

"Everything's going to be fine. Don't you trust me?"

"As far as I can throw you." He laughs, or tries to anyway, I think. A sick sort of noise croaks on its way out of his mouth.

I reach over and squeeze his bicep. "That's pretty far. And you trust Igor, don't you?"

"The man with the master plan. Yes."

"Then you know Igor's already planned a way to succeed with this." I want to tell him so much. But as we turn onto our street, I'm distracted. There's an eerily familiar black sedan parked in front of our houses. And a navy SUV. And a white van, with its window open and a camera lens sticking out.

Gabe jerks the car to a stop in his driveway. "America's sweethearts."

We've got our own paparazzi. For a second, I forget about the quad. If the reporters are watching, we'll have to play the part, won't we? I reach for Gabe's hand.

He ignores me and gets out of the car. "We're going into our own houses. Don't touch me or talk to me any more than you need to."

"What?" I follow him as he lifts our bags out of the trunk. "But—"

"We've already been named to the World team, we don't need to pretend anymore. It's the only way to lose them, Mad." He nods at me to take my bag, then grabs his own and rolls toward his house.

The last thing I want is pictures of me looking like an idiot, so I yank my bag toward my own house.

"See you tomorrow," Gabe calls out.

"Yeah, good *practice* today," I holler back without looking at him.

I let the side porch door slam itself shut after me. Inside, I melt myself into a puddle on the floor. Pretend. Practice. We're right back to the beginning and I'm tired. I don't want to do another run-through of the "What are Gabe and I?" program.

My phone rings. "I Need You Now." The ringer I set for Gabe's calls. But I don't need this, this whatever we are, on again off again, hiding then pretending then hiding bull crap. I ignore the call.

It rings again. It keeps ringing. I pick up.

"Mad, I'm sorry," Gabe says before I can even yell at him.

With the chance to yell sucked away from me, I cry instead. "Why? Why would you do that? It's an excuse, Gabe. To be out."

"It's an excuse to *pretend* to be out. I don't want to be just a show for the camera."

"Me, either," I whisper.

"I let them use sick kids. Terminally. Ill. Children. For personal publicity. I'm losing myself." He chokes. "I can't lose you, too, Mad."

"So let's stop pretending. Let's *tell*. Maybe it's good publicity, but it's true, isn't it? It's real, isn't it?"

He's quiet.

"Gabe. Tell me this is real."

"It's not that easy. What'll happen if we tell? Say I come over to your house and get you right now. Say we walk down to the hiking park for a winter stroll. What'll happen?"

They'll follow us. All the way there. All the way through the park. It's public property, we can't stop them.

"Driving lessons with your dad. How much fun was that, camera crews in the backseat? And those were people your dad hired to make you guys look good. This time they're not going to want to catch us looking good."

In any moment of decision, the best thing you can do is the right thing. Theodore Roosevelt. If it means losing our privacy, maybe keeping the secret is the best thing we can do. Telling the

♥ 241 ♥

truth should be easy, but something else is bothering me about Dad and Boston. Something that's scraped away the happy thoughts of Mom and Dad getting along again for a change. Dad doesn't know anything about me and Gabe. Honest Bill arranged a photo shoot that he thought was completely dishonest. "It's going to be okay," I say. Us. The quad. My parents. Everything's going to be okay. It has to be.

32

I'm falling, my body speeding for the ground. I jolt awake. Just a nightmare. I close my eyes. *Crack!* I pop my eyes open again, but I can still see the broken tree branch. I rub my left arm and look at my alarm clock. I can sleep for another twenty minutes. I shudder. Or dream for another twenty minutes. I get out of bed.

"Relax," Mad tells me at the car. She wiggles a full set of gel crash pads at me. "I came prepared."

For a crash. My stomach does a backflip.

I feel even sicker when we pull into the rink. There's too many cars here for five thirty in the morning. At least Igor stops the reporters at the door. They flash their badges at him, but he says, "Sorry. Closed practice."

I'm relieved until I realize the only reason Igor wouldn't want reporters around would be that he doesn't want them to see us if we mess up the quad.

We do our off-ice warm-up, then Igor gives us five minutes to get our legs under us. He takes Mad aside, speaking quietly to her at the boards. Changing his mind? Please? *Please?*

No, the triumphant smile on Mad's face smashes that dream into shards. "A nice big triple to warm up," Igor announces.

That I can do. The triple Salchow is our best throw. It's why Igor keeps it in our program, even though most of the other throw triples have a higher base value. He's told us before that it's so big and beautiful it seems effortless, rare praise from Igor. And he's right. I watch Mad sail through the air, neatly completing the three rotations and checking out into a textbook landing. There's a reason we always earn two positive grades of execution on that move.

"Very good," Igor says. "One more." He turns to me. "The highest you can. You must be ready to tackle the quad next."

We're gaining speed when Mad stops abruptly.

Igor puffs a cloud of breath. "Madelyn."

"Just a sec, I think my lace is loose." She bends over, unhooks her tights, and fiddles with her skate boot.

"Everything fixed?" I wring my hands, but that only makes the nervous tingles spread into my arms.

She stands up. "*I* don't need to fix anything," she says, keeping her voice low. "But *your* hands are shaking. No thinking ahead, remember? Focus on the now; there'll be enough to worry about when we get to the quad."

Once again, we set up for the throw. Step, cross, step, cross, Mohawk. I put all of my strength into the element and watch Mad complete one-two-three-*what-the!* My heart stops as I realize she's already going for the quad but I can't tear my eyes off her. Four. She crashes. But it was a fully rotated throw. She was right, we're already very close.

Mad bounces back up and skates toward me. "Sorry. We didn't see any other way."

She tricked me. No. *We* didn't see any other way. She and Igor both. I'm stunned for a second, but it was a good trick. And it worked. I breathe low. "It's okay." *We can do this. We're going to do a quad.* Confident now, I set up another attempt. And another. And another. On the fifth try, Mad makes three and a half rotations, touches down with her hand, and cheats the last quarter out in a shaky landing.

Flying high from our success with the quad, I don't even care that the reporters follow us to school. They won't be allowed in the building. Unfortunately, the news is. I walk into my first period gym class to a chorus of "Woo-hoo, Nielsen!"

Chris pantomimes clicking snapshots. "He shoots . . . this time he doesn't score." He laughs and bumps me in the ribs. "When are you gonna get on that?" Some of the other guys call out about how the only girl I can keep is one I'm not really dating.

The locker-room banter follows me around all day, the other guys mimicking Chris's fake photog skills every time they see me in the hall. In English, though, someone is a little too focused for a joke. Kurt's staring me down the way he stares down the puck in a face-off. Suddenly I have yet another reason to keep my secret. There's no way to win here.

33

Gabe was right about the reporters. Without any fire, the news freezes up fast and they're gone within a couple days. I wait until Sunday night to be sure, but after spending Saturday's families movie night sharing a throw blanket but not being able to do anything else besides brush fingers with Gabe in the popcorn bowl, I can't wait any longer. Maybe neither Gabe nor I know what to do about our secret mess, but Boston was about more than a show. Visiting the library, walking in the Public Garden, Gabe knowing just what to say to calm my nerves . . . all of that was *us*. I miss us, miss Gabe. With the reporters hanging around, we haven't gotten even a few minutes in the garage together since Nationals. And we qualified for Worlds. We landed the *quad*. I want to celebrate.

I set my cell phone alarm for midnight, put my phone on vibrate, and slip it into my pillowcase so it won't wake my parents. I didn't need to bother. I lie awake in my bed, watching the moon outside and feeling as though it's Christmas

Eve again and I still believe in Santa Claus. At eleven thirty I rise. From my bedroom window I can see Gabe's house, the single light on in the kitchen and the rest of the windows dark against the bright porch lights.

I slip my arms into the sleeves of my robe, pull on a pair of thick socks, and pad downstairs. I ease open the hall closet and slip on my boots. In the kitchen, I look at the rack beside the door. There it is, hanging from a thin red ribbon.

Our whole neighborhood is white and peaceful as I slip through our side yards, stepping in Gabe's footprints in the snow to hide my tracks. The key to the Nielsens' side door grows warm clenched in my fist. I unlock the door, slowly and carefully turn the knob. Relocking the door behind myself, I take off my boots and hold them tight against my chest so I won't leave puddles.

I could climb the stairs to Gabe's room in my sleep, even though I haven't gone up there in ages. When we were little, Gabe and I loved bouncing on the squeaky sixth step, but I skip it tonight. Our parents let us have sleepovers when we were kids, too, but those stopped the year Gabe turned nine. Our last one was at my house and Mom came to wake us for breakfast and found Gabe and I huddled together under my covers.

Mom called Mrs. Nielsen over. My lip quivered and Gabe couldn't look either of our moms in the eye. "I'm sorry," he said. "I know we weren't supposed to." He rummaged through my sheets until he found my gaming system and handed it over to my mom.

"Was that all you were doing?" Mom asked. She and Mrs.

Nielsen started laughing so hard that tears streaked from their eyes.

If I get caught this time, though, neither set of parents will be laughing about it. Nor will they believe that Gabe and I were playing video games again, even if that was what we were really doing before. Outside Gabe's bedroom door, I strain my ears for any sound of movement but I don't hear anything. I reach for the knob.

Then, out of the corner of my eye, I catch a door opening down the hall. I glance around, but the hallway doesn't offer me anyplace to hide. I press myself as flat as I can against the wall.

Something furry brushes against my leg and I almost drop my boots. Then I hear the purring. Axel rubs himself against Gabe's door, then back against my leg, almost as though he's asking what I'm waiting for. I pray the door will stay quiet and turn the knob to Gabe's room. Axel darts between my legs, almost tripping me as I step inside.

My heart thuds against my chest. I haven't been in Gabe's room since seventh grade. In middle school, the amount of time we spent in practice increased and we just hung out at the rink instead. Could I have misremembered which room was Gabe's? The Batman bedspread's gone, as is the twin bed with its trundle. Did he switch rooms? No, he signals from the same window.

Axel waltzes over to the bed and leaps onto it, curling himself up next to the mass of loose blond curls. I step over the pile of dirty clothes next to the laundry hamper and follow him. I'm in the right place.

The mattress is firm as I sit on the edge of Gabe's bed and watch him sleep. His new bed is bigger than my full-size bed, probably a queen. I realize that I'm still clutching my boots and I set them down beside the bed, then toss my robe on top of them. Rethinking that move, I shove them both under the bed skirt, just in case.

Gabe is deep in sleep. He lies on his back, one arm stretched across the sheets, almost as though he was expecting me. I slip under his covers and cuddle against him, laying my head against his bare chest. His heart beats slow and steady against my cheek, but mine races as I trace circles down his body. Usually when we're fooling around together, Gabe mostly touches me. Tonight's my turn to be the explorer.

I ease the covers aside, lift my head, and look him over. Batman pajama pants. I smile. Some things never change.

Gabe stirs in his sleep, and I gently pull the covers back over us and lie down in the crook of his arm. More can wait for another night.

34

Gabe

God, that ear thing Mad does is—

My eyes pop open. It's not Mad. Axel's licking me, again. "Thought I shut you out last night," I grouse. But it's not his fault he ruined another awesome dream. I reach over to scratch his chin, then stop mid-reach. I blink, but the vision doesn't change. Mad's in bed with me.

No, she's not, my brain says. *You're dreaming. Again.* I turn on my bedside lamp and stare. Slowly I stretch my hand out and pat lightly at her body. I pat her all over. That feels really . . . real.

Mad stirs, opening her eyes. She sits, looks at the clock, and plops back down in my bed, yanking the covers over her head and muffling her voice. "Gabe, it's only quarter to five. We've got fifteen more minutes of sleep!"

"You're not real. You can't be real. I'm dreaming this again." I resume patting.

"Knock it off," comes her still muffled response. "I'm real."

She slides her hands across my pajama pants and just when I'm thinking this is the best dream ever, she pinches my inner thigh. Hard.

I yelp.

She pulls me under the covers with her and silences me with a kiss. "Shh, your parents will hear!"

My parents were so relieved to get out of playing taxi for our early-morning skating practices that they bought me the Viper for my sixteenth birthday. Before then, I had to pound on their door to wake them for rides. It would take something major to get them out of bed before seven, possibly an earthquake. A fire, at the bare minimum. It's burning hot under here with Mad, but I think we're safe. From my parents, anyway.

I toss the covers off us and eye her knit tank top and shorts. Mad's got the lean and slender type of body that can make almost anything look sexy, but it's not the outfit I would've chosen. In my mind, she'd be down to at least her underwear if not already naked. If she's really here, though . . . "How'd you get in?"

Mad curls onto her side facing me and my eyes run along the line of her hip jutting up so temptingly. "Climbed the tree."

"You didn't. Do you realize—?"

"That I could break my arm?" She reaches to the nightstand behind her then dangles a metal object in my face and laughs. "We have a key to your house."

I vaguely remember my parents saying something about

leaving a key at the Spier house years ago, in case I was ever locked out. With Helen around, I've never needed to use it. But, now that I think of it, we have a key to Mad's house as well. Fully awake now and in a good mood, I pull her on top of me and kiss the tip of her nose. "Did we . . . ?"

The corners of her mouth twitch up. "In your *many* dreams, maybe."

I roll, pinning her beneath me, and nip at her ear. Pressing myself against her, I can't hide the hopefulness in my voice. "Can we?"

"Nope." She giggles and wiggles out from under me, but she lets me catch her again that quick.

I trace a fingertip from her chin down her chest, gently teasing the neckline of her tank top down between her breasts, and whisper, "Can I at least sneak a peek?"

"Mmm . . . nope." She slides away before I can block her escape again and nods at my clock. "Five o'clock. Time to skate."

During both the morning and afternoon practices, I'm shameless. Every time Igor isn't looking, I beg. Just to hear her laugh. On the way home, I drive under the speed limit to get a few extra minutes talking to her. "Mad, you know I was just teasing today, right?"

She smiles. "By the twentieth request I'd connected the dots." When I pull in the drive, she checks that the coast is clear and pecks my cheek. "Tonight, Romeo."

* * *

That night, when she doesn't come over, I flash her: JULIET?

Her answer comes back: ROMEO, OH ROMEO! WHEREFORE ART THOU, ROMEO?

Favorite class or not, somebody's been paying more attention to *me* in English instead of to her assignments. Wherefore means why, not where. But why *not*? I rummage through the extra keys in the drawer by the side door. One's labeled SPIER.

35

Moonlight streams through the sheer curtains in my windows and bathes Gabe and I in its soft light as I let him sneak the peek he wanted that morning and . . . a lot more. We roll together under my covers. Our extra practices have been steamy before, but this is another level of heat completely. Gabe's skin burns against mine and I feel feverish.

He throws the blankets back and sits up. "I want you."

"No, really?" I giggle. "I kind of figured that out on my own. You've been begging like a puppy all day."

He doesn't answer me. Instead he pulls me to a sitting position, reaches for the sides of my camisole, and draws it over my head. Silent now, I let him undress me. Gabe looks at me, at *all* of me. I drop my head, look down at my small chest and barely-there hips. They're advantages for skating. But for other things?

Gabe traces my chin with the edge of his finger, tipping my head to make me look back at him. "You're beautiful, Mad." He reaches into his pocket, then sets two silver-wrapped squares on my nightstand. "I brought . . . supplies. Just in case."

The winter air is chilling my exposed skin. I shiver. I've already gone a lot further tonight than I meant to. I know Gabe's not a virgin. Even when we were kids, he didn't always wait for me. He always let me catch up, but am I ready to catch up this time?

Gabe sheds his pants and I look at all of *him* as he climbs back into my bed beside me. He draws the sheets back over us as we lie together. Naked. I feel him hard against me and oh my God am I really going to—

"I'll be gentle." He kisses my neck below my ear. "I know how to make it good."

I squirm. *So gentle, so careful, so good.* I've heard the whispers in the school hallways. So gentle. So careful. So good. With so many *other* girls. *You won't be able to resist.* With the places his hands and mouth go next, I know why they say that, too.

"Please," he whispers.

If I don't stop him now, *right–this–millisecond–now,* I won't be able to. "Gabe," I manage, choking on his name. "We can't." He rolls away from me, but I hear the quietest of groans escape his lips. "I'm sorry."

His voice sounds strangled. "Give me a minute."

It probably isn't even a minute, but it feels like an hour before I dare open my mouth. "Are you mad?"

"No." He groans again, more loudly this time. "Just hormonally challenged. It'll pass." He's quiet again, then he says, "It's okay if you don't want to."

"I do, but . . ." How do I explain this? If I let him, the

longing will be answered. This need can't be satisfied. "It has to show in our skating. The longing, the need."

Lying on his back now, Gabe laughs. "You sound like Igor."

"Well, it's true. Besides, Romeo married Juliet first."

Gabe rolls back to face me. "I already married you, remember?"

I remember. Late summer, in the small overlap when we were both six years old. Under the maple tree, with a lace tablecloth for a veil and a bouquet of dandelion fluff. And a gorgeous, antique engagement ring that got Gabe into megabig trouble when his mother caught us playing with it.

He tickles me. "It's been what, eleven years? Time to consummate that marriage." Then the smile slips from his face. "Sorry. I shouldn't make a joke of it. I don't want you to do anything you're not ready for. But . . . do you trust me?"

On a daily basis, I let him lift me over his head one-handed and throw me through the air. This is a different kind of trust, but . . . "Yes."

"All right." He draws me to him and holds me tight. "Because I know how to make it good without going all the way, too. And Mad? I want to make you feel the way I feel about you."

I cling to him, trembling once again, but this time my trembling isn't from the cold. I pull away from him, get my panties off the floor, and put them back on. I trust Gabe, but I don't trust myself.

36

Next day at school, I'm nodding my way through English. Across the room, Mad is, too. I grin at her. Last night was totally worth falling asleep in class. At the rink after school, I can't even handle our jump rope warm ups. Looking at Mad has me melted into a puddle of slush.

Igor stomps into the lobby. I wipe the doofus grin off my face. But he's not upset with us. Doesn't even notice me slacking on our warm-up. He growls, "Where. Is. Christopher?"

"I don't know." The truth. I didn't see Chris in the locker room at all.

Igor stomps off. Mad and I can't help it, we lose it laughing. "Chris stole his door again, didn't he?" Mad says.

"Probably."

Mad and I get our skates on and head for the ice. I want to work on our transitions, just for an excuse to touch her, but Mad cuts me off after one program run-through. "We have second lesson today," she says. "Let's work on your Axel."

Not inspired. Mad's gone from landing the jump to landing

it consistently. I haven't made any progress at all. And today? Forget it. I'm way too distracted. Then we hear Igor yelling again and we're both distracted. Poor Kate is late, too, and in Chris's absence she's bearing the wrath of the Russian herself. By the time Chris slinks onto the ice, Igor's worn out his voice.

Not surprisingly, Kate doesn't speak to Chris the entire session. Doesn't even look at him unless Igor specifically directs her to. It takes awhile, but they crack the KGB. Igor gives up and makes them practice pattern dances on opposite ends of the rink from each other.

"What'd you do this time?" I ask Chris in the locker room after.

"None of your business." He doesn't even change, just stuffs his bag and hauls out of Dodge, slamming his locker door so hard as he leaves that it bounces right back open.

In the car, I ask Mad. "You know what's going on with Chris and Kate?"

"Besides the fact that they're going for the gold at the World Fighting Championships?" She hesitates. "I got my acceptance letters last week. Wichita State and Riverview Community."

"Me, too. What does that have to do with anything?"

"Maybe . . . Kate started getting hers." Mad pauses. "She told me she wants to go to school in New York or California."

Chris's grades won't get him anywhere other than Riverview Community. I'd be seriously pissed if Mad went California or bust on me. Could they be breaking up for real this time? The thought makes me a little sick and I glance at Mad. She smiles at me. "Don't worry, I'm going wherever you're going."

I laugh. "Yeah, because I'm driving."

"Seriously, though," she says. "I think we should go to Wichita State. Close enough for training, far enough for some privacy."

"Privacy, huh?"

"Shut up, Gabe." Mad blushes.

Good. I'm not the only one looking forward to tonight.

37

That night, I lie in Gabe's arms, blissed out. I can't think of anything and yet I'm thinking about everything. Skating's always soared me to skyscraper heights, but Gabe touching me is like I'd imagine the Pacific Ocean, the waves of feeling rolling over me. I nestle even closer to him. I don't need New York or California, I'm a Kansas girl. The heartland, that's where my heart is. And Gabe and I, we're not Chris and Kate. But . . .

I reach across his chest and run my fingers through his hair. "Gabe?"

"Yeah?"

"About Wichita State . . . if you wanted to go somewhere else . . . I'd go with you."

He rolls toward me and kisses my forehead. "I'm good here. I'd really rather not leave Igor, anyway."

"You don't want to leave Igor?" I giggle. "That's what you say to me in bed?"

He pulls me on top of him. "Forgive me if I'm not

thinking straight. You're a little distracting." He kisses my lips this time.

Lying on top of him, I can feel his distraction. Suddenly I feel so selfish. Gabe's touched me everywhere, made me feel everything. But . . . "Gabe?" I move off him and slide my hand to his leg. Across his leg. And this time, I touch him. "Show me what to do?"

He gasps deep. "God, Mad."

"What?"

"Do that again. Please."

I do. His hands find mine, curl my fingers around him and set a rhythm between us. We've had thirteen years of following each other's movements, it doesn't take long. This time, I bring the ocean to Gabe.

After, he's a mess. A wet, sticky mess, and so are my hands. I go to the bathroom and wash up. I bring back a warm washcloth for Gabe. He wipes his stomach up, then he pulls me up against him. "Mad?"

"Yeah?"

"When can we do that again?"

Several sleep-deprived yet seriously fun nights later, I'm yawning in the produce department with Mom when her phone buzzes in her purse. "Maddy?" Mom calls out from across the bags of apples and grapes. "Could you get that?"

I dig through Mom's mammoth bag but I'm not quick enough. MISSED CALL flashes on the screen. Harold Ziegman. "Just Harold."

Mom places her armful of fruit into the cart. "If it's important, he'll leave a message or call back."

As if on cue, the phone begins to vibrate in my hand. I pass it off to Mom as we head for the checkout aisles.

"Harold. What's up? . . . Just a sec, I can't hear you." Mom cups her hand around her cell. Her face twitches. "You're kidding."

With everything going on with Gabe and me, I'd almost forgotten my worries about Mom and Dad. But this is it. The reporters have found their next story. Whatever Dad's been up to, it's out. I move closer to Mom.

Mom steps away from me and walks faster. "That's terrible. Of all the—" She stops short. "I've got to go. We'll talk later."

"What's terrible, Mom?"

Mom pushes the cart into a checkout lane and grabs a copy of *Good Housekeeping*. She leans against the magazine rack. "That cake recipe looks delicious."

Unless it's somebody's birthday, Mom never makes cake. She knows I have to watch what I eat and tries not to keep sweets around the house. There's something here she doesn't want me to see, something Harold would look at. I dart into the vacant checkout lane next to us and start scanning the magazines.

I haven't found it yet when I feel Mom grip my shoulders. "Maddy, please."

I freeze as I see it. I was looking for the wrong thing. What Harold found this time wasn't about Dad. "America's Sweethearts: Not So Sweet?" reads the headline. Underneath it, Gabe's smiling and laughing. With Kate.

38

Gabe

A hand touches my shoulder and I startle. "Jeez!" Yanking my earbuds out, I turn to see Mom. I scoot my desk chair away from my window, praying she doesn't put it together that I was looking at Mad's curtains. "Sorry, you surprised me. I was just . . . visualizing program run-throughs." In bed.

"It's a good technique." Mom smiles but her lips are sucked into her mouth so they don't show.

I don't like that look. At all.

Mom says, "I need to talk to you . . . about you and Maddy."

Shit. So busted. I fake innocence anyway. "Yeah?"

"Cynthia called me and . . ."

Double shit. Better Mad's mom than the Senator, but how much do they know?

Mom doesn't notice my wince; she's not even looking at me. "I'm sorry, sweetheart. We shouldn't have pushed you into it. I wanted you to have that opportunity for Worlds, that opportunity I never got, but . . ."

I breathe a sigh of relief. She doesn't know.

Mom takes her other hand out from behind her back. She's holding a magazine. I'm on the cover. Dancing with Kate. The picture's been Photoshopped. Kate's nightgown costume from the Christmas show wasn't that short and I never touched her ass. In the corner, there's a grainy shot of Mad alone on a bench.

Quadruple-triple combo shit. Mad's going to be *pissed*.

My parents are all apologies at families night but they're not the ones Mad really needs an apology from. I've been a begging puppy lots of times with Mad. Tonight though, after our parents all go to bed, I slink over to her house with my tail between my legs, ready to be swatted with a rolled tabloid.

Mad's waiting for me in her bedroom, but she doesn't swat me. It's worse. She cries.

"I'm sorry," I say.

"I know," she sobs.

"I didn't," I say.

"I know," she sobs again.

"I . . ." I still can't say what I really need to say. I curl my body around hers and hope the rest of me can say what my mouth can't.

It's an easy call that, innocent or not, I need to do something more to make it up to her. Pinterest is no help; a search for how to make up only brings me tips on applying eye shadow and creating my own custom lip gloss. I'm desperate enough to ask Chris for advice. Who better to ask than the king of make-ups? I figure that before gym class, I'll make up some hypothetical situation. When I get to PE Monday morning, though, the guys are at it again. Next to mine, Chris's locker has the cover photo of me and Kate taped on it. I rip it down and crumple it before he sees.

When he comes into the locker room, though, it's pretty obvious he already has.

"Sorry," I say. "You know I didn't."

He does know. It doesn't fix anything.

After a lackluster practice, I make myself a sandwich and take it to the study. Dad's computer is already on. I swallow my first bite and wipe my hands on my pants, then open the browser. "How to make up" gives me the same cosmetic advice from Pinterest. I type in "how to talk to girls" instead. Study the hits. Maybe this'll be easier than I thought. Howtotalktogirls .org is an actual Web site?

When I click on the link, though, there's a picture of a girl unzipping the back of her dress. A seduction ad pops up over top of it. Maybe howtotalkgirlsoutoftheirpants.org would've been a better name. Note to self: Clear browsing history and cookies.

I check out some of the other links while I eat, but most of them are about similar things. A couple that initially look promising turn out to be too simple, suggesting things like making sure you have good hygiene. I stop and think for a minute, remembering Mad's long-ago crack about my feet. I had a shower at the rink. I sniff my toes anyway. Maybe they don't smell like roses but they aren't that bad, either. Are they?

I look at the next link, a review for a book. Written by a nine-year-old. If only I could be nine years old again. Things with Mad were so much easier when fantasy and reality could blend in the land of make-believe.

Make believe. Suddenly I know what to do. I open the browser again. Just like I thought, there's tons of info. I'm going to have to run to more than one store, but it'll be worth it.

The side door bangs open. "Gabe?"

Mad? I minimize the browser before she sees what I was looking at. "In the study."

She bursts into the room. "Is anybody else home?"

Am I forgiven? Maybe I don't need plan W after all. I smile. "Mom and Dad are at work and Helen has camera club."

Mad's not smiling. Her voice trembles. "I can only stay a few minutes. Mom thinks I'm getting a homework assignment from you."

"What's wrong?"

She grabs the mouse from me and maximizes the browser. For a split jump second I worry how I'm going to explain away the bouquets, but Mad's so intent on typing into the search box she doesn't even notice the pictures. "I have to show you . . ."

My stomach drops. Not another tabloid story about us. "Mad, I don't care what they wrote this time. I'm not going anywhere."

"*You're* not." Mad stabs the enter key and stands, her whole body shaking. "My dad is."

With Mad's body out of the way of the screen, I see what she's typed. "Senator Spier Spied." The screen displays a full-color shot of her dad.

I lean toward the monitor as though moving closer will somehow change the picture in front of me. It doesn't. There's Mad's dad. Leaning on the arm of another guy. The accompanying text announces that Senator Spier's been kissing more than babies lately.

Mad clicks through link after link and I see her dad's been caught with this guy in more than one place. In a lot of the shots, he's wearing a hat and sunglasses and it could be someone else, but one photo is inside a bedroom. The Senator's wearing a hat in that one, too, but he's also down to his undershirt and there's no denying his bicep tat from his Navy days. Nor the fact that the other guy was closing the blinds as the photo was snapped. Mad turns her face toward mine. "Mom's more than enough *woman* for him, he said. Guess that was the truth."

I stand and pull her head against my chest. "Oh, Mad." But I can't help looking back at the computer screen. There's something weirdly familiar about that other man, like I've seen him before. In another photo.

Leaving my embrace, she yanks her phone out of her pocket. "I texted him. He still won't even admit it."

I squint at the Senator's reply text: *Truth will ultimately prevail but there is pain to bring it to light.* "Which president was that?"

"George Washington. But it's a misquote." Mad takes her phone back and shoves it in her pocket again.

Mad's dad can wax political all day. Why misquote something? "What should it be?"

"*Truth will ultimately prevail* where *there is* pains *to bring it to light.*"

Where there is pains to bring it to light. This, whatever this is, isn't the truth? The real truth is . . . worse than an affair? Where have I seen that other man before?

"Why couldn't he just tell us the truth?"

We haven't told the truth ourselves. For a lot of reasons. Telling the truth should be easy, but some secrets are really hard to come clean about. "I don't know, Mad." I don't. I don't know what to do, I don't know what to say.

Mad presses her face into my chest. "I don't need you to say anything. I just need you to hold me. And to listen. And to . . . be there for me."

Shit, double shit. If determined, dedicated, driven, Senator Spier can't keep his love life under control, what the hell do I think I'm doing?

39

In the library at lunch, I give up on studying. I can't take the whispers anymore, the sympathetic glances from the librarians. "We're a family," Mom said to me last night. "We stick together. And it's not true, anyway, Maddy. It's tabloid smut, like what they printed about you and Gabe." But I know where Gabe spends all his nights. Wrapped around me. And I know where my father's been spending his nights. On the couch or in D.C. And I know Honest Bill isn't always honest.

With our own relationship status still on secret mode, Gabe and I haven't altered our separate lunch and hallway routines at school. But today I need to talk to him, need him to calm me down. I push through the library doors. He's across the hall, rifling through his locker with his back to me. But he's not alone, another girl's with him. I step closer. It's just Kurt's girlfriend, Mouse. She's probably waiting for Kurt; his locker's right next to Gabe's.

Or is she? Not acting very mouse-ish at all, she leans into Gabe. "So I've heard some intriguing things from Anita.

Rumor has it your talents at the arena extend beyond the ice?"

"Mm-hm." Gabe shoves a pile of books onto the top shelf of his locker and something small clatters onto the floor.

Mouse kneels at Gabe's feet and picks his pen up. She holds it lightly to her lips, then out to him, still on her knees in front of his crotch. "Beyond the ice, and under the bleachers?" She rises to stand face-to-face with him.

He takes his pen from her fingers. "Anita lies."

"Piper, too?"

"No," Gabe says slowly. "Piper doesn't lie."

Mouse moves closer still, brushing her hand against his hip. "There's a hockey game tonight. Want to go?"

My vision blurs and I spin away. Smack into a pair of freshman girls, their arms loaded with art supplies. The girls scramble to steady themselves and manage to hold on to most of their load. But a giant canister of beads falls off the top of the pile. The plastic container hits the floor with a loud *pop* and the glass seed beads rain onto the tile. I slip on them as I run down the hall and fall, but that's a move I'm used to and I'm back on my feet in an instant.

"Mad!" Footsteps behind me.

I run faster, feeling as though my heart will explode in my chest. I know where he's been spending his nights, but I also know his attention span for girls. Is this why he's wanted to keep us secret?

The footsteps behind me increase their speed as well. We've played chasing games for years, but the only place I could ever outrun him is on the ice. It's pointless to keep running. I slow to a brisk walk, staring ahead down the hallway.

Gabe falls into step beside me. He reaches in front of me as though to stop me and I bristle before I realize he's opening the door for me. "It's not what you think," he says.

What isn't what I thought? The hallway scene? Or me and Gabe? I stalk up the stairs and stride into English class.

My usual spot isn't taken yet, but Kurt's alone at his table as well. I grip my backpack to keep from shaking. "Is this seat taken?"

Kurt swings his legs off the chair next to him and pushes it out for me. "All yours."

I sit, pull out my book, and bury my face in it, blinking rapidly. Kurt tugs on my book. I tug back. "What are you doing?"

He puts his hands over mine and loosens my fingers, then turns my book right side up. "Try that, Juliet," he says softly. His eyes wet, he glares at Gabe.

I'm not the only one who saw Mouse and Gabe.

40

After what just went down in the hallway, I need Chris's advice worse than ever. Next to me, he has his head buried under his arms. Probably sleeping. I poke him.

"Lemme alone," he mumbles, his face still plastered to the table.

"Come on. I need some help."

He groans. "I'm failing this class, dumb ass. Ask someone else."

"Not with class stuff," I mutter. "I have a . . . girl problem."

Chris lifts his head and looks at me. He's as gray as the winter sky out the window. "Join the club. I'm the treasurer and I'm collecting dues." He slumps back down and lays his head on the table again. When Miss Xander calls him for roll, he asks for a pass to the nurse.

Alone now, I slump down in my own seat. I already knew he had girl trouble. And this time, his girl trouble is *my* fault. I look over at Mad. She's passed on her normal spot today and joined Kurt at a table in the middle of the room. I watch Kurt inch his chair closer to Mad's. He glances back at me. I scowl and flip him off. Like it's my fault that his new girlfriend came on to me in the hallway. I assume Chris's position and watch the minutes drag by on the wall clock. Instead of taking notes, I ink swirling black clouds across my paper.

With a minute left to go, I toss my book in my bag. The bell begins to ring and I shoot across the room. I'm at Mad's side before the chimes even finish.

"We're playing tonight." Kurt picks up Mad's bag for her. "If you want to come."

I take hold of Mad's bag. "Sure." Jerk. I lock eyes with Kurt until he lets go. "See you there."

With Kurt ruffling my feathers, our afternoon practice is stellar. Igor singles me out for praise. "You attack elements today. Yes. Do this always." But by the time I get through the shower, I've lost my strut. Forget baby steps, I've let Kurt push me into dangerous territory.

Music blares over the speakers as Mad and I take our seats in the home section after our showers. At least I was spared making excuses about showing up somewhere with her since we were both already at the arena. I pick the breading off my chicken tenders bit by bit and pile it in the paper basket. The game's started but I don't know who won the face-off. I can't even keep track of who has possession. "I'm going to the bathroom," I tell Mad.

In the men's room, I pace in front of the sinks. One of the taps needs tightening, and the water drips against the porcelain with a tiny but urgent *plink, plink, plink plink plink*. I force the handle all the way off but the *plinking* echoes in my brain.

BAM. The bathroom door slams against the wall.

I turn. A black-and-yellow janitor's cart is squeaking into the room. Behind it, a hooded figure bops his head in time to the low thumps of the rap music coming from his earbuds. As the cart clears the door frame, I move toward the hall.

I see Chris's face at the same time that Chris sees me.

He pulls his earbuds out, and the music gives one last pound before it's silenced and shoved into the front pocket of his hoodie. "What are you . . . ?" I trail off as I realize he's asking the same question.

Chris grabs a squirt bottle off the cart and begins spraying the mirrors. "I work here," he says to the glass, his image blurred by trailing tears of cleanser.

"Since when?"

"Since now."

Since now. I shrink down even smaller. Since he has to get Kate some ridiculous make-up present after I got him in hot water.

Chris looks over his shoulder. "Don't tell me you came to watch the hockey game."

I shrug. Pick at my nails. "Mad wanted to."

Chris switches the bottle for a clean cloth. "So are you going to watch the game with Maddy or hang out in here all night?"

I stop picking my nails and bite them instead. "I've got trouble with Kurt."

"Yeah? Me, too." Chris scrubs at a stubborn spot. "He saw me walking into the ladies' room. Never mind that it should be obvious I'm going in to clean it." He rubs the glass so hard it squeals. "You know what girls do? Kiss the freaking mirrors. It's a bitch getting their lipstick off."

"Kurt's after Mad."

"You slept with *his* girlfriend."

"Mad's not—" I stop. I can't say she is, but I can't say she isn't, either.

Chris begins to spray down the sinks. "I'm only surprised it took him this long. When were you with Anita? Like, two years ago? But if you want to retaliate, someone's waiting outside and I'm pretty sure she's waiting for you."

I peek around the janitor's cart that's still propping the door open. There she is, sitting on a bench in the lobby. Mouse.

41

I lace my fingers and stretch my arms out in front of me. Rolling my shoulders, I wish I'd brought something to cushion my rear from the ice-cold bleachers. I wrap my arms around myself, tucking my hands in the sleeves of my coat to keep them warm. My hot chocolate's long gone. What's taking Gabe?

The first period's halfway over and Riverview's already leading 3-0. We're trouncing Palisades so badly it isn't even fun to watch. The goal light flashes. Make that 4-0. "Ri-ver-view! Ri-ver-view!" chants the crowd around me. I rub at my temples.

The score is six to nothing and there's only a couple minutes left in the period by the time Gabe slides back onto the bench, setting his plastic cup between us. "Sorry."

"What took you?" The screams drown out his reply. Riverview's scored again. I sigh and stare out onto the ice.

A giggle. A girl's voice, breathy. "Excuse me." Mouse

practically sits on Gabe's lap as she squeezes past. Shrew. I feel like tripping her, but I swing my knees to the side to let her through. She picks her way to the far end of the bleachers. Her cheeks are flushed and one of her barrettes is sliding out of her thin, mousy hair.

Oh, no way. I wheel to face Gabe. "You didn't." As the crowd roars, I grab Gabe's soda to throw it in his face.

"Didn't what?" Gabe throws his hands up in defense. "Mad, what the hell?"

"You messed around with Mouse."

"No! She just came up to me. There's *nothing* going on. My bleacher days are over."

The cup shakes in my hand. Gabe can lie like a politician, and . . . "You think I'm just like my mom? That I'm going to close my eyes while you fool around?"

"I'm not your dad, Mad. I'm your . . . boyfriend."

Did he just say what I thought he said? Out loud? Here? I grip the plastic cup so tightly that its lid pops off. The sharp scent of ginger ale pricks my nostrils as the sticky liquid drips over the edges of the cup and runs down my hands.

Gabe hands me a napkin, takes the cup from me.

I hide my shaking hands under the napkin. Once I wanted Gabe to be my boyfriend out loud and in public, but right now I just want the truth. "Why is her hair all messed up?"

"I don't know. Maybe she was with Kurt."

"*Kurt* has been out on the ice the whole time." I stare back out at the rink, where Kurt has a breakaway and is headed for goal number eight. "Why were you gone so long?"

"I told you. I went to the bathroom, ran into Chris and got talking."

I crush the napkin into a ball. "What were you talking about?"

Gabe's eyes drop to his lap. He's lying, I think, but he looks back at me. "You."

"Me? What about me?"

He leans in closer to me so I can hear him. "Mad, you need to stay away from Kurt."

I narrow my eyes at him. "Like you stay away from Mouse?" It's a snappish remark and I feel bad as soon as I say it.

Gabe doesn't snap back. "Please. Even if you're mad at me. You don't know what he does."

"Maybe not. I know what *you* do."

"I'm afraid he's going to do something to hurt you."

"Like what, try and screw me under the bleachers?"

I'm being an ice queen, but Gabe doesn't call me on it. "I'm not like that anymore. I swear on my skates. I don't want any other girl. Only you."

I want to believe it, but right now I don't know what to think or who I can trust. I let Riverview rack up a couple more goals, then I casually remark, "You know, I always thought that mole of hers was so cute."

"Really? The one—" Gabe's face turns crimson and his shoulders creep up to his ears.

"I knew it. I knew you were lying. There's no way you've seen that mole unless you've—"

"Seen her naked." He pushes his shoulders back down and looks at me. I pause. I didn't expect him to admit it. "She's on Kurt's phone. He took pictures of her. Showed them to all the guys in the locker room."

"You looked?"

"It's hard to avoid when someone's sticking the phone right in your face."

"Does she know?"

"Doubt it. From the looks of it, she was either asleep or passed out. I don't want pictures of you on his phone."

"You think I'd let him take nude photos of me?"

He looks at me sharply. "What do you remember about New Year's?"

Puking in front of Gabe. In the bushes and at the rink and all over his car. "Thanks for reminding me."

"Not New Year's Day. New Year's Eve."

"The party being not canceled." I can't help it, I cut back at him again. "You hiding our glasses."

"You got drunk."

"I did not." But as I say it, I try to remember what else happened that night. New Year's Day I was so embarrassed about almost puking *on* Gabe that I didn't think about New Year's Eve. And now . . . I don't remember anything else. I don't even remember if I watched the ball drop or if I got my midnight kiss. That awful headache the next day . . . was a hangover.

"Kurt spiked the punch. You couldn't even stand up and you were holding on to his arm and he was going to . . ." Gabe's fists clench. "I shouldn't have messed around with Anita, okay? I got sick of Kurt running his mouth off that I quit the team because I was gay. It bugs the shit out of me when he does that because I know one of the guys on the team *is* gay and won't come out because he's afraid of what Kurt will do. So when Anita asked me if *I* was, I told her I didn't know. Asked if she'd like to help me find out."

"And what did you find out?"

"That Anita isn't worth fighting over. Listen, I don't know what Mouse is playing at. But I'm not playing this time."

The buzzer sounds. The period's over and, as the crowds file past us, so is the conversation.

When I get home, Mom's wrestling her suitcase out of the hall closet. "Oh, good, you're back. I was hoping I'd get to say good-bye to you."

Good-bye? I trail after her as she heads into her room. "Where are you going? I need to talk to you."

Mom's never been the obsessive packer that Dad is, but this time she's literally throwing clothes into the suitcase. "Didn't you see my note this morning?" She closes the suitcase and latches it, not even noticing that a piece of clothing is caught and sticking out the side. "I'm going to D.C."

To D.C. "You're going to help cover this up. Mom. He's cheating on you. How can you—"

Mom grabs me tight, almost knocking me off balance.

"No, Maddy. He's not. It's not what you think it is. That man is an old friend of your father's. He's just . . . helping out with something."

"With what?" *Truth will ultimately prevail where there is pains to bring it to light.* "Please. Please tell me the truth."

She doesn't say anything for a minute and I think if I just stay quiet maybe she'll cave. "Maddy," she says finally, "I can't. This is bigger than you know. They're starting to talk about your father for the presidential nomination and this could ruin everything."

"Secrets suck."

Mom squeezes me harder. "Yes, that's the truth." She pecks my cheek, fierce, then she releases me and grabs her suitcase and her purse. "I've got a plane to catch. I'll call you when I get in. Grab what you need and take it next door. Jensine's expecting you."

Next door? I can't, not tonight. I need some space from Gabe. I need to figure things out. I want to believe him but I'm not going to be my mom. "I'll just stay here."

"Not okay."

How many times have I sneaked over to Gabe's and now that I don't want to go, I have to? "I'm seventeen years old, Mom. Kate's parents let her stay home alone."

"It's not a choice, Maddy. I don't know how long I'll be gone and I've got enough to worry about without worrying about you home alone, too."

"Kate. I want to stay at Kate's."

Mom kisses the top of my head. "This isn't on the floor for debate, dear. This is an executive order."

Late that night, the door to the guest bedroom cracks open and Gabe's blond waves peek through. He tiptoes in, easing the door shut behind him. I still don't know what I want to do about us but suddenly I don't care. If Dad gets to do whatever he wants, then I'm going to do whatever I want. When Gabe walks up to the bed, I grab him by the waist of his pants and go for his drawstring.

"Whoa," he says. "What are you doing?"

His drawstring's stuck, I've accidentally pulled it into a knot. My fingers pry at the strings. "You. I'm doing you."

"No. Not tonight."

"Why the hell not? I thought you wanted to be my boyfriend."

"Yes. Your boy*friend*. Which is about a lot more than sex. This isn't about us, it's about your dad." He takes my hands in his. "I don't want it if it's not about us. I've done that too many times before and I'm not doing it again."

Too many times before. No more secrets. "Tell me. Tell me about all of them."

"No, Mad."

"Yes. We can't have any more secrets. Gabe. I can't take any more secrets."

"That was before *us* and you already know, anyway. You already know about all of them."

His phone. I do know. Gabe hasn't kept secrets from me before, even about the worst parts of his past.

We don't talk anymore. We don't have sex, either. Gabe

curls himself around me. *I'm not going anywhere,* his body says. But I need more than that. I need three little words.

The next morning, new pictures start cropping up everywhere. Dad and Mom present a united front, *so* happy together. They deny the stories of an affair. They even let themselves be photographed kissing, something they've never allowed before. JFK's Camelot on the surface, but I'm a good history student. I know the truth about Camelot.

42

Three nights I spend just holding Mad. Three days Mad fights for every element at practice, trying to hide how much her parents are cracking that rock-solid exterior she presents to the world. Three evenings my parents sit somber and sympathetic with us at dinner and I realize that even though they don't have a clue about Mad and me, they knew about the Senator. They knew the whole damn time.

But even before three days, I've figured out what Mad needs from me. And I think I'm ready. It's time for plan W, and an unseasonably warm first Monday in February is the perfect day.

"Is that Igor? What's he doing outside?" Mad shades her eyes from the sun as we pull into the arena parking lot.

"Enjoying the weather, maybe?" But the KGB isn't the type. The colder the better, as far as he's concerned. Curious, I pull the car up in front of the building.

It *is* Igor, a stack of neon-green papers tucked under one arm and a roll of tape in his hand. He says something I can't quite make out. Something about noise?

I roll down the window. "What's going on?"

"No. Ice." Igor repeats himself, his scowl a contrast to the cheerful weather. "The compressors, they are broken. Is fixed for tomorrow morning." He turns his back to us and slaps a paper against one of the arena doors. CLOSED FOR REPAIR.

"Want some help?" Mad asks.

Igor frowns over his shoulder at us, his hand flapping as he tries to shake off a piece of tape stuck to his glove. "No. Go." He rips it loose and waves us off. "Take a hike."

I roll the window back up. Sounds perfect to me. Now initializing plan W.

Mad laughs. "For once he got the expression right. Sort of, anyway. A hike in February?"

"Why not? My legs aren't used to doing nothing after sitting around all day at school. Let's go home, ditch these uniforms, and go for a hike."

"A hike." She leans back against her own seat. "This is an afternoon of surprises."

I fight to keep the grin off my face. The surprise is only beginning.

At home, I trade my school blazer and khakis for a T-shirt and my favorite jeans. I throw my coat back on, toss my scarf around my neck. In my haste to tie my hiking boots, I catch my fingers in the laces more than once. I grab the bag I prepared and double-check it. I've got everything.

I wait for Mad by her side door. Still zipping her purple parka, she steps out and eyes my backpack. "How long of a hike were you planning?"

I tug her hat down over her ears. "Only a couple of days."

The hiking park's two miles from our houses. A long walk by most people's standards, but we exert more energy doing our daily jump rope warm-ups. We get the place to ourselves. Sure, it's nice out. Even if it's February, people are thinking about taking their Christmas lights down or getting caught up on their shoveling, not about hiking. I bounce on the balls of my feet as I walk.

Mad laughs. "Sheesh, you weren't joking about your legs, were you?"

Even after she teases me, I can't stop. The rose-cubes can't hold a candle to this. Practically jumping Axels now, I walk her past the playground. Nestled to one side near the beginning of the trails is a grove of pine trees. Remnants of last week's snowstorm decorate their branches and sparkle in the late afternoon sun.

Mad's eyebrows rise as we head for the trees. "Thought we were going for a hike?"

"We hiked here, didn't we? Come on." I take her hand and pull her into the clearing. At the back is an arch formed of an ivy-covered trellis. In summer, this is a favorite spot for weddings. Winter might not be a great time to gather large groups of people outdoors, but the trellis looks pretty in the snow, too.

"We could have done this at your house, you know," Mad says. "Your parents don't get home until dinnertime anyway. It would be warmer."

"Here's better." I dig my iPod out of my backpack and thread the wire from my earbuds through the trellis to support its weight.

Mad giggles. "You brought mood music?"

"Yeah." Not the kind she thinks, though. I sneak a glance at her. Turning the volume as high as it'll go, I press play and the soft strains of Pachelbel's "Canon in D" float out from my makeshift speakers. Not just any arrangement—I listened to a dozen versions before finding this perfect duet. The piano strong and steady, the violin's notes soaring above it, it mirrors our partnership. Simple and elegant, it's mood music all right. Exactly the kind needed for a quiet wedding at the park.

43

I know the music from the first gentle notes, my favorite piece to play on my violin. "Canon in D." A classic wedding piece. My heart skips a beat. A classic *wedding* piece. And we're standing under a wedding arch. Staring at Gabe, I feel something ticklish press against my hands. I look down. He's given me a bouquet of silk flowers, a mix of white and cream roses with berries and twiglike stems peeking out from between them. I clasp it in my fingers and feel light-headed. These are no dandelions.

"Mad?" Gabe's smile wobbles. "Breathe, okay? You're going to start turning blue." He takes his own blue scarf and drapes it around my neck. "There, something borrowed and blue. Just in case that was a superstition instead of, like, shock."

Taking a gulp of air, I look into his eyes. This is happening. This is really happening.

His eyes looking into mine, his voice solemn, he proclaims, "We have gathered here today to celebrate the union of Gabriel Nielsen and Madelyn Spier."

If this is a joke, it isn't funny. Searching his eyes, though, I find no trace of amusement. He's serious. Oh God, he's serious.

"Have you not read that the one who made them at the beginning made them male and female and said, 'For this reason a man shall leave his father and mother and be joined to his wife and the two shall become one flesh? So they are no longer two, but one. Therefore what God has joined together, let no one separate.'"

The memorization, the music, the wedding arch. They all work together to create the wonder, the magic of the scene before me. I feel that rush of anticipation, like my heart's flying down the ice for a triple Lutz.

Taking my hands in his, Gabe asks, "Do you, Madelyn, take me, Gabriel, to be your husband, promising to cherish me, forsaking all others, from this day forward?"

Since we were young enough to play house together I've wanted nothing else. Softly but firmly I answer, "I do."

His gaze is unwavering, a strong, left back outside edge. "Then I, Gabriel, take you, Madelyn, to be my wife, to have and to hold from this day forward, for better or worse, for richer or poorer, in sickness and in health, until death do us part."

No flutzing, this time the Lutz is clean. He loves me. He really loves me.

He tucks the loose strands from my ponytail behind my ears. It's started to snow, and soft white flakes stick in his hair and on our coats as though we've been pelted with rice. He leans forward and places his lips against mine in a tender kiss. A perfect landing.

Untangling his iPod, he offers me one of the earbuds. We walk out of the park, a flute and gentle harp playing Mendelssohn's "Wedding March" in our ears.

On the walk back, I'm the one who's bouncing. And stealing glances at Gabe only about every two seconds. Smiling so big I can't believe my face doesn't split open from pure joy. Giddy doesn't even come close to describing it.

Back at my house, Gabe lets his fingers linger against my cheek, taking back his earbud as slowly as he can. "I know your mom's coming home tonight. But come over after? Please?"

I nod. I'm beyond words. I float up the steps to my house, peeking over my shoulder in the doorway. Gabe's watching me, a smile on his face, too.

In my room, I hug the pillow Gabe uses when he sleeps over to my chest and breathe him in. I can't wait until tonight.

Tonight.

I take another breath of salty Irish Spring, Gabe just a little bit sweaty. Gabe didn't want to before; he said it wasn't about us. But if today wasn't about us . . . Tonight I'm going to Gabe's house and tonight . . . I'm going to give myself to Gabe.

Mom texts me that her flight was delayed. It's past eleven when she tiptoes into my room and kisses my pretending-to-be-asleep forehead, almost midnight by the time I'm finally able to tiptoe over to Gabe's. But it's worth the wait. A few carefully chosen props give his room the feel of a reception hall. He's draped a tablecloth over his desk and set a white frosted cupcake, complete with miniature bride and groom, on a china saucer on top of it. We cut it together and feed each other bites by candlelight, a collection of Nat King Cole's love songs playing in the background. Gabe pulls me into his arms and we take our first dance to "When I Fall in Love." We're still slow dancing when the playlist starts cycling through again. With my head against his shoulder and his arms around me, I feel the rise and fall of his chest, breathe in his Irish Spring, and know I could be happy to live in this moment forever.

Gabe kisses my forehead, his lips as light against me as the snowflakes at the park that afternoon. "We should go to bed."

I get snuggled under his cozy flannel sheets as he stops the music and blows out the candles. He crawls under the covers with me and I wait for his fingers to tease at my pajamas. It's time for my surprise for him.

Gabe gives me a peck on my cheek and rolls over.

44

Gabe

Click. Mad's switched my bedside lamp on. I squint in the bright light. I'm not getting out of it that easily. She props herself up on her elbow and looks at me. "Don't tell me that's all I get on our wedding night."

I sit up and lean back against the headboard of my bed. "It wasn't supposed to be about sex, Mad." Okay, maybe that's a teeny bit of a lie. All right, a horrendous lie. I've been thinking about sex ever since Igor assigned me the Romeo role. But it's not a lie now. I didn't expect to feel like this. I can't explain why the urge isn't here tonight. Because of Mad's parents, or is it just that our mock wedding was a little too real?

Mad sits up, too. Her nipples perk through her thin tank top. Underneath, she's got nothing on.

My body fights my mind.

She climbs into my lap and whispers in my ear. "What if I want it to be?"

No.

Yes!

NO. I can't take it that far when our entire relationship is a secret. I want to take her on dates, kiss her without worrying that someone will see us. It isn't that our mock wedding was a little too real, it's that it was too *un*-real. I wanted to show her I wasn't playing around anymore but even six-year-old me knew a real wedding needs rings. "Not tonight." I put my arms around her, groaning at the warmth of her pressed against me. I lie. "I don't have anything."

Mad's mouth is against my ear. "What happened to your, what did you call them? Supplies?"

I think fast. "They expired."

She sits back a little and looks at me with narrowed eyes. "You had time to pick up a cupcake but you didn't have time to go to the pharmacy?"

"I . . ." I sigh. "I didn't want there to be any pressure."

Her face softens, then she turns and reaches for her robe on the floor. She digs in its pockets. "Well, it doesn't matter if you don't have any. The ones you left at my house were still good, so . . ." She presses two condoms into my hand. "I do."

That's my trouble. Those two simple words of hers. The very essence of a wedding. I thought I was ready, but with everything that's passed between us, even during the ceremony this afternoon, I haven't once told her—

"I love you," Mad says.

I love you. I can't say it out loud, can't let go of that last bit of fear. Falling in love is so much scarier than falling on ice and, hell, I'm chickenshit.

45

Gabe sets the condoms on the nightstand. He puts his hands to my face. His thumb hops along my cheek, just like it did that time he made me pinkie swear to leave the romance on the ice. "Mad, I can't."

"Why?"

He drops his hands and looks at his lap. "It wasn't real."

I take his hand in mine. "It felt pretty real to me."

"And . . . there's no reskates on V-cards."

No reskates on V-cards? I can't help it, I giggle. He turns away, and I stop. Was *he* sorry about losing his? "We've never been asked to reskate anything," I say softly.

"First time for everything," Gabe whispers.

"But I'm ready. I'm sure." I climb back into his lap.

He doesn't say no this time. He kisses my lips. Gentle. Soft. His mouth moves to my neck, traces down from my ear to my collarbone. He kisses the tops of my arms, the insides of my elbows, the backs of my wrists.

My whole body feels warm and tingly. He's driving me insane. I reach for him.

He moves my hand away. "No thinking ahead. You're rushing. Focus on the now." His hands go to the sides of my waist and he eases my tank top up as though he's unwrapping the most fragile of gifts.

He draws my bare chest to his, presses his face into my neck and there's nothing but the warmth of his skin against mine and, when he pulls back again, the sound of his breathing coming just the slightest bit faster.

He lays me back in his bed, puts his hands to my waistband and slides my pants down, his fingers lingering over my hips. He reaches for the drawstring of his own pants.

"Wait. Let me."

He does this time, then lies beside me and pulls the covers over our legs.

"Gabe?"

"Mad?"

"Should we get something?"

He picks up a condom.

"No. Well, yes, but I meant . . . for the bed. If I bleed?"

"Probably you won't. Most girls don't. And before you think too much of me, I learned that at the Nielsen School of Gynecology, not from personal experience." Gabe reaches into his nightstand drawer and pulls out a tube that looks like lotion. He clicks open the lid, squelches something out into his hand, snaps it closed again. He rubs his fingers and blows on them. "The bleeding is usually from the guy being too rough. I promised I'd be gentle."

I feel him touch me then. Warm. Wet. I hear his breathing, the crinkle of the wrapper, the latex unrolling. He kneels beside me. Leans over me, runs the fingers of his other hand through my hair.

We breathe together. He positions himself above me. Lowers himself toward me, and then—

We are together.

After, I hug him to me, content in the feeling of his weight pressed against me. He pushes himself up, and I cling to him. "Stay here."

He pulls away. "I can't."

"Please," I whisper.

"Just a second." He removes the condom, balls it in a tissue. He lies down again, on his back this time, and pats the space beside him. "Come here."

I nestle into the familiar crook of his arm.

He kisses the top of my head. "That was—"

A little bit awkward, maybe. A little bit messy, maybe. But still . . . I look up at him. "So far beyond incredible?"

He smiles and strokes my hair again. "Good night, Juliet."

I lie back down and drape my arm across his body. I listen to his heart beat within his chest, feel his breathing slow and even out. "I love you," I say again.

He doesn't answer me.

I prop myself up, look at his closed eyes, and trace my finger over the rise and fall of his chest. He's already asleep.

46

Gabe

My alarm goes off, the soft yet still overly enthusiastic voice of the morning-show host, but I'm already awake. I turn it off, wonder how many cups of coffee that deejay drinks to be so chipper in the wee hours. I close my eyes, but thinking about the deejay can't force the more worrisome thoughts from my brain. I slide my hand sideways under the sheets until my fingers meet the warmth of Mad's body. She stirs at my touch, but her breathing stays slow and even. Still asleep.

Last night, I made love to Mad. I don't care if that's a prissy, girl way to describe it, that's what it was. But after? I curl in a ball, feeling like I'm going to hurl. I pretended to be asleep. Mad told me she loved me, and I pretended to be asleep. I just couldn't say it. I never had a two-week rule. I never had a problem with the word "girlfriend." I've always had the problem that as soon as I get in a girl's pants, it's over. I thought I could change, but I couldn't say "I love you" before we had sex. Am I going to want her at all anymore?

Mad stretches. Yawns. I feel the covers pull away from me as she sits up. The comforter rustles, then her lips brush against my cheek. "Wake up, sleepyhead. We've got practice." I hear her feet touch down on the floor and then a rush of cold air hits my body as she pulls my blankets all the way off. She giggles. "Well, part of you is awake, anyway."

I open my eyes. There she is. And, I still want her. In fact, not only do I want her, I'm desperate for her. It doesn't matter that it's five in the morning and I've had less than four hours of sleep.

I grab her hands in mine, pull her toward me. "Please? You still have one, right?"

She looks at my clock. "Yeah, but wouldn't tonight—"

Before she can say no, I cover her lips with my own. "Two minutes."

"Two minutes?"

She's laughing, but I'm serious. Last night was careful and slow. I took as much time as I could stand. Last night was about her, but this morning is about me. Being just careful enough not to hurt her, I let my sense of urgency drive me and make good on my word.

At the rink, I slip a CD of last night's playlist into the music box and join a glowing Mad on the ice for warm-ups. I'm grabbing a quick drink at the boards when Chris snaps off his skate guards, in a foul mood once again. "Man, bad enough to be up at this ungodly hour. What is this drivel?"

"Nat King Cole." I grin.

"*You* put this on?"

I have to tell someone. "Well, turns out it's true about male figure skaters. You know, like you always say? You're either in bed with your partner or pitching to your own—"

"Yeah, do me a favor and don't stand next to me in the locker room again." Chris swears. "Ever." Then he sees Mad. Even from across the rink, there's no missing the dreamy smile entrancing her face. "Oh, f—," he begins before dissolving into laughter. "I mean, for real! It was about time, anyway." He pulls it together. "Just . . . be careful, all right?"

If he says anything else, I don't catch it. Screw careful. I've discovered fearlessness and it's freaking awesome. Halfway across the rink, I catch Mad in my arms and sweep her into the swing dance pattern. We follow with our own improvisation, almost missing Igor's arrival. We snap to attention.

Igor smiles.

I rub at my eyes. Mad and I stayed up way too late last night. I'm tired. I'm imagining things. But when I stop rubbing, the smile is still stretched across Igor's face. I gape.

Igor brings his hands up from his sides, probably to shake some sense into me. Slowly, though, he begins to clap. "Yes, yes. Very good. Everything is in place. New exhibition piece I think, do you not? Let me see again."

As Igor goes to start the track over, I shake my head. This is too good to be true. Last night, this morning—I must have dreamed it all. I pinch myself. It hurts. I turn to Mad. "Did he just say what I thought he said?"

Mad's turning blue. I shake her until she breathes. She nods. "He did."

Before, we dreamed of *going* to the senior World Championships. But if Igor's going to let us do a new exhibition piece, he isn't just planning on going. He thinks we can *win*.

47

Maddy

Our afternoon practice is one of those rare but wonderful sessions where everything goes as smoothly as freshly cut ice. I land the quad throw every time we attempt it. Gabe and I skate clean double runs of both our short and long programs. Igor smiles again. Twice. He even allows us more time to play with choreography for our new exhibition piece. Wiping the shavings from my blades as we step from the ice, I hum the music under my breath: *"When I fall in love . . ."*

Gabe notices and smiles at me. As we walk down the corridor, he takes my hand in his. "This morning?" His fingers squeeze mine, strong and warm. "I had the most awesome dream that wasn't a dream."

I squeeze his hand back. "Me, too."

He stops suddenly, jerking my arm. "The music!"

"You forgot to give it to Igor so he could cut it."

He holds up his other hand in a confession of guilt, his pointer finger sticking through the middle of the CD. He scowls, imitates Igor's voice. "That was not part of plan."

I giggle. "What was?"

Gabe's body presses mine against the wall. I feel his kiss all the way down to my toe picks. He steps back. "I better take this to Igor before he comes looking for it."

"Want me to go with you?"

"No, I wanted to ask Igor something anyway. Take a long, hot shower. I'll meet you at the car."

Still thinking of Gabe's kiss, I float to the girls' locker room. I open the door and am greeted with the sound of retching. Kate's bright orange skate guards peek out from under one of the bathroom stalls. The tangy smell of vomit hangs in the air. I pinch my nose and knock on the stall door. "Kate? You all right?"

Her voice is weak. "I'm okay. I think I just ate something bad. I feel much better now." Rumblings from the toilet-paper dispenser are followed by flushing, and she stumbles out of the stall.

"You sure?" I take a step back. With her red eyes and white face, she doesn't *look* better. Now's not the time for me to catch some bug. I need to clear this locker room ASAP.

Kate nods, and that's all I need for clearance to ship out. Figuring I'll wait for a shower until I get home, I change my clothes at warp speed. Mom keeps the dress shop open late on Tuesday nights and, as usual, Dad's in D.C. If I catch Gabe before he gets to the locker room, maybe we can sneak in a shower at my house together. Feeling the steamy water already, I zip my jacket and head for the south corridor.

Igor's office is open as always but the corridor's quiet. Did I miss Gabe? Then, just before I get to the door, I hear Igor's voice. "Everything goes to plan, yes?" he asks, his tone low and serious. "But yesterday . . . no, what do we say, *preparation* . . . How do you forget this?"

I suck in my breath and press myself out of sight up against the wall. I'm not supposed to be listening to this, that much is obvious, but I can't stop myself. Yesterday? What are they talking about? We didn't even have practice last night because of the broken compressors.

The frightening thought shoots into my skull and freezes my brain. Igor couldn't know what we did yesterday, could he?

Peering through the cracked door, I see Igor slide a box across his desk. The box itself isn't that large, but its Trojan label grabs my attention like a spotlight.

He knows.

How does he know?

"Two is pair, three is crowd, yes? A baby is not part of plan. See me if you need more." I see Igor begin to rise, hear the chairs scraping against the concrete floor, and dart down the hall. *I don't have anything,* Gabe said last night. I feel sick to my stomach. Igor met us outside yesterday— Were the compressors really broken? I didn't go inside to check, I took Igor at his word and . . . oh, God. *Take a hike.* Were Igor and Gabe planning this all along?

I remember how Igor and I conspired on the throw, the media ambush he must've arranged at Sectionals. Igor's an incredible coach, everyone says so, but here he is out in the middle of Kansas nowhere. He doesn't have any national recognition yet. I know Gabe and I are his prize stallions, know coaches are ranked based on the achievements of their students. Even more than Gabe and I want to win, Igor needs us to win.

Ducking into the deserted maintenance corridor, I sink into a corner and put my head between my knees. The stench of hockey equipment turns my stomach even more as my mind races back through the many stolen moments of the past couple of months. The feel of Gabe's arms around me, the gentle stroke of his hand, his lips against my skin just this morning. Last night, and the nights before. That first night, at the ballet.

The ballet. I groan, feeling the ache deep in my abdomen. The memories I treasured five minutes ago now make my skin crawl. Of course it was too perfect, Igor giving us private box tickets. Those don't come cheap; why not gallery seats? And assigning us romantic movies to watch outside of practice?

I remember yesterday's wedding and make it to the trash can just in time to avoid being sick all over the floor. How could I have believed that Gabe could come up with that on his own? I replay his words that day in my head and realize that even then, reciting vows, he managed to avoid telling me outright that he loved me. *It wasn't real,* he said. All this time he's wanted to keep us a secret, all his lame excuses. Of course he would never tell me it was because we were *Igor's* secret.

I should have known that very first day, all their "go-work on-your-brackets-Madelyn" hushed conversations. When Gabe wouldn't even look at me until Igor made him. I saw what I wanted to see, believed everything because I wanted so desperately to believe.

I curl into a ball against the wall and let the tears flow.

I've no idea how much time has passed before I cry myself dry enough to notice the buzzing of my phone. Ignoring Gabe's text and tossing the phone back in my bag, I go wash my face. I'm not letting him see me cry.

48

Gabe

I'm toweling off by the time Chris gets into the locker room. "What did Igor want?"

Chris frowns. "Same old. I screwed up. Story of my life. Don't make it yours, Romeo." He flips a box of Trojans onto the locker room bench in front of me. "Here. A return for the times you've hooked me up."

I shove the condoms in my jacket pocket before any of the hockey players come in and see us tossing them around. "Um, thanks?"

As cool as not having to fake a run to the pharmacy is, the situation is . . . awkward. I speed dress, then head for my car. Load up last night's playlist. As the car heats up, so do my thoughts. I instant replay this morning: Mad on my lap, as close as we can possibly get. And damn, I wish I hadn't told Mad to take a long shower. I groan. I forgot it's Tuesday.

When Mad finally emerges from the arena, I've been waiting twenty minutes. I get out to help her with her bag. "Okay," I tease. "I know I said to take a long shower, but seriously?"

"You said you had to talk to Igor, I was chatting with Kate."
Mad slams the Viper's trunk.

I open the passenger door for her, then get in on the driver's
side. "Your mom works late tonight, right?"

"Yeah."

I show her the box of condoms in my pocket. "Do you want
to—" I stop, seeing her face twist up. "Are you okay?"

"No."

I scrunch up, stuff the box back in my pocket. *So* romantic,
Romeo. "Sorry." I reach for her hand. Wrong move again. She
yanks her fingers from mine. "Mad?"

"It's . . . nothing," she says. "I don't feel very good, that's all."

She doesn't look very good, either. She looks like she's about
to hurl all over my car again. "Um, do you need a bag or something?"

"Just take me home." She closes her eyes and leans against
the car window. "Please."

49

Maddy

It takes everything I have to suck it up for the car ride home after seeing those Trojans. I can't handle homework tonight. In my room, I throw myself onto my bed and sob into my pillow. It smells like Gabe and isn't a comfort. I get up and strip the sheets and haul everything downstairs to the laundry room.

When Mom comes home, we have dinner together. Or rather, we push food around on our plates together. She doesn't offer any information about her trip and I don't ask. I understand now why she doesn't want to talk about Dad. Some things hurt too much to talk about.

That night, I lie miserable in my bed. I washed *all* my bedding but I may as well have washed it in Irish Spring. Gabe's scent lingers, teasing me with the memories of the nights we spent teasing each other. I can feel his body curled around mine, his fingers soft in my hair.

Stop it, I will myself. But I'm still wanting his hands on my back, knowing just where to knead to ease the tension practices always leave in my muscles. I whip my pillow across the room. Maybe I'll go sleep on the couch.

Standing, I see the flash from Gabe's window. Out of muscle memory, I cross the room to my desk. The flashlight's in my hand and I've given my reply signal before I can stop myself.

CAN I COME OVER?

NO. DON'T FEEL GOOD.

SORRY.

Tucking my flashlight away in the drawer, I almost miss the rest of his message: I LOVE YOU.

I pulled my hamstring once in ballet class, slid down into the splits without properly warming up. Heard that quiet ripping noise, felt the pain move from *what just happened* to crippling, ohmigod, going to pass out. That's happening to my insides right now. For years, I've wanted those words. But not now. Not when I know what they really mean. My eyes blur against the flashing light.

I LOVE YOU. Because Igor told me to.

I LOVE YOU. Because that will make us win.

I LOVE YOU. Because that's the *plan.*

I lay my head down on the desk and cry.

My alarm clock sounds distant. I start to sit and realize my cheek is cemented to my desktop. Prying my face loose, I try to shake the stiffness from my neck and then remember. I close my eyes but I still see the light flashing over and over. I LOVE YOU, I LOVE YOU, I LOVE YOU. Shuffling across the room, I turn off the alarm.

For once, Gabe's waiting for me. "Feeling any better? You look like hell, Mad."

The bags under his eyes don't look super hot either. "Good morning to you, too."

"Hey." He catches me by the shoulders. "I didn't mean it like that. I'm worried about you. I love you."

Hearing the words out loud only makes me feel sicker. I brush him off, climbing into the car. "I'm fine. We already missed practice once this week. Let's go. You know I hate to be late." Slamming the door, I crank the radio and stare out the window.

We've had better practices, to say the least. The short program goes all right, I can still play the role of a temptress. I know the biblical story. Delilah didn't really love Samson. For eleven hundred pieces of silver she seduced him to learn the secret of his strength. She facilitated his capture by the Philistines, who gouged out his eyes. And since I feel like doing exactly that to both my partner and my coach at the moment, I stay in character.

The long program's another story. Igor has us run section after section to no avail. "We stop," he says finally. "Is not good to push so hard on off day. I see you this afternoon."

The afternoon's no better. Igor's playing the cut from "When I Fall in Love" as we come out to the ice. I have to excuse myself to the ladies' room. I'm flushing the toilet when Kate's orange guards run into the stall next to me.

"Sorry," Kate mumbles, still wiping her mouth as she exits the stall.

I give her a sad smile. "Just doing the same thing myself. Maybe I have whatever you have."

Kate looks my body over. "No. You're too perfect to have what I have."

Too perfect? I look down at my thin body. I remember Kate pinching her flat stomach at the mall, saying dress after dress made her look fat. Throwing up today, throwing up yesterday. She didn't eat something bad, doesn't have some stomach bug. "You're bulimic."

Kate walks to the sink and starts washing her hands.

I turn off the tap. "Kate, that's serious."

"I know." She turns the water back on, finishes rinsing, and turns to leave without even drying her hands.

I stand in her way.

Kate sighs. "Maddy, I've already got an appointment with the doctor, okay? I know I've got a problem." She gestures toward the door behind me. "Isn't Igor waiting for you? You'd better get your rear end on the ice."

I do just that. I haven't fallen so many times on a single session since I learned my first Axel. Igor dismisses us after only an hour, but my practice clothes are still soaked from my many wipeouts.

In the locker room, I peel off my sopping tights and examine the deep purple and blue marks already forming on my legs. It'd make a good police shot; I look like a battered woman. Screw that, I *am* a battered woman—only the marks are someplace no one will ever see. My body as numb as my heart, I realize it has to stay that way. I'm going to have to hide how sick Gabe makes me feel. I'm going to have to be like my mother, covering up everything, because if I don't? I'll have to kiss my gold medal dream good-bye.

That evening, no flashes come. Gabe comes instead. I stifle my groan.

"Hey." He sits on the edge of my bed, leans over, and brushes my hair back from my face. "Sorry you had such a rough practice today."

"It happens. I'm really not in the mood, Gabe."

"I didn't expect you to be." He slides under the covers next to me. "Where does it hurt?"

I release my groan. "Everywhere."

"Roll over. I'll take care of you."

I comply, if only to hide my grimaces in my pillow. Yesterday, I couldn't sleep for wishing for him. Tonight, each seemingly caring touch makes me want to flinch.

Gabe works his way over my muscles, his fingertips working deep into the tissue and managing to avoid all the bruises. As he finishes my massage, he says, "You know, I should've written it into our vows: in landing and in falling. Just for the record, though? Even if you skate like today at Worlds, I'll still love you."

"I bet Igor told you to say that."

"Igor did not tell me to say that. In fact, I'm pretty sure

he'd kill me if he found out I told you that." Gabe pulls my head against his chest and I want so desperately to believe this is real. Then he continues, "Skating like that at Worlds is definitely not part of his plan."

I'm glad that he can't see my eyes. I scrunch them tightly to keep back the tears. I count the seconds until I can reasonably pretend to roll away from him in my sleep and pray for morning to come.

50

In the morning, I watch Mad swing her legs from the bed. My ears strain for any noises from the hall. It makes me nervous, being at her house. My parents sleep like cadavers, as though they'll never catch up on the sleep they lost in med school. Hers? Not so much. And if I'm caught here, *I'll* be the dead body. Even if the Senator's not home right now, he knows where I live. I keep my voice low. "Hey, come here."

Mad stops but she doesn't turn around. She sits on the edge of the bed with her shoulders curled forward.

The bruises must be even worse than I thought. I sit up and scoot beside her. Hook my thumb under the elastic waistband of her flannel pajama pants. "Let me see."

Still hunched over, she crosses her arms over her chest and drops her chin down toward her knees as I pull at her waistband to expose the ugly yellow mark peeking out from under the edge of her panties. I ease her pants back up. Put my arm around her and tuck her head under my own chin. "Got your hip pads for today, right?"

Her head nods, brushing against my chin. I feel the wetness against my bare chest. Mad leans forward out of my embrace and wipes her eyes with the backs of her hands. I hate seeing her hurt like this. All the same, this isn't my Mad, crying over bruises. Something else is wrong.

Mad walks over to her dresser. She pulls her uniform skirt right over her pajama pants, then wiggles the pants out from under them. She changes into her blouse with her back to me. The flinching. The distance. It's not the bruises. Not about skating at all. It's *me*. When did all this start? The damn Trojans in the car. No reskates on V-cards. Dammit.

I scramble for the right words. "Sorry. Maybe it wasn't the best plan."

Mad turns and looks at me. She's buttoned her blouse all the way up tight against her throat. She turns away again. "Maybe not," she says to the wall. She picks up her school things and leaves me in her room.

I yank my pants on quick and follow her, even though I'm only half-dressed. "I love you, Mad. Even if we're not . . . I would've waited for you."

She stops and looks back at me. Softly she says, "Some things you don't get a reskate on."

At the arena before morning practice I sit in the chair across from Igor's desk and bounce my knees up and down. Igor lifts his nose out of his notebook. I put my hands on my knees to stop them.

"Yes? What?" He's still holding his pencil.

I take a deep breath. "Something's wrong. With Mad."

Igor gives me the KGB equivalent of a no-shit-Sherlock look. "It needs to."

It needs to what? He doesn't finish and my mind takes a few more seconds to figure out that he meant it needs *two*. It takes two. This I know, but . . . "I don't know what to do."

"You did something wrong."

"I think so. Yes."

"Then you *fix*." If Igor were my mother, he'd be blowing his bangs up right now. Since he doesn't have bangs, the fur on his hat flutters up instead.

I don't know how to fix it. Worse, I'm not even sure I *can* fix it. I blink hard and leave the office. It's only because I'm staring straight ahead, willing myself not to cry, that I see Mad's gray-and-purple Nikes disappearing around the end of the corridor into the lobby.

51

Maddy

I would've waited for you, Mad. Another line I almost believed until I saw Gabe in Igor's office again this morning. And to think, I—

"Maddy? Hey, Maddy? *Allo?*" Jonah waves his hand in front of my face. "Could you maybe save the spacing out for astronomy?"

"Jonah, I'm sorry." I look at the tiny print on the page full of instructions for our experiment, then give up and look at him.

He hands me two pencils with their erasers removed. "Sharpen these on both ends, please."

That's about where my concentration level is lately. The only part of the project I can be trusted with is sharpening the pencils. But when I get back to the table, Jonah takes the pencils from me, pokes them through a piece of cardboard over a glass of water, and starts connecting them to a battery with wires and electrical tape. "Are you sure that's right?" I ask.

He flips the directions over so I can see the diagram on the back and keeps taping.

Huh. I flip the paper back, curious now. What's this experiment about? Electrolysis. *Splitting* molecules. "That's it!"

"Where?" Jonah asks. "I don't see the bubbles yet."

I don't care how or where the bubbles were supposed to appear. I've made a better scientific observation. I can still take control of this situation. I don't have to be part of a pair. After all, how long have I been keeping notes on my single skating peers? Sure, it's too late to qualify for any major competition this season as a Senior lady. But the Worlds are only a few weeks away. I can make it through a few weeks. And after that, I'll retire from pair skating.

I wear my crash pads during practice that afternoon, just to be on the safe side, but it doesn't matter. I'm back. At home I help Mom chop vegetables for quick salads before Dad's town hall meeting. I scrape the freshly grated carrots into the salad bowl and decide to skate my idea out with Mom. "Do you think I could make it as a singles skater?"

Mom scrapes chopped celery in with my carrots. "What?"

"Singles skating. Do you think I could be competitive?"

She rests her chin on her thumb. "Maddy, you've got your father's drive. I think you could make it at whatever you decide to do," she says finally, going back to her slicing and dicing, with an onion this time. "But what makes you ask that?"

"I was thinking, maybe next season, you know, after Worlds, that maybe I'd just skate by myself for a while."

Her chopping slows, then stops. The knife trembles in her hands. She sets it aside. "What would you want to do that for? You and Gabe are doing so well. Worlds this year and maybe someday even the Olympics, just like you always dreamed. And you always wanted to skate with Gabe, ever since you were a little girl."

I shrug, my eyes still on the knife. Why is Mom acting so odd? "Some things change."

Mom rubs her eyes, then swears.

I wince. "Onion juice, ouch."

She walks next to me and hugs me tightly. She holds me for a few minutes. "God, I wish it were only that. Sweetheart . . ."

The edge of my forehead is getting wet. Mom's crying. I pull away from her, and it's not just the onion. "You're starting to scare me."

"I'm so sorry. . . ."

For what?

Mom's voice shakes. "We should've told you. I knew we should've told you. We should've told you a long time ago."

I step back from her. Honest Bill, ha. Try Dishonest Dad. "Told me what?"

She looks at the floor. "Daddy didn't want you to feel self-conscious about it."

"Mom! About what?"

Her eyes are still on the tile. In a dull voice, she says, "You can't skate on your own."

"What? You just said—"

She jerks her head up and looks at me. Two angry dots shine from high on her cheeks. "We can't afford it."

"It wouldn't be any more expensive than it already is." My chest tightens. Maybe she doesn't really believe . . . "You said you thought I could make it."

Mom takes a ragged breath. She holds her arms out, but I ignore them. Finally, she drops them again. "I do think you could, Maddy. But Daddy and I never paid for your skating apart from buying skates and material for costumes. Test fees, until that last test. Jensine and Richard have always paid for ice and lessons for you and Gabe both."

I study her for a sign that she's joking. Nothing. For real? In a world where so many girls are desperate for skating partners that mothers import Russian male skaters for their daughters, Gabe's parents pay for *me* to skate with their son? "Why?"

"Jensine felt bad, that day she took you both to the rink. She thought you'd have a good time, obviously. She didn't expect you to fall in love with skating the way that you did. She'd skated competitively herself, knew how expensive the sport was even as a hobby. Your father was just starting his political career. And the dress shop? Little black profit margins. She knew we couldn't afford it, and Gabe wanted to skate with you. So the Nielsens offered to pay for your lessons as long as you wanted to skate with Gabe."

"So that was it?" I stare at Mom. Igor's betrayal was bad enough. I always liked Gabe's mom, thought it was cool how she used to let me play dress up with her old skating costumes and medals, how she always complimented my skating. But she used me. She saw how good I was, and she *bought* me so Gabe could have a better skating career.

And my own mother . . . my own mother *let* her? So there'd be money to fund Dishonest Dad's campaigns? A business deal. The memory of Gabe's words starts my body shaking. Everyone was in on this. Everyone but me. *How badly do you want to win? Money can't buy a gold medal, but it can get you damn close. It's part of the game.*

"Would you have wanted it any differently? Would you have wanted me to tell you that you couldn't take private lessons? That you could only skate a couple of public sessions a week and you'd have to wear rental skates?"

"If we can't afford it, what about our house? How do we afford that? What about the rest of my school tuition?"

Mom sighs. "This is your grandmother's house, you've always known that. And Grammy pays what your scholarship doesn't cover. I'm sorry, baby."

I blink back my tears. This is worse than before. First I lost Gabe. Now the ice. What's left?

In Palisades High's auditorium, waiting for my father's town hall meeting to begin, I slouch in my seat with my arms folded over my chest. Applause fills the room, but I only pull one hand loose and pick at my nails with my thumb. Mom can make me listen. She can't make me look.

But the shocked gasp, so collective it sounds like an audience cue card, can. As I lift my head to the noise, I see my father being lowered to the floor of the stage by two of his aides, his entire body twitching freakishly.

52

I'm not supposed to answer my dad's phone, but the location ID is flashing Washington, D.C. Who would be calling from there except Mad's dad? "Hello?"

"Dr. Nielsen?" My dad and I sound a lot alike on the phone, but before I can correct the woman she continues. "This is Linda Ashman. I'm calling with the update you requested on your patient, William Spier?"

Senator Spier? What? The Senator isn't my dad's patient, is he? I clear my throat. "Yes?"

"His next appointment will be Tuesday, February 11, at six o'clock. We've made arrangements for him to use the staff entrance, as he requested."

"Thank you," I say in my most professional Dr. Richard Nielsen voice. "Anything else?"

"If you can just reassure him that the few members of our staff who know have agreed to secrecy."

"I will." To make sure there isn't some mistake, I add,

"The Senator appreciates the continued discretion of your office."

"You're welcome."

I press END just as another call starts to beep in. "Dr. Nielsen? This is Pat at County. William Spier's en route from Palisades High; he had a seizure."

I grit my teeth. "I'll be right there." I grab the pin and pop the lock on my parent's bathroom. "Dad!"

Dad pushes the edge of the shower curtain aside with the water still running. "Gabe? Can't it wait?"

"Senator Spier had a seizure. They need you at County, now." The water stops immediately. Dad grabs his towel, then his pants. "I know he's your patient. I'm going with you," I say.

He pulls on a shirt and shoes and runs downstairs. "You're not supposed to answer my phone," he says as I follow.

I get in his car.

"Gabe, you can't come along. Patient privacy."

I'm not moving.

I burst into the ER with Dad. Mad and her mom are waiting in chairs. I slide into the seat next to Mad. "Hey."

Mad's mom hustles off after Dad, but Mad doesn't move from her chair. She blinks at me. "You *knew*."

"I just found out, Mad, I swear. Besides, would it have changed anything?"

She looks right at me. "I can't trust you at all, can I? I heard you in Igor's office. You think this is something you can fix, just draw up a new plan?"

"No. Yes. I mean, it's something I *want* to fix. I love you, Mad."

Her head turns to the wall. She doesn't speak, but her words echo in my brain. *Some things you don't get a reskate on.*

53

Mom takes me home an hour later. I head for bed, but I can't sleep. First I lost Gabe, then the ice, and now . . . Dad? My father has brain cancer. A pineal astrocytic tumor, grade one . . . slow growing, hasn't spread . . . highly treatable. None of Mr. Nielsen's words are a comfort.

The words of Dad's newest speech, the one that will air tomorrow and that Mom and I read over tonight, spin in my head:

To quote one of our great presidents, Franklin Delano Roosevelt, "This is preeminently the time to speak the truth, the whole truth, frankly and boldly." Recent photographs have caused much speculation about my new right–hand man. Desmond Everts is an old Navy buddy of mine, who's been helping me with a covert operation of sorts . . . as a nurse. Since October, I've been receiving chemotherapy treatments to recover from brain cancer. Following my requests, my office staff and my wife have kept my battle private. I did not wish anyone to think me too weak to be a leader. I did not realize at the time that to make such a choice, to choose dishonesty, makes me no leader at all. I'm so proud of my daughter, Madelyn, whom many of you have seen in the news for her figure skating accomplishments. Maddy and I have talked many times about how in sports, it's not about whether you win or lose. It's how you play the game. I have not played well. The only limit to our realization of tomorrow will be our doubts of today. I cannot ask the people of Kansas to elect a leader that they might doubt. It is with great regret for my lack of faith in you all . . . that I withdraw my bid for reelection.

"The only limit to our realization of tomorrow will be our doubts of today." That's the line that bothers me because it's also a quote from FDR. From a speech he never delivered . . . because he died the day before he was to give it.

I get out of bed and creep down the stairs. On the island in the kitchen, I pick up Dad's wig that Mom tossed there when we got home. Every hair is still perfectly styled. Dad apologized for not being honest with me. He wasn't forthcoming, but he didn't lie to me. *Truth will ultimately prevail, but there is pain to bring it to light.* I get that misquote now. He didn't want me searching for the truth because he was trying to protect me.

I touch the strands, brown without a touch of gray. How many months ago was it that I brushed Dad's real hair off my hands to the ground? Dad's loss of appetite, his crankiness, his weird sleep patterns, all the evidence was there. I fold the wig and place it back on the island.

In the front hall, I take my skates from their bag in the closet. I sit on the floor with my skates in my lap and trace my finger over the scratches, the gouges, and the scuff marks covering the once-pristine white leather.

In the kitchen, I hear the door click open. Gabe's blond

hair appears ghostlike in the dimness of the hall. He takes my skates from me and puts them away. "Come on." He scoops me up in his arms and carries me upstairs. "Your dad's going to be okay." He tucks me in and lies down beside me.

But neither one of us sleeps.

54

Next morning, Igor starts our lesson right away. His gray eyes scrutinize our warm-up. I skate through the patterns. Mad keeps pace beside me. The skating's technically correct, but the mood's off from the very first strokes. Romeo pines as ever, but Juliet's already dead in his arms.

When we're done warming up, Igor pulls Mad aside at the boards. Whatever he says, Mad only shakes her head. Igor puts our music on.

We move from our opening pose to the triple twist. I launch Mad into the air, my heart breaking into a million pieces when I catch her. I want to hold her forever. I want to be there to catch her always.

But, stiff in my arms, she doesn't want me to catch her. Doesn't want to even look at me. Kristen. Piper. Lisette. Is this how it feels?

Distracted, I've lost time with the music. I rush into our side-by-side jumps. Lose my check on the three-turn before the flip. I can't complete the rotation. Scrambling back to my feet, now I start our combination spin too early and we can't get enough speed to hold all our positions. It's over. "I'm sorry," I whisper to Mad. "I'm sorry. I'm so, so sorry."

The music pounds, echoing my desperation, as Mad sets her left inside edge for the throw, her back to me. I put my hands at her waist. Bend my knees. Turn. Lift.

The timing is wrong, very wrong. Mad's body is heavier than it should be. Dead weight.

"Stop!" Igor shouts.

But it's too late, I'm in too deep to stop now and she flies out of reach into the air and all I can do is watch the horror show that is "Mad!"

55

Hip-first fighting a fall only hurts wor-

56

Already crumpled before she even hit the ice, Mad's body slides into the boards with enough force to send our water bottles tumbling. I reach her side at the same time as Igor.

"Kate!" Igor yells. "Call 9-1-1. Then get Ms. Rasgotra. Now." He shoves my hands away from Mad's white face. "Do not touch her." He feels for her pulse, checks for breath movement. "Madelyn? Can you hear me?"

Kate's skates clang up the stairs as she runs for the lobby. The twisted tune echoes through the arena. I can't stand here and do nothing. I hurt Mad. She lies there, broken. I caused this. I beat my fists against the unbreakable glass barrier.

Chris pulls me away. He grabs my fists in his own. "Stupidest damn play in the whole fucking world. I'm not letting you be a real-life Romeo. The tragedy stops here. She fell. It happens. Shit happens. It doesn't mean you give up. Now an ambulance is coming for Maddy. Are you her partner or not?"

Her partner. She's so much more than my partner. Skating's never mattered, really. It's always been about Mad. All those years she chased me across monkey bars. I've always been bigger, faster, stronger. I could've easily outrun her. I never did. Now I know that deep down I've always known. Like boot and blade, we were always meant to be a pair. Meant to be together.

"Then get yourself together and go." Chris glances at my knuckles. "Hell, they'll probably make you go, anyway. Looks like you need stitches."

Igor doesn't want me to ride along but, like Chris said, the paramedics take one look at my hands and tell him where he can shove it. I follow in silence as they carry Mad's stretcher into the parking lot. The last time an ambulance came, it was for me. The day of the tree. I remember lying on the ground, gazing up at the bare branches of our maple tree cracking the perfect blue sky into pieces. I called out for Mad. She leaned over me, her face making all the cracks disappear. "I'm here," she said. "I'm okay."

This time, I hold her hand as the sirens cry. "I'm here, it's going to be okay." Because I have to believe it, I add, "You're going to be okay." *And please,* pleads my heart. *Please let* us *be okay.*

When we unload at the hospital, I chase after the stretcher. A nurse catches me just inside the emergency room. "Not so fast. You need some attention yourself."

Mom bursts through the doors, almost knocking into both me and the nurse. "Gabe! Igor said there was an accident, that Maddy fell—" Her eyes drop to the bloodstained gauze the EMT wrapped around my hands. "Did she clip you?"

I shake my head. "I broke her."

Her eyes meet mine. "No. No, you didn't. Falls happen in skating, we all know that. Igor thinks she hit her head but your father's with her."

My father. Dr. Richard Nielsen. Nationally known, award-winning neurosurgeon. "It's bad," I say. My body shakes this time. "How bad is it?"

"Gabe." Mom puts her hands on my shoulders. "It's going to be okay. It's probably a concussion. Serious, yes, but we know how to treat them. And your father is very, *very* good at his job." She takes my hands, peels back the gauze, and looks at my knuckles. "Call a plastic surgeon," she says to the nurse. She ushers me into the sutures room and takes a closer look at my wounds. "These aren't cuts from a blade. What the hell happened?"

The rest of me hurts so badly I don't even feel anything in my hands. But I have to tell. The tragedy stops here. "I slept with Mad."

"What?" Mom snaps her gaze away from my hands, right to my face, and I can see my words hit her one by one. "You didn't." She looks at my face for a moment, then sinks down into a chair. "Oh, Gabe . . ."

The door to the sutures room opens and a silver-haired doctor backs his way into the room, snapping on gloves. He looks at my hands and whistles. "I'd hate to see the other guy."

"Safety glass," I say. "I beat up safety glass."

The doctor tips his head to the side, evidently not sure if I'm joking. "Well. Guess I wouldn't recommend that in the future."

"Me, neither," I say. "Turns out it's not all that safe." For some reason, this is crazy funny and I begin laughing out of control.

The doctor looks at Mom. "You, uh, want a psych consult, Jensine?"

She shakes her head, still collapsed in her chair. "Not necessary."

I stop laughing.

Mom straightens and lifts herself from her chair. "Give us a couple minutes, Jack, will you?"

"This won't take long." Dr. Jack Whoever pats something that stings against my cuts.

I flinch, but not from the stinging feeling on my hands. I don't want to be alone with Mom just now. "Let him finish, Mom."

"Please."

The doctor stops and looks at her. "All right, Jensine." He snaps off his gloves and leaves the room.

Mom gets up and starts pacing back and forth, the tiny room requiring her to turn about every five steps. She stops and stares at the ceiling. "I hate having to ask this. But honestly, Gabe. What. Were. You. THINKING?!"

The tears overcome me again. "I love her, Mom. For real this time. I'm in love with her."

Mom doesn't say anything for a long time. Just sits and wrings her hands. Finally she asks, "How long?"

It was never about two weeks. It was never about the word girlfriend. Hell, it wasn't even ever about sex. It was always about Mad. I couldn't ever make another relationship work because my heart's always belonged to Mad. "Forever."

Mom says quietly, "I should've known."

57

I lie still in the hospital bed as Gabe's dad touches my cheek. "Buck up, kiddo. CT's clear. You'll need to lay off any training for a couple weeks, just to be sure, but you're going to be fine. A little more sleep at night and no more skipping breakfast, okay?" He rises from his seat in the chair beside my bed, his white coat falling crisply into place. "Anything you want right now?"

"No." I stare at the foam ceiling tiles. One of them has a pale brown stain right in the middle. I look away from it but all the little dots and cracks make me feel as though everything could crumble down on me at any second.

"Hey," he says, still standing beside my bed. "It's a lot to handle. I wish I had pushed harder for them to tell you earlier, but it's going to be all right, Maddy. You and your dad both." He gives my hand a quick squeeze. "I'll send your mom in."

Tap, tap, comes the knock on the door frame a couple minutes later.

I sigh. "Come in, Mom."

No answer, only a rustle of plastic. It's not Mom. I whip my head toward the door. It better not be— I put my hand to the side of my head. It wasn't a good idea to move so quickly.

Kate steps into the room and gives a shaky laugh. "No, just me." Her sneakers squeak across the floor, the torn ends of her over-the-boot tights flapping against the laces. She's still wearing her practice clothes. She sets a bouquet of flowers on the bedside table. "How are you feeling? Dr. Nielsen says you're going to be all right."

I pull the covers further over myself. "He doesn't know anything. I'm not."

Kate clunks her purse onto the floor and shudders. "God, I hate the smell of hospitals." She sits on the edge of the bed. "I know what's going on with you and Gabe."

Even the mention of his name makes me wince. "I don't want to talk about it."

"Maddy, it won't go away just because you don't talk about it." She takes my hand. "I was upset, too, when I found out. I'm sorry, I shouldn't have compared you two to Romeo and Juliet. Yeah, it sucks and it's not what any of us planned, but it's not something to be suicidal about."

"I fainted. And . . . Igor planned it."

"What? Are you crazy? There's no way."

"I heard him. Talking to Gabe in his office."

"No," Kate insists. "Why would he do such a thing?"

"Because he only cares about winning."

"That's not true. Anyway, how would you being pregnant help you win?"

"I'm not preg . . ." Wait. Ohmigod. If I were a doctor, I'd misdiagnose everything. All the clues about Dad that I missed. And Kate, all nervous twitches at Sectionals. A *mistake*. She and Chris weren't on edge because of colleges or poor skates. She's not bulimic. I look at her. "You're pregnant? Oh, Kate . . ."

"But . . ." She falters. "You were throwing up . . . and New Year's Eve . . . you and Gabe . . ."

"That's what Igor planned. Gabe sleeping with me. Of course he wouldn't want me knocked up. He was pissed at Gabe for forgetting condoms, even gave him a whole box."

Kate looks directly at me. "Did you *see* Igor give them to Gabe?"

"No, but he told me he was going to Igor's office. I know it was him."

"They were Trojans, weren't they?"

I cock my head at Kate. "Yes. How did you—?"

"Because Igor gave them to *Chris* after reaming him out because he caught us fooling around. He doesn't want us pairing up off-ice, no way he wants his star students doing it. Just what he wants, drama before major international competitions and enough skater babies for a parent-tot class."

"Kate, Gabe had the box."

"Chris probably gave it to him." Her face crumples. "Like we need them now." Footsteps echo in the hallway outside the door, and Kate stands. "I need to go." She slings her bag over her shoulder and heads for the door as Igor and Ms. Rasgotra enter the room.

Igor and Ms. Rasgotra sit by my bed. "Madelyn," Igor says,

his face looking gray even without his fur hat, "I know there is something wrong. You must tell me."

Ms. Rasgotra says, "Gabriel did something to you."

Did he? Or did I do this all to myself? All this time I wanted Gabe to trust me about our relationship, but I wasn't really trusting *him*. Have *I* been Romeo, ready to let everything die because of a misunderstanding?

Igor takes my hand in his. Off the ice, his fingers are warm. "World medal is very special thing, yes? But—at finish, that is all. Thing. A lesson more than one of us learns difficult way." He takes Ms. Rasgotra's hand and gives it a squeeze before letting go. "I am sorry. I did not think Gabriel . . . sadly, I am wrong before." He looks at me. "You do not have to skate with Gabriel. We find you different partner, or you skate as single lady. I have always known you could do either."

"Did you . . . ?" I scrunch my eyes closed, then open them. I have to know. "Did you give Gabe a box of condoms?"

"No," Igor says. His face grows even more gray. "Should I have done this?"

He thinks I'm pregnant, too. "No! No. Did you . . . tell Gabe to pretend to love me?"

"That first day, I tell him to pretend, yes. On ice, nothing more. I am sorry, Madelyn. I did not mean to open can of sardines."

Worms, I think, but I worm myself out from under the covers. High heels clack in tandem across the vinyl floor of the hospital room and Mrs. Nielsen and Mom approach my bedside.

Mom leans over and hugs me. "Maddy, I'm so sorry. Your father and I got so caught up in our own troubles that we didn't see what we should've seen. I love you. No matter what."

Mrs. Nielsen is next. "I love you, too," she says. "I love you like you're my own daughter. I always have." She pulls back to look me in the eyes. "I paid for your skating because I know what it's like to have to give up on a dream. I would still pay for your skating, even if you didn't want to skate with Gabe anymore. And I will still love you even if you don't want to skate anymore. But Maddy . . . Skating or not, I think you still want to be with Gabe."

I do. I've always known how Gabe felt about me. Gabe and I aren't a real-life Romeo and Juliet. We're not star-crossed, we're star-matched. Like boot and blade, meant to be a pair. "Can I see him?"

"Um," Mrs. Nielsen says.

Ohmigod. When I fell, "Did I hurt Gabe?"

"No," Mrs. Nielsen says. "No, it's not that—" She looks at Mom.

Something like a grimace stretches Mom's face. "He's talking with your father."

58

Gabe

When I told Mom what I wanted to do, she cried. The Senator's next on my list, though. My turn to cry. I steel myself before stepping into his hospital room. "You," he says. The shine on his head, now bald without his wig, glares at me along with his eyes.

Yeah, somebody briefed him already. But I've done my homework. "Teddy Roosevelt. *The only man who makes no mistakes is the man who never does anything.*"

"Are you calling my daughter a mistake?"

Okay, this performance isn't going quite how I envisioned it. The Senator reaches for his IV. Before he can pull it out and strangle me with it, I continue. "No. I'm in love with your daughter, sir. What I meant is, how I handled things was a mistake. And I'd appreciate it if . . . you'd let me try again."

"And what exactly are your intentions this time?" He's still holding his IV. Twisting it, actually.

I don't wait to see what Navy SEAL maneuver he might be up to. I show him my plan.

"No," he says.

"Yes." I've learned a lot from Mad. How to be dedicated. How to be determined. And I've never been more driven than I am right now. All those years Mad never gave up on me, always trusted that someday I'd see what had been right in front of me all along. Shit happens, Chris said. But I'm not giving up. I'm never giving up on Mad. I'll stall this debate as long as I have to. I grab the hospital directory from his bedside table and start reading it out loud.

The Senator stares. "You're going to read the whole thing."

Yeah. "And I'll read every one of Shakespeare's plays next if I have to. Because, Senator Spier? Shakespeare himself didn't have enough words—"

He's not smiling, but he's not frowning either. "All right, Gabe. I recognize a filibuster when I see one. Let's talk."

When I finally make it to Mad's room, she's not alone. Igor, Ms. Rasgotra, Mom, and Mrs. Spier are all crowded around the bed. But sometimes you can't take baby steps. Sometimes, you just have to jump. I take a deep breath. Push my heart onto that left outside edge. And I vault. "I love you, Madelyn Spier. I am hopelessly, endlessly, head over skates in love with you. And if I'd just stopped being chicken and said it when I should've, maybe none of this would've happened. Can you ever forgive me? Can you still love me?"

Mad looks right at me. "I've always loved you. That day in the tree, I fell because I was reaching for you. I wanted you next to me."

"I want to be, Mad. Always."

"I'm sorry I doubted you."

Doubted me? "What?"

"That I thought you were only pretending because Igor told you to."

Wait a sec. "That's what you were upset about? I thought you were upset about—"

"Nope. No, definitely not." Mad blushes. "We're good there."

Yeah, that convo can wait. Secrets might not be so great, but there is such a thing as too much information. I take the ring on its chain from its box and put it in her palm. "Forget about being just America's sweethearts. I want the whole world to know about us."

Mad lifts the chain and looks at the ring. She tries to sit up and swoons back into her pillow. "Oh my God, Gabe, is this . . . ohmigod, it is."

It is. We're not six anymore, but the ring is the same. Great-Grandmother Nielsen's ring. Because I know what love is now. Love is an intricate filigree band. Complicated but beautiful. Love is three diamonds. For past, present, and future. Love is never giving up even through the Great Depression and two world wars.

Mad looks at Mom. "Does—"

I chuckle. Mom does, too. "Yeah, I asked her this time. I'm in enough trouble after 'fessing up to your dad."

Mad winces. "How'd that go?"

"You didn't want kids, did you?"

She smiles. "We could adopt." She reaches for my hand and finds the bandages on my knuckles. Her eyes pop. "Please tell me you didn't get in a fight with my dad."

"No. It was Plexiglas." I squeeze her hand. "It's a long story." I take the chain from her hand and fasten it around her neck. "Your dad won't let me make it official until after graduation, but this is my promise. In landing and in falling. I love you, Mad."

She smiles. "I love you, too."

"Oh, and while you're recovering? I could really use some extra coaching on my triple Axel."

"Oh, really?" Her smile switches over to a grin. "You're going to jump this time?"

I'm going to jump. She makes me want to be brave.

Epilogue

Mom's outdone herself with this dress. Delicate white lace over a sweetheart bodice, with a flowy chiffon skirt. No, it's not my wedding dress! Gabe and I want to do college and maybe a couple ice tours before we permanently knot our skate laces together. But I smile up at him as he stands beside me on the ice in Shanghai. He smiles back and squeezes my hand. His promise, Great-Grandmother Nielsen's ring, hangs on a chain around my neck for all the world to see.

Igor freaked about changing music a month before Worlds, but I couldn't skate *Romeo and Juliet* with Mad anymore. I'm not going to be her Romeo and I won't let her be my Juliet. Shakespeare didn't have enough words to describe what she means to me. It was time to choreograph our own story.

The piano sounds, strong and steady. Our song. "Canon in D." We dance across the ice. Each edge deep. Each turn precise. As the first violin notes soar, I raise Mad overhead into our star lift.

We sail down the rink into our triple-toe, triple-toe

combination. Leap into our flying camels. Glide into our spiral sequence, Mad's body tucked tight against mine even through the change of edge.

The music builds. We take our back crossovers. Step forward onto matching left outside edges. Vault into the air. One-two-three and there's the extra half rotation. This time it's my leg that's so bent, but I fight for it. Stand up. And I've done what I never could've done without Mad. We're the first pair to pull off side-by-side triple Axels.

Maddy

We set up for the quad, Gabe's hands firm on my sides. Just at the top of the crescendo I spring from the ice, feeling the release as he launches me. My arms cross tight against my chest, elbows down, ankles crossed. I spin through the air, the skirt of my new dress a white whirl with the rotation. As soon as I land, I know we've won.

Our pair spin is a blur of camel, sit spin, layback. My body arched back, skate drawn to my head, I smile up at the rafters of the arena. In our lasso lift, I'm so high I could float right through those rafters.

Gabe

We finish with our death spiral. We present, arms locked out, free legs extended. And I take an extra stroke toward Mad, my face right up to those barely-there freckles. "I love you." With my eyes locked on hers, I don't even care about anyone's reaction. This time was exactly what Mad and I wanted.

The crowd is a dull roar beyond my ears, a blur beyond my eyes. All I need is right here, holding my hand. And this is about so much more than choreography. When I kiss Mad, it's beyond something. It's everything.

Hand in hand, we head for the kiss and cry. Today, we're going to kiss. Sometimes, we'll cry. There'll be broken tree branches. Misunderstandings and crash landings. It turns out all relationships are like Axels. They take a leap of faith and they have their ups and downs.

But it's not about falling, it's about what you do after the fall. Whatever happens, we'll pick ourselves up. Brush ourselves off. And circle around for another attempt.

Acknowledgments

Thank you first to my parents, for raising me on love and stories, and to my husband, my real-life love story.

Thanks also to my fabulous Flurries and the other members of the Lake Effect FSC, especially Mel, for being my technical caller on this project, and Duane, for braving a pair test with all five foot, nine inches of me.

Many thanks to the members of SCBWI-MI, especially Sarah and Kristin, for supporting a newbie; Tracy, for saying the hard words when they needed to be said; and my FLAG critique group members, Amy, Dan, Roxanne, and Wendy.

I am also blessed to be part of an incredible community at VCFA and am especially thankful for the support of my mentor, Lori Goe, and my first semester advisor, Betsy Partridge, who both influenced this project more than they know.

Thank you to the Swoon Reads community; your thoughtful comments made this story both a finalist and a better novel. Special thanks to the Swoon Reads staff, especially Holly and Jean, for your patience and guidance.

Finally, thanks to Mrs. Rocker, for being the Mrs. Mason of my own senior year and for never settling for less than my best.

Turn the page for some

Sw♥♥nworthy

Extras...

A Note from the Author

Maddy and Gabe's story is fiction, but I had a lot of fun setting it in a real world that I love: the world of competitive figure skating.

Highly competitive skaters like Maddy and Gabe who hope to represent the United States internationally qualify through a competition structure organized by the U.S. Figure Skating Association (USFSA).

Most skaters compete at one of nine regional competitions before advancing, there are limited numbers of high-level pair and dance teams, and these skaters can start directly at one of the three sectional competitions. Sectionals are held in November and the top teams from each sectional advance to the Nationals in January. The World Figure Skating Championships are typically held in March. The time between competitions allows skaters to recover and also to adjust and improve their programs based on the judges' scores.

Though Maddy and Gabe only attend qualifying competitions in the book, many skaters try out their new programs at non-qualifying competitions held by skating clubs all over the country. Recreational skaters can compete at these competitions, too. The USFSA offers many types of programs for skaters of all levels, from beginners to seniors and from preschoolers to adults—it's never too late to learn how to skate.

If you would like to learn more about the sport of figure skating or find programs in your area, please visit usfsa.org.

A Coffee Date

with author Katie Van Ark and her editor, Holly West

"About the Author"

Holly West (HW): Do you have a favorite fictional couple? It doesn't have to be in novels, it can be any fictional couple.

Katie Van Ark (KV): I do. It's Julie Taylor and Matt Saracen from *Friday Night Lights*. At the end of that series, I was just like, "Okay, this has now become my favorite TV series ever, ever, ever, ever." I loved that they ended up together at the end. I re-watched the first season recently and he's just so sweet to her in the beginning. Not that he doesn't stay that way, but just going back to the first season especially when Julie gets the idea she needs to sleep with him because he's the quarterback and he sees that she's not really ready and they just end up leg wrestling on the floor? It was a really cool way for a teen guy to react.

HW: I, personally, have not watched *Friday Night Lights*, since I'm not usually drawn to sports stories, but I've had many people on the Swoon Reads team tell me, "You have to watch *Friday Night Lights*, you have to!"

KV: And it's really not a football show. Is that a funny thing to say? But, it's not. It's totally a girl's show because it's all about the characters and their relationship drama and that type of stuff. So, football is part of the story, but it's not the story itself. *Catching Jordan*, a favorite book of mine, is the same way. It's a football novel, but it's about the relationships that are going on in that setting.

Swoon Reads

HW: Do you have any hobbies? What kind of things do you do for fun?

KV: My husband made the mistake once of calling figure skating a hobby. He's a fast learner, that man, one of the things that I love about him, and he never, ever did that again. I have this issue with hobbies. They become compulsive. Skating was a hobby in the beginning and very quickly, it was a passion. And writing was a hobby in the beginning and very quickly, it was a passion. So, I really have a problem with hobbies. I don't know when to stop.

"The Swoon Reads Experience"

HW: Let's talk about Swoon Reads as an experience. How did you learn about Swoon Reads?

KV: I came across it in the *Bulletin*, which is the national newsletter for SCBWI, the Society of Children's Books Writers and Illustrators. There was an article there with Jean, a great interview about her vision for the site.

HW: And that timing seems to have worked really well. What was your experience on the site like before you were chosen?

KV: Well, I came to the site first as a reader. I would recommend that anybody who is interested in submitting a manuscript do that, just poke around and see who's there, what types of manuscripts are there, and what types of comments people are leaving. As for the actual upload—from what I've heard from others, too; I'm not the only one who felt this—was an "Oh, my gosh. This is my baby and I just put it out there for everybody to see" moment, which can be a little bit scary when you don't know what's going to happen or what the end result is going to be. As I got to know people on the site better and we were commenting on each other's manuscripts and I saw the kind of feedback I was getting, I had come to a point where I was like, "You know, I'm okay with this." I looked at it as more about the value of the feedback. Before the first list was announced, I was still happy even with the thought that my manuscript might not be chosen. It had still been a valuable experience. Then, of course, the phone call was extremely exciting.

"About the Book"

HW: Now, let's talk about the book itself. Where did you get the idea for the book?
KV: People say you have to write what you know, right? That's very old writing advice, but I think in some cases, it's more accurate to say to write what you *feel* and *think about*. And the idea for this book came from, in a lot of ways, a hole in my heart. Because I had thrown myself into skating with such passion that when my husband and I decided we were ready to start our family, and I got pregnant that I suddenly had . . . issues. You know, you get to a point where you can't skate anymore, and I made it until month seven, but then I sat down on a chassé, which is a really easy-to-do move, just like a stepping move, no turns, no jumps, no nothing. I was like, "Okay, my balance is too far shot. I can't do this anymore." It sounds melodramatic maybe, but I came home and I just sobbed my eyes out because I was missing my skill level so much. And I hadn't even missed a practice yet. I had already gotten to skate that day, but just the thought that I still had months left to go with pregnancy and . . . I thought, I can't do this anymore; what am I going to do?

SwoonReads

HW: I'm impressed you got to month seven.

KV: I don't recommend that. I wouldn't do it again. What happened actually was that my skill set adjusted to my new center of balance, so that after I had the baby and I went back, I had to readjust to a new center of balance all over again. I did go back to skating a week after I had my baby because I just had to. And I had to wait for my mother to leave because she wouldn't let me do it. How awful is that? But, it's true. And when I stepped on the ice again, it didn't even matter. I knew all the work I was going to have to do, but it didn't matter; I could breathe again. For all these months, I had not been able to breathe and then to step out there and be like, "Okay. Life is going to be okay." Yeah, I'm too intense about things. I have this hobby problem. That's where the story came from, though, that emotion and that longing. I thought, "I'm going to make this character who is faced with the prospect of this skating life that she loves, this boy she loves, and what if she loses them forever? What would that be like?"

"The Writing Life"

HW: Do you have any writing rituals? Do you write in a specific place?

KV: My writing ritual is to write. You can't make excuses about it. It doesn't matter where you are or if you don't have your computer or what's going on or how busy you are. I make myself writing notebooks and I take one pretty much everywhere I go. Because if you don't make that a priority, then you're never going to get finished and you're never going to get to your revisions. So, that's my writing ritual, really. When my girls are in school, that's my blocked-off writing time and I have a cup of tea and I sit my butt down. And if I'm stuck on something, I'm allowed to switch. If I need a change-up, I take my notebook to the park or the beach. I can work on another project if I'm stuck, too, but that's writing time. It's on the calendar. So, I try and be as faithful to that as I can during the week. It's a job, really. It's a very fun and awesome job that I feel incredibly blessed to be able to have.

HW: What's the best writing advice you've ever heard?
KV: It's old SCBWI advice: Butt in chair. A writer must write. Until you put it down on paper, you're not a writer.

The Boy Next Door

Discussion Questions

1. The story of *Romeo and Juliet* appears often throughout the book. What parallels can be drawn between Shakespeare's famous lovers and Gabe and Maddy?

2. Near the end of the book, Maddy considers taking her skating career solo, but her mother says they wouldn't be able to afford it. If you had to choose between continuing an activity you love with someone you dislike or giving it up altogether, what would you choose?

3. Maddy's parents hide her father's illness from her so she won't be distracted from her skating. Do you agree with their choice? Why or why not?

4. There is a lot of wedding imagery near the end of the book, and Gabe even gives Maddy his grandmother's ring. Do you think Maddy and Gabe are too young to be engaged?

5. Gabe and Maddy's skating programs progress from *Romeo and Juliet* to the story of Samson and Delilah to "Canon in D" (a popular wedding song). How do you think this mirrors their off-ice relationship?

6. If you were a figure skater and could pick any song or story to use for your program, what would it be and why?

7. Chris and Kate's relationship is an interesting foil for Maddy and Gabe's. What makes the two of them different?

SwoonReads

8. Gabe changes a lot over the course of the novel. What was your initial impression of him? Is it different from how you feel about him at the end? Do you feel like Maddy goes through a similar transformation and growth?

9. Maddy is very hurt by the secrets that have been kept from her, and feels as if everyone is lying to her. Do you think a secret is the same thing as a lie?

10. Gabe and Maddy look at the world very differently. How would the story have changed if it had been told through one perspective?

Want to host your own
Swoon Reads Book Club Party?
Download our *free* event kit at
www.swoonreads.com/partykit!

Words are strong.
Love is stronger.

Can Jordyn find the courage to tell Alex how she really
feels—and the truth about her family
—before he slips away forever?

*C*rammed like a sardine in the small, upper lobby waiting for the homeroom bell, I feel strangely alone and disconnected. Then, I catch sight of something familiar, propped against the foot of one of the old wooden benches. It's a worn black Jansport with "Alex" written in Wite-Out across the front pocket. I perk up at once, instantly feeling more grounded. Alex is around here somewhere. He'll throw me my favorite smile—the one that makes it seem like we're laughing at some joke no one else gets—and this place won't seem as serious or intense.

Suddenly, I can't wait to see him. We haven't talked much in the past few weeks, because his family was on vacation and he stopped working at the club when two-a-days started for the football team. Sometimes, I'd see him down by the field after our evening practices, but most nights, he seemed kind of distracted, über-focused on football, I guess. Alex isn't the best player in the world. No matter how many wind sprints he runs or how much time he spends in the weight room, he's perpetually second string. You can tell it annoys the crap out of him, this one thing Mr. Perfect can't be perfect at. I find his frustration sort of endearing. And the rest of the team must find his persistence admirable, because they elected him co-captain, second string skills and all. He's just got those natural leadership genes, like a young, half-Hispanic Barack Obama or something.

Alex is good people. And as if to prove my point, he walks through the door closest to the teacher lot, barely visible behind the tall stack of books he's carrying for Mrs. Higgins, our ancient librarian, who hobbles alongside him, smiling up in admiration.

I bite my lip to keep from giggling. My friend is such a Boy Scout. Seriously. I'm not kidding—he's an *actual* Boy Scout who's been working on this big Eagle Scout project in whatever spare time he has, which isn't much. But on a daily basis, he seems to go around earning merit badges in Helpfulness and Nobleness and all that good stuff.

"I'll be right back," I tell Erin and take off in his direction.

He notices me over the top of the books and grins instantaneously. "Air Jordan—there you are!"

I smile in response to today's selection from his litany of ridiculous nicknames . . . Air Jordan . . . M.J. . . . Twenty-three . . . or as he called me for a while in Spanish class last year, Veintitrés.

I can't think of a single thing I have in common with Michael Jordan, the basketball icon, other than my name, which is Jordyn Michaelson. I'm five-foot-three, with hazel eyes and wavy, dark, shoulder-length hair cut in layers. Female. And white—sadly so, being that summer just ended. But for whatever reason, Alex is amused by stupid nicknames. Thing is, as stupid as I find them, it's impossible to look at his face when he's busy cracking himself up and not feel amused, too.

His brown eyes get all sparkly, and his wide grin of even, white teeth gets all goofy. Combined with the close-cropped black hair and a slight widow's peak, all I see is a little boy looking for mischief. Alex is one of those people who looks right *at you*, for real, and practically dares you to make mischief with him.

Hurrying toward him, I realize I'm opening my arms to give him a hug, even though hugging isn't something we usually do. There are unspoken boundaries we have not dared to cross, not even dared to *approach*, since last year. I'm so focused on Alex that I don't even notice Leighton Lyons, our other hockey co-captain, trotting across the lobby from the opposite direction, until we have a full-on collision. Our shoulders slam into one another's and I stumble backward, off balance, my heavy backpack nearly pulling me down.

I right myself and rub my shoulder, grumbling inwardly. Girl really needed to learn that other people inhabit this planet. Where was she headed in such a hurry?

When I look up, I get my answer, even though it's not one that makes sense. Not. At. All. I see her arms wrapped around Alex's torso, beating me to the punch with a hug. Then I watch as she does one better and plants a quick, flirty kiss upon his lips. "Hey, babe."

I stand and stare in disbelief, like an idiot, waiting for it to compute. Which it doesn't. Leighton hugging Alex. Leighton *kissing* Alex. Leighton calling Alex "babe." What? When? How?

But none of it cuts as deeply as him casually looping his arm around her waist and turning to talk to me like none of this requires an explanation. Like none of this should bother me in any way. At least he has the decency to ask if I'm okay, which Leighton does not. "You alright, Jordyn?"

"Yeah, I'm fine."

Even though suddenly, I'm not. There's a sick feeling in my gut, as the realization sinks in that suddenly everything is different.

"Please," Leighton interjects. "She takes harder hits than that on the field every day." Pinching Alex's side, she smirks at him. I notice how they stand exactly eye to eye, the same height, and I feel small and insignificant. "We're just as tough as you guys, right, Jordyn?"

"Umm, sure."

"It's so good to see you," he says, smiling all the while, but rubbing her hand with the pad of his thumb while he says it. "I was so pissed I had to miss the staff party. You'll have to give me the recap."

I swallow my feelings and try not to bat an eye. "Yeah, it was quite the event. They added karaoke this year. And to be honest, I really would have been okay with summer ending without having to see Mr. Jacoby perform 'Happy' in a bathing suit."

Alex throws his head back and laughs, his full belly laugh, the one that always makes me feel like tiny seeds in my heart are blooming. His laughter nurtures some kind of longing that has no business being rooted there. His arm around her waist makes those little sprouts of wistfulness wilt and topple as quickly as they sprung up.

"Please tell me you were a backup dancer for him at least?"

"Absolutely." I smile in spite of myself, in spite of the Leighton-shaped elephant in the room, and shake my head. "You know me so well."

"Did Petersen show up really drunk again?" he asks, referring to the president of the club. "Hit on any of the lifeguards who aren't even legal yet?"

Leighton tugs on the bottom of Alex's shirt before I get a chance to answer. "Hey, listen. I need to talk to you about some athletic council stuff real quick and I've got to run to the ladies' before homeroom, so can we . . ." She's talking to Alex but looking at me, waiting for me to make myself scarce.

"Yeah. Sure, babe," he nods quickly, the word sounding even more wrong coming from his lips than hers. Alex tightens his grip on her and turns in the direction of the side hallway, where there's some space. He talks over his shoulder as they walk. "We'll catch up in History, okay, Michaelson?"

I nod, ignoring the tightness in my throat. Before, his use of my last name used to feel intimate. Now, it reminds me that I'm a buddy and nothing more.

Looking for something else to make you swoon? Check out these other great

 Swoon Reads titles!

Fourteen viewpoints.
One love story.

Even her guardian angel
might have trouble
saving Cara . . .

Katie Van Ark is a member of SCBWI and RWA and a student at Vermont College of Fine Arts. She enjoys reading, writing, and of course, figure skating. She lives in Michigan with two daughters, two cats, and one very patient husband who was also her high school sweetheart.

The Boy Next Door is her debut novel.

Swoon Reads